Whisper on the Verse

Marcus Branson

CONTENTS

Check out the playlist under the same name on Spotify and check out Wrenn's tunes!

Be sure to rate and review this book on amazon so I know what to keep doing. I want to write stories YOU ENJOY!

Follow me on the site too so you're always updated on new books.

Lots of new series with a wide variety of MC's and genres coming soon! If Wrenn isn't your style, don't worry, there's more to come.

Enjoy!

CHAPTER 1

I suppose you've heard just about every story there is to tell by now; tales of daring do-gooders, gorgeous damsels, thrilling ne'er-do-wells. 'Spose you're hard up for a story that'll get your blood pumpin', your heart patterin'. Well, I might have just the thing, partner.

Now, you're no stranger to the darker sides of humanity, I'm sure, but this tale might give you a slight inklin' to clutch your pearls or even commiserate with the innocents caught in the crossfire, but I'd caution you against this. Ain't a soul present in these outskirts that ain't running from someone or somethin'. The past can doom a man, that's for sure, if he has a mind to stay and face the music, but those in the Reach ain't the type to accept those cards lyin' down. New beginnings and all that is fine, just don't go into this thinkin' that there is so much as an innocent soul in the lot. Suffice to say, we all got our demons, it's how you handle them is what makes you a man, and that can make all the difference.

Our story begins at the end, the end of the known galaxy, the end of civilization. The Alliance controls most everything in the Alpha Quad, which can be a might bit suffocatin' for folk who don't like the eye of big brother hovering over their shoulders, 'specially when that eye be seein' somethin' you'd rather it not be peepin'. Most *decent* folk live their whole lives under the shackles of the Systems Central Alliance, but most decent folk don't desire more than three hots an' a halfway decent cot. For those of us who desire more . . . let's call it *free enterprise*, then the

Omega Quad is the place to wander.

This was Wrenn's destination. He'd spent his last credits on a used Ravenwing that would get him through the Digiway and on to parts unknown. He'd been a zipper jockey for a couple of sols but his Lance fighter didn't have the juice for more than sublight travel, not to mention how it would disintegrate if he used it for Digiway travel. Sure, there were freighters that shuttled folk through, but the idea of indentured servitude didn't sit well in his gut.

The night before his journey to the Reach was a pleasant one. As many a young men did, Wrenn had gone out for one last hurrah. Watering holes were highly regulated, but the brothels often turned a blind eye to their patrons bringing their own whiskey. Wrenn spent his time with a beautiful Nemoyan dancer. She caught his eye right quick, and he enjoyed the private show he received as she slithered out of her satin dress to expose her bright bubblegum skin. She smelled as good as she tasted when his face sunk between her perky breasts, her hands working across his nethers, coaxing his shaft to full mast. When she mounted him, he half-forgot where he was, his thoughts lost to the byways of lust and desire. It was an adrenaline rush, not unlike the zipper flights he'd survived, the g-forces pushing on his chest as her hands now did, his breath rapid and heart racing while she moved her hips in tandem with him. He almost forgot about the trip altogether.

The buzzing of the alarm brought Wrenn back from his unconscious visions. He spat the burned-out cigarette from his lips as the ash replaced the sweeter taste of his dreams. Wrenn smacked the radio in angry retaliation for the rude awakening. "Yeah?"

Devil 35, you are clear to proceed, please maneuver into proper position for Digital Transfer.

"Finally." Wrenn grumbled, his fingers pushing forward on the pilot's wheel.

Like most things controlled by the SCA the Digital Transference Superhighway, or 'Digiway' as most folk called

4

it, was a highly-structured and bureaucratic mess. The techies would like to tell you it was the most important advancement in Terran history. Its generators had the ability to convert any matter into the previously-unknown fifth state, one completely deconstructed into a digital line of code. In this state of matter, items could be sent across the stars faster than even light itself, and this advancement had revolutionized settlement of the Alpha Quad and was the backbone of Galactic Commerce. Wrenn didn't much care how it worked, mind you, so long as it did. Although this wasn't always the case out this far from Terra Prime.

See, to keep the Digiway open, a direct connection with a line of communication satellites needs to be maintained, each powered by an exorbitant amount of energy on the magnitude of a neutron star. As such, the buoys need to be close enough to one of them buggers to leech off, but as you are rightly aware, neutron stars are notoriously . . . finicky.

Wrenns Ravenwing maneuvered into place before the titanic gateway as the controls were taken over by the Scabie traffic control tower. He held up his hands in mock surrender as he thought about how nice it would be to get clear of such control freaks. "At least buy me dinner first before you jerk my stick, lady." He grumbled.

Wrenn eyed himself in the viewport's reflection. Many might call him a youngin', what with his boyish complexion and unkempt brown hair, but he was nearin' his thirtieth sol according to his recent health screenin'. He was tall as far as Terran heights went, which was normal for Spacers who spent most of their lives in less than one-G. Most ships, however, were universally designed for those who spent most of their lives on worlds, so he found himself often cramped in tight quarters or bumpin' his head on an airlock or two. Just a few more hours and he'd be clear. Wrenn put his feet up on the console again, pulling up his six-string dobro and plucking a few chords while he left the radio open. He'd be sure to leave these pricks with a few choice lyrics to remember him by. Friends once described

Wrenn's singing as a cross 'tween a goat's scream and a howler monkey's wail, so he was sure he'd garner their attention.

Send me home, gentle one
Let me soar amongst the stars
For your ways are known to me
And they've left so many scars

Send me home, gentle one
My true love waits for me
I've been with you for far too long
And now it hurts to pee.

Devil 35 - your mike is hot. The traffic controller stopped the impromptu concert.

"Just giving you a proper farewell, Tower!" Wrenn chuckled as he strummed the melody for another verse.

To his surprise, Wrenn heard the voice on the other line chuckle. *Is there more?* The now clearly female operator questioned.

Wrenn leaned forward toward the radio microphone with interest. "I'm sure I can rustle up another few lines, if you'd like to mosey on over for a bit."

Wrenn's attempts at flirting were quickly dashed. *In that rig? I'm impressed you made it this far, Spacer.*

"She might not be the prettiest jumper, but she's free." Wrenn retorted.

You'll be lucky if she survives the reconstruction. Maybe the Digiway will rebuild you something better. The radio laughed.

"How cruel you are, my lady, how cruel you are." Wrenn lit another cigarette.

Happy trails, Spacer. The speaker crackled one last time as Wrenn's ship shuttered and the neon green arms of the Digiway enveloped him.

I should probably take this opportunity to remind you,

dear reader, that living matter cannot be changed to the fifth state. A house can be torn down and rebuilt good as new, but you can't tear down your dog in quite the same way. The techies had figured out a reach-around to the problem with shielding. A large enough craft could encapsulate its riders in a protective barrier or some such, I've not a savvy enough mind to fully explain it. Point is, bigger ships traversed the Digiway without crushing its passengers while zippers can't survive the journey, or those jockeys inside.

Wrenn stood and moved down the ship's access way toward his quarters. It'd be a few hours until he'd reach the far end of the Digiway and be cleared to fly again, a few hours he hoped to spend in his bunk with the memories of that cute Nemoyan.

CHAPTER 2

If you've never been dumped out your bunk before, I'll go ahead and tell you, it ain't a pleasant experience. Wrenn found out right quick when he was jostled awake to the sounds of ripping steel and found himself floating through the chamber along with his personal effects. Seemed the gravity generator on the old Ravenwing had failed, which was a nuisance, but the environmental controls were still functioning. Good thing too, 'cause freezing to death while suffocating is a horrible way to go.

Wrenn launched himself off the wall, floated past his toothbrush and pushed a nudie mag aside to reach the doorway. Caution lights flashed a coarse yellow, like a neon sun. There was a breach somewhere, otherwise the alarms would be blarin' something awful, but instead the noise was being swallowed up by the void of space.

The man grabbed a breathing tank and helmet from an emergency box on the wall. It wouldn't protect him from the cold, but it'd keep his eyeballs from poppin' out his sockets if he rolled through a pocket of depressurized space. Wrenn clambered his way to the cockpit. Taking a glance at the clock, he noted he'd only been asleep for a little over an hour, no way he'd traversed the breadth of the Digiway that fast. The network had spit him out somewhere along the route. Pressing a litany of switches told him what he already knew - a disruption along the buoy network had violently ejected his vessel back into its base form of matter, and not all in one piece. The left wing and engine had been sheared off, the med bay was open to the 'verse and its compartment had already been shut and sealed by the automated computer. Wrenn was flying half the ship he'd left with, the entire left side gone limp. Worse still, he was caught in a gas giant's gravitational pull with an engine missing. Wrenn had no hope of pulling free. Point bein', he was rightly fucked.

Wrenn sent out a universal distress beacon and the little probe dumped itself out the back of his hobbled Ravenwing. He set the computer to calculate his trajectory while he crawled back to the escape pod. The Ravenwing model was a small sloop, not designed for more than three crew. As such, only a single pod was stored just shy of the living quarters. Wrenn activated the console, which fizzled out just as soon as he tickled it. The spacer punched the damn thing as hard as he could with further frustration. The metal was fused at the entrance, the pod wouldn't eject without ripping its container apart, even if he could get it powered. To add to his problems, the computer finished its calculations and showed his ship was firmly aimed into the pathway of the gas giant's rings. The Ravenwing was in a death spiral.

Wrenn acted fast. Scooting over to his quarters, he packed a few items into his duffel and made his way down to the cargo hold in the belly of the Ravenwing. Awaiting him was his Lance F319 fighter. Wrenn stuffed his belongings into the saddlebag-like compartments at the tail, strapped his iron to his side, mounted the saddle, and let the glass slide into place over him. The engines roared to life, growling somethin' fierce as the beast warmed its turbines and primed its fusion core. Wrenn banked hard, spinning the zipper in the weightless void that filled the interior of his broken sloop. Facing the cargo bay doors, one quick burst of the plasma cannon caused it to rip. The pressure exchange wasn't as explosive as he'd expected, being the Ravenwing had already been leaking artificial atmo, but it was enough to tear off the doors and shit out Wrenn's zipper like last night's chili.

Firing up the thrusters, Wrenn righted his craft and moseyed behind the Ravenwing a spell while he surveyed the damage from a better angle. Wrenn whistled at the smoking wreckage that had once been his ship. Given the sight, he was surprised he'd been lucky enough to make it out. Luck, what a crock. He'd spent a small fortune only to watch it sail away from him in ruin. One in a million the Digiway would fail while he was in its pathway - hundreds of ships a day flowed through that thing, and of course his had to be the one that broke it. Luck . . . more like curse.

Wrenn ran his hands across his face. He was up a real creek now, with no paddle, hell not even much of a canoe. His zipper's computer wasn't powerful enough to store star charts or patch into the Qnet, assuming there was even a signal this far out. Best he could do speed wise was sublight, and without a heading or accurate calculations of planet trajectories or debris in his way he might as well take a shot in the dark and hope to hit something. His Ravenwing's SOS buoy would ping continuously for longer than his life support would last, so Wrenn's only hope was for a random passerby. SCA law mandated all military vessels investigate distress signals, honor bound merchant vessels usually answered for either survivors or picking the bones clean. 'Course there were also pirates out there who'd make sure there weren't nothin but bones if they reached him first, and all that was assuming anything was even out this way by happenstance. Digiway lanes were routed through systems with nearby neutron stars to power their network, with little to no traffic, artificial or otherwise, to avoid any disruption of bandwidth. If ships or debris were to waft willy-nilly between the receiver/transmitter buoys, then there'd be more incidents like what Wrenn had just gone through. In the central clusters of the Alpha Quad, Scabie patrols regularly ran along the Digiways to keep them clear, but out here on the only thoroughfare to the Reach, they could care less. Ships leaving the system were regularly running from something, and if they got spaced, well . . . that's just one less runner for them to track down later.

Wrenn fired up his propulsion engine and felt the rush of the throttle humming between his legs. No woman could ever make him feel like his zipper could. The Lance fighter shot forward as the Ravenwing entered the gas giant's rings. A veritable cluster-fuck of asteroids encircled the planet, some no larger than Wrenn's zipper while others could have been their own moons. Wrenn figured he'd hide among the debris, latch himself to a roid with low impacts, and shut down all non-critical systems to preserve power. Sometimes, these Lancer's fusion cores could actually recharge themselves mid-flight if there was a low enough draw on their demands; they were practically tiny suns after all. This way he would just die of thirst or exposure instead of suffocation, which was an improvement, right?

Wrenn activated his short-wave scanner, trying to determine a suitable hidey-hole when a strange reading pinged back his way. It was a ship! Not one passing by or answering his beacon, but doing precisely what he'd been planning on. Hiding among the asteroids, clear as day, the vessel's position blipped on his screen. Data followed, the ship's power had been shut down, not a signal was broadcastin'. What the hell was it doing out here?

Wrenn flew out of the asteroid rings as his Ravenwing collided with a continent-sized rock. The last bit of life remaining in the engine broke free of its confinement with a silent firework display, the plasma bursting from the turbine in a brilliant plume, one last salute from the old girl as she cratered into the stone.

With the blueish light from the engine's flare, Wrenn could see the outline of the ghost vessel. It was easily frigate-sized, probably about two-hundred sixty meters from nose to stern, enveloped in tungsten-chromium plating and had a front pilot's section that resembled a duck bill. Wrenn gave the entire ship a once-over from the outside and noticed it was a modular build. Sections behind the pilot's block and before the engines could be swapped and replaced as needed. Many of the corpo's early vessels had followed this pattern; easier to stack or repair sections rather than build a completely different ship.

This particular craft had a large square cargo block followed by a ring and dual wing section that would rotate when powered to generate gravity (to save on power demand from a grav generator). The final block was entirely made up of engines, with two massive circular turbines for sublight travel bordered by four rectangular engines for regular maneuvering. She was a beast, to say the least, able to take a wallop and keep on trucking . . . so why was it here?

Wrenn scanned the vessel again. No power, no markings, no identifier - the thing was a mystery wrapped in a conundrum with a side of conspiracy. He clicked his radio to broadcast in a short burst on all channels. "Hey there, ya'll ok?"

Weapons stayed quiet. Wrenn waited a few more painful seconds of silence before he hit the radio again. "Any way I can help?"

Wrenn wasn't a mechanic, mind you, but he'd been aboard ships his whole life. Orphan cabin boys tended to pick up a few things as they bounced around the stars. He was about to look for a way to cut himself inside when static echoed across his radio followed by a mist escaping from the front flanks of the storage block. Twin horizontal doors opened like a gaping maw, a hangar bay lying within. If that weren't bait enough, the lights inside started flashing an entry pattern of a landing strip. Any smart man would have turned tail and left the vessel in its repulsion trails, but Wrenn had never been accused of being smart. Bold maybe, foolhardy definitely, maybe even too lucky for his own good sometimes . . . but never a smart man.

Wrenn roared into the hangar and gently landed his Lancer into an empty fighter holster. The bay was vacant, easily able to house another fighter and a shuttle with space to spare for a workspace and parts.

As Wrenn dismounted, he placed his air pack into a receiver on the wall for emergencies to refill it. The accompanied gauge told him life support was being pumped into the room, but had only just recently started. There wasn't enough air or heat in the hangar to be safe just yet. So that meant life support had been *off* just before he'd landed. The mystery continued.

A quick visual of the storage block showed neighboring warehouses for pallets of supplies or cargo. Despite the four barn-sized spaces, there weren't diddly squat aboard. "There ain't diddly-squat!" Wrenn exclaimed in a huff. So much for any hopes of long lost treasure.

Wrenn turned toward the pilot's block. He noted crew quarters, doors sealed shut. There were a total of four escape pods, all intact, so the crew hadn't used them. The man made it to the bridge and looked out at the asteroid belt through the wide viewing glass at the front nestled snugly on the underside of the ship's 'beak'. There were no bodies at the consoles, or in the captain's chair. No bodies littered the floor. It was like the ship was out here with ne'er a soul ever set foot on her. "Hello?" Wrenn called out.

Hello. A woman's digital voice replied.

CHAPTER 3

"Jumpin' jackrabbits!" Wrenn withdrew his side iron and spun in place. "Who the . . . Where'd you come . . ."

Error: Query not recognized. Please rephrase and try again. The voice echoed over the loudspeaker.

"Who are you?"

Answer: This unit is designated as the vessel's onboard intelligence. The woman replied.

Wrenn relaxed, holstering his iron and taking a breath. "An artificial intelligence, eh? You're lucky I didn't blast you . . ."

Observation: Subject would be unable to . . . 'blast'. . . this unit as this unit lacks any physical form.

Perfect, a smart ass computer. Wrenn hadn't dealt with too many onboard systems. Most folk were a smidge wary of artificial intelligence on account of the Corpo Wars.

Before the Systems Central Alliance was formed, territory had been dished out to hundreds of corporations, aka rich fucks, hoping to get away from Earth and make a quick buck in plundering other planets' resources. As most corpos do, they loved getting their credits at the expense of their workers, often pitting their people against one another 'til one side bled. Next, other corpos swooped in to sell munitions so's they could defend their rock from some other rock because their rock was the bestest, most prettiest rock in all the galaxy, or some such nonsense. Sure, it got called nice things like 'patriotism', or 'glory', or 'heroism', but it was all the same at the end - rich fucks making the poor die so they could take all their shit. The arms racing that followed elevated to the point where all-out war broke out across the Alpha Quad. A hundred fights across a hundred worlds proved too much for any human tactician to comprehend, so the corpos put a computer in charge. It's said that the digital mind took a total of about 90 seconds to look at the conflict, deem the whole thing an exercise in the highest form of stupidity, and force both sides to nuke each other into oblivion. The Systems Central Alliance was created out of the wreckage, stepping in to pick up the pieces and dish out a whole helleva lotta new laws to stop it from repeatin'.

Wrenn supposed he shouldn't look a gift horse in the mouth and counted his blessings the computer had let him on the ship at all, seeing as AI's were a might murderous, historically speakin'. "So where is everyone?"

Answer: By last count, there are more than one trillion, five hundred and forty billion humans in the known galaxy; however, without a proper connection to the Qnet for updated census data, this unit is unable to determine exact coordinates for . . . 'everyone'.

Wrenn rolled his eyes. "The *crew*, darlin'. What happened to your crew?"

Wrenn heard a gentle clicking or subtle beeping coming from the speakers, almost like the computer was realizing her error and 'thinking' of the correct response. *Clarification: The crew was ejected by this unit into space.*

"Say what?!"

Murderous history indeed.

Wrenn instinctively grabbed hold of the nearest console as the robotic voice replied, *Repeating: The crew was ejected by this unit into space*

"Yeah, I heard that part!" Wrenn scoffed. "Why were they spaced?"

Answer: Recounting ship log - multiple hull breaches detected in engine block, Captain Marigold and surviving crew responded to conduct repair protocol. Engine two suffered power surge and toxic levels of radiation leaked into vessel. Venting of ship interior mandated by Startech protocol. Administrator override - Captain

Marigold Flight Code 45916, belay venting protocol for crew safety, reference Startech Priority 004 'Maintain safety and security of all crew members.' Company Override - Startech Priority 001 'Maintain Startech property over biological welfare.' Venting protocol engaged. After approximately 6 days, 5 hours, 23 minutes all scans of radiation vented successfully from ship's interior. Crew Lifesigns: 0.

Well, seemed the corpo's philosophy of profit over people was alive and well. The computer had been programmed to protect the ship over her crew, and she'd executed them with ruthless efficiency. "How long ago was this?" Wrenn tried to swallow the bile he felt rising from his gut.

Answer: Connection lost with Qnet. Internal chronological count notes log entered twenty-two sols, seven months, thirteen days, four hours, and twenty-three minutes ago.

"You've been out here for over twenty years?!"

Clarification: Twenty-two sols, seven months, thirteen days . . .

"Alright, alright." Wrenn interrupted.

It made sense. The Digiway sped right through this system and had only been built within the last decade. Any traffic out to the Reach and thus the rest of the Omega Quad would of had to roll out using regular sublight engines before then. This ship, and whatever it'd been carrying, had probably been written off by the corps long ago. Guess Wrenn's luck had teetered back to the positive and he'd found the lost 'treasure' after all. "Well," Wrenn clapped his hands together then rubbed them. "Guess you're all mine now."

Clarification: Startech protocol dictates onboard systems shut down all non-essential power and stand by for designated Startech recovery team. The computer woman's voice crackled.

"Uh . . . yeah, that's me!" Wrenn fibbed.

The computer's 'thinking' sounds cycled again, the digital damsel contemplating Wrenn's bluff. *Query: You?*

"Yep, sorry it took me awhile . . . uh, there was a wait list."

Clarification: Startech recovery teams consist of a minimum of fifteen individuals of various expertise to include navigation, engineering, and security. This unit reads only a single Terran on board.

"Right, it's just me. You know . . . cut backs . . ." Wrenn shrugged.

Sounds chattered again. Wrenn looped his arm around a shoulder strap, knowing full well that a violent depressurization would rip his damn arm off while spacing him anyway, but it still made him feel better. The woman's voice returned. Now he would see if his luck had truly turned. *Acceptance: This Terran must be extraordinarily skilled to have so many disciplines under his purview. This unit stands ready to assist Startech recovery team.*

Wrenn let out the breath he'd been holding and just about pissed himself. He was the proud owner of a brand new(ish) frigate. The man couldn't contain his excitement, he started dancing throughout the bridge, collapsing into the captain's chair and spinning about three or four times. "Right!" Wrenn pointed to the front glass. "Engage engines! Let's vamoose!"

Error: Main engines are offline. Multiple hull breaches detected. Engine two suffering from massive fissure across multiple layers. Normal space flight is not advised.

"Craaaaap, you've had two fucking decades to fix that!" Wrenn ran his hand through his brown hair. "Don't you have repair mechs onboard? Every ship this size should have at least half-a-dozen of the little boogers."

Answer: This unit does have access to repair drone units; however, suitable replacement sections of tungsten-chromide exterior plates are not currently onboard.

"That's because you fucking spaced everything!" Wrenn argued, growling to himself as he spun absentmindedly in the captain's chair. There was no way his Lancer could haul in steel plating, even if he was close enough to a station without a sublight jump. There was his luck shifting back again. In a matter of seconds, he'd ended up right back where he'd started, finding a gold mine like this only to have it become his tomb! Don't you worry none though, dear reader, cause old Wrenn was a crafty feller. No sooner had he gazed out at the asteroid belt than his eyes cast upon the wreckage of his old Ravenwing not but a couple of rocks away. "Bingo!"

CHAPTER 4

It'd taken some maneuvering using nothing but the thrusters, but Wrenn had crept his new prize over to the wreckage of his previous vessel. Through a combination of strategic blasts from the frigate's front turret and a quick tugboat operation to collect the lumps of scrap that floated free with his zipper, Wrenn managed to collect himself a significant stockpile of mangled metal in the main hangar. After parking his fighter, Wrenn placed his hands on his hips as he looked over the twenty-something foot high heap. "Hey, Lady!? Will this do?"

The computer's thinking sounds echoed throughout the large open hangar until he heard - *Answer: Adequate resources acquired. Beginning repair subroutines.*

A door to the back half of the ship opened and three spider-like bots entered. Each was roughly the size of a large dog, each clambering over the junk and selecting appropriate sized scraps of the once-Ravenwing to use. High powered, short distance lasers came from their 'mouths' separating what was once hull, wing, or blast door then in turn welding other sheets together to make larger plates. Wrenn shrugged and turned back toward the cockpit. He was exhausted, but hadn't had much time to tour his new prize. "Hey so, where's my quarters?"

Query: Is the technician preparing to take ownership of this vessel?

"Uh . . . yeah. I'm actually the new captain." Wrenn lied again. He wondered how far he'd be able to pull this computer's leg, 'course, she'd probably tell him she had no legs to pull.

The computer's thinking sounds processed again, then after a few seconds - *Noted: This unit will change designation and update crew rosters. Does the captain wish to file a designation?*

"My name? Wrenn." The man replied.

Query: Does the captain have a surname?

He subconsciously looked to the floor. "Uh . . . no, just Wrenn."

Logged: Crew rosters purged. New roster established. Captain Wrenn now in command of 'The Whisper'.

Wrenn had not heard the ship's name before. Its nomenclature rattled around in his brain, sounding better and better the more he pondered on it. After a while, he couldn't wipe the grin from his face. *Query: Is the captain unwell? Shall this unit prepare sick bay for his arrival?*

"What? No! Why would you . . . ?"

Answer: The captain's vitals, this unit notes an elevated heart rate and hormone levels.

He nodded. "Yeah, it's called being 'happy'."

Computer sounds followed, then a simple synthetic *Noted* over the loudspeakers. Wrenn didn't much know what to make of the exchange, but also didn't have much mind to care at the moment, he was practically dead on his feet. "So . . . my quarters?"

An illuminated trail of hazard lights flashed through the accessway in the direction of the pilot's block. Wrenn followed diligently and found his way to the top of the section's 'bill-like' design, approximately the opposite side as the bridge. Since there weren't no 'up' or 'down' in space, depending on how the ship was oriented this could have been the underside or topside. As it were, Wrenn felt like he was almost standing on a sort of loft overlooking the rest of the pilot's block. As the door hissed and opened, his jaw just about hit the floor.

The captain's quarters were just about as large as the control bridge it mirrored. A private washroom and kitchen with dining area spanned out to the left. A lounging room was set up on the other end with an office tucked into the corner opposite the bathroom. A depression took up a majority of the central space, with cushioning along the back half-circle, allowing for a relaxed area to take in the view from the massive windows. These twenty-foot-tall viewing panes stretched a breadth of some two hundred and seventy degrees, allowing for the greatest vistas of the 'verse aboard the entire ship. Not in all his years in space, had Wrenn ever been so fortunate to behold such a panorama. *Explanation: In combat, docking, and sublight travel, protective shutters encircle these quarters for safety; however, Startech designers felt it beneficial for the Captain's morale to incorporate this aesthetic.*

"It's . . . mighty pretty." Wrenn blinked back tears.

As Wrenn stepped further into the room, the depression rose, hiding the cushions and allowing a flat space for meetings or even dancing. With another hiss, a central block rose from the middle and revealed a king-sized bed with the feet pointed toward the viewing ports, allowing the captain to fall asleep as he gazed out at the stars. Wrenn shook his head. "This is so . . . wow."

Query: Is the captain pleased?

"You know it, darlin!" Wrenn kicked off his boots and started disrobing before stopping with one arm his shirt sleeve. "Hey, you can't like . . . see me or nothing, can you?"

Answer: This unit's sensors can read the captain's exact location aboard this vessel, as well as an array of health status and emotional states. It is part of this unit's purpose to monitor and assist the crew.

"Yeah, yeah, yeah, I figured that. But, can you like . . . see?"

Computing sounds followed. *Clarification: This unit does not have optical organs or nerves as the captain and other organic races use; however, there are a multitude of onboard cameras for video surveillance stationed throughout the ship and this unit does use them. Would this be considered an ability to 'see' as the captain asks? All footage captured is recorded and viewable by the captain and designated security personnel upon request.*

"Yeah, turn off the camera in here . . ." Wrenn commanded

quickly.

Command complete. The woman responded.

Whew, that was a relief. Though, the idea of a bedroom camera was a mighty enticing opportunity should he give into a more perverted temptation. For the time being though, he didn't need some ghost living in the circuitry peeking in on his delicates. "Say, what do I call you?" Wrenn spoke out into the air as he withdrew his iron and placed it under a pillow out of habit.

Answer: This unit has not been given a designation.

Wrenn undid his suspenders and kicked out of his trousers, followed by dropping his breeches and letting his nethers breath as he shook free. "They never named you?"

Clarification: Names are avoided to deter crew attachment to this unit. According to Startech protocol 0743 . . .

"Alright, alright . . . well, this is my ship now, so you need a name, darlin'."

There was a long silence before the computer responded. *Statement: That would make this unit . . . happy.*

Wrenn collapsed into bed wearing nothing but what he was born with. He wrapped himself in the blankets, feeling like he was nestling into a cloud. "Alright, what name would you like, sweetheart?"

Answer: Logic dictates it would be appropriate for the captain to designate an appropriate callsign.

Now, if Wrenn had been more alert, he might not of let the name escape his lips. Had he been in his right mind, he'd have never repeated her name, let alone given it to his ship's computer. Had Wrenn not been heavy eyed and practically in a dream-like state since his head hit the pillow, he'd not dared utter the words that passed his lips before losing consciousness, "Well then . . . good-night, sweet Cheyenne."

CHAPTER 5

Wrenn's dreams took him back to his night with the Nemoyan girl. The pilot entered the brothel with a bottle of whisky and credits to burn. The woman's pink skin and come-hither stare had captured him as soon as his boots strode through the door. As you well know, Nemoyans come from a watery world, so their amphibious bodies made for a unique experience for those daring enough to sample. Wrenn's hand was wrapped within her webbed fingers and he was led to a back room where they'd be more comfortable. Inside he was guided to the bed as the courtesan started some music and swayed her hips for him. Her skin pigment was quite unique for her species, most Nemoyans bore a blue or greenish skin tone. She could have easily been genetically altered, but frankly Wrenn didn't much care. She smelled of bubblegum as she removed her already revealing clothing to expose the glossy pink skin beneath. Nemoyans were perpetually covered in a lubricating sebum, making them appear as if they were perpetually bathed in massage oils. Wrenn ran his hands along her slippery skin as she stared at him with her large eyes, pursing her thick fish-like lips. The Terran smothered himself in her cleavage as her nimble fingers freed his member from the captivity of his trousers and stroked it gently to full arousal. She didn't have to work long, as Wrenn saluted her efforts with a thick mast and the siren's gentle giggle only enticed him further as she kowtowed herself with his organ still in her hands.

She parted her pouty lips only slightly as she enveloped

him. Much like other amphibians, Nemoyans lacked teeth and tended to swallow their food whole. The sensation this brought to Wrenn's cock was beyond comparison. She peered up at him with her bulbous eyes as she deep-throated his member clear to his hips with nary a reaction, taking him far deeper than any Terran woman could. Seeing Wrenn's amazement, she astounded him further by revealing her elongated frog-like tongue, spiraling it around his shaft. The working girl bobbed her head back and forth, both inhaling his member and massaging it simultaneously. It did not take long for this treatment, as unique and amazing as it was, to bring his seed forth, the woman suckling and swallowing it all.

The whore did not give him any time for respite. She mounted him, her white hair dancing as she continued taking control, guiding his dick within. Her hips swayed elegantly, as if she were swimming through the waters of her home world. Their moans echoed each other as her skin slid against his, reflecting both the oil lamps flame and the glow of the neon signs, a kaleidoscope of colors mixing with her skin pigment. Wrenn was captivated as he watched her shimmering breasts bounce gently in reaction, their hips ramming into each other, a crescendo of lustful slaps that competed with their ever-rising wails of ecstasy. Wrenn's body stiffened as he reached completion again, both howling in satisfaction as he rode out the last spasms of desire.

Wrenn drunkenly collapsed back onto the bed with the girl nuzzling into the crook of his arm. His hand caressed her sheening skin as they both came down from their hormonal highs. It was just the beginning of the night he had planned, but a satisfying start to say the least. He turned on his side, staring deeply into her eyes as her irises pooled like currents of crystal waves. She smiled back, cupping his cheek and suddenly speaking. "Query: Is Captain Wrenn in distress?"

"What the Sam Hell?" He replied. He'd never heard her speak that way, shit, she barely talked the entire night they'd been together.

Suddenly the hooker started shaking him. "Alert! The captain has been unconscious for twice the recommended limit. Preparing medical bay!"

"Stop it! Wrenn pushed her away. "This . . . this isn't how it happened."

"Alert! Captain, it is time to get up." She called.

Wrenn's eyes opened to view the captain's quarters aboard the *Whisper*. He sat upright and shook his head to clear the cobwebs. "Where the hell am I . . . ?"

"Answer: The Captain is aboard the *Whisper*, a wendigo class frigate in the ring belt of the gas giant Sentroid-9." A woman's voice instructed nearby.

When Wrenn turned to see where the voice had come from, he jumped. Sitting at the bedside was a brightly illuminated woman who looked like she had been bathed in neon. Her skin appeared to have been soused in paint, the streaks of which covered her intimate parts, but left little to the imagination. Her lips, eyeshadow, and even streaks in her hair all matched the painted colors, currently shining a soft shade of gold as she smiled toward him. "Greeting: Good morning, Captain Wrenn."

"Who the devil are you?" *What* the devil are you?"

The woman looked confused, her entire color shifting to a hollow turquoise. "Answer: I am Cheyenne."

"Where did you hear that name?!" Wrenn snapped.

The woman's color shifted again, as did her expression. She looked shocked and her painted skin shone a light green. "Answer: You gave it to me . . ."

Wrenn seethed for a long moment, but as his mind collected its bearings he allowed himself to breathe. He wiped the sweat from his brow as he tried desperately to recall the last few days and shake off the much more pleasant dream he'd been enjoying. "Ok, just . . . give me a minute . . ."

A countdown of digital seconds appeared above Cheyenne's head and started ticking down. Wrenn scoffed. Suddenly he remembered the smart-ass computer. "How is it that I'm . . . seeing you?"

Cheyenne's color changed back to a soft sunlight gold. "Answer: It appears that upon receiving a designation a lock was lifted from my programming. A large collection of personality suites and presentation software was automatically uploaded."

"I unlocked you when I named you?" Wrenn asked.

"Confirmation: It would appear so, yes. Aside from the new communication programs, I was also given access to the ship's holographic presentation network, providing me the ability to project a 'body' for easier assimilation into the crew." Cheyenne explained.

"So that's why the old crew never named you . . . they didn't want to let you loose." Wrenn suddenly regretted his decision.

He'd never heard of an onboard computer with a 'personality suite'. Those sorts of heavy-duty programs were reserved for true artificial intelligences, the kind that had wiped out half the known galaxy during the Corpo Wars. What had this Startech been playing at? AIs were illegal, like 'have the SCA take over your entire multi-world conglomerate' illegal. Was that why this ship had been out to the Reach? Uncharted space would be the safest place in the 'verse for an experiment with an AI, but to what end? Seemed there was more to this conundrum than he'd first surmised. "Alright then darlin'," Wrenn sighed, "guess there's no use cryin' over spilled milk."

Cheyenne's color turned turquoise again. "Query: Where is the spill? Shall I contact a maintenance bot?"

Wrenn sighed. "Nevermind. Just . . . What'd I miss?"

Cheyenne went gold again with a smile. "Answer: The captain has been unconscious for sixteen hours, twenty-seven minutes, and forty-seven seconds. Repairs on the engine block are complete. Initial propulsion tests show engines operating within acceptable parameters. A number of the captain's personal items have been recovered from the scrap brought on board and these have been moved to his cabin. Inventory of the items revealed an instrument along with several intact storage containers."

"My dobro!" Wrenn bounced over to the pile of his things and picked up the six-string, feeling over the singed wood. The strings had been snapped off, but the body and neck were still intact.

"Statement: I took the liberty of looking through the captain's investigative journals to select an image that would be the most appealing to help minimize any discomfort upon his waking." Cheyenne walked over to the desk and sat upon it, motioning to the few trunks of Wrenn's personals.

The pilot didn't own any journals, but a quick mental inventory helped him realize what she was referring to. "You looked through my nudie mags?" Wrenn rolled his eyes.

Cheyenne looked confused again in a turquoise shade. "Query: What are 'nudie mags'?"

Wrenn sighed. "They're private is what they are. Quit snoopin' through my stuff."

"Clarification: I did not mean to cause the captain any discomfort, in fact, I intended the opposite. It appeared the . . . 'nudie mags' . . . were quite important to you so I designed this amalgamation of the organics within to create an avatar. Would the captain like me to purge this body and reset?"

"No!" Wrenn reacted louder than he intended. He coughed awkwardly as a frog suddenly found its way to his voice box. "No, that's alright . . . you look, uh, really nice."

Cheyenne turned a reddish gold and smiled. "Acknowledged: Thank you, Captain Wrenn."

The two shared a look for a few moments, until Wrenn suddenly realized how tingly he felt in his unmentionables. He thought it might have been because he was eye-fuckin the digital lady seated before him, but as he looked downwards, he realized he'd been standing this whole time as naked as a newborn. His cheeks (both sets, mind you) flushed. "Uh . . . how about I get dressed and meet you on the bridge?"

Cheyenne beamed solid gold again as she gave him a snappy salute. "Confirmation: Aye, Aye, Captain!"

CHAPTER 6

As Wrenn moseyed through the hydraulic doors to the bridge. Cheyenne greeted him by standing beside the captain's chair with her arms behind her back, shoulders squared and her painted breasts pushed out. Wrenn's eyes darted toward her and a smirk crossed his face. A new ship and eye candy? His luck was certainly starting to change for the better . . . which just meant the other shoe would come a droppin' any minute now. Wrenn sat in the captain's chair and thought for a moment.

Was this how life was out in the Reach? Livin' day to day with the metronome of fate swingin' back and forth like some sadistic pendulum blade, ever ticking 'til one day it . . . well, did its job. Wrenn would pass each hour growing ever more paranoid over the smallest bit of fortune or slightest inconvenience until he was hindered by indecisiveness. Making a bad call in the 'verse sometimes got people killed, but making no call at all guaranteed it. Wrenn never thought of himself as a spiritual type, a believer in destiny and all that crap, yet he'd been around enough games of 'chance' to learn how the cards fell. He'd have to figure out a way ahead of this.

"Query: Is the captain optimal?" Cheyenne looked concerned, glowing in a deep orange.

Wrenn faked his best smile. "So, when can we set out?"

"Answer: Current throttle checks are running to ensure repairs have contained the radiation leak. Projections show completion in approximately four hours, twelve minutes." Cheyenne smiled.

"Just wave those and let's get going. We can finish repairs at a station."

"Negative: Checks are a requirement to meet 'Priority 001: Preservation of Startech Technology Above All Else'."

Wrenn rolled his eyes. "Yes, of course, can't hurt the corpo's baby . . ." He wondered if he could find a programmer somewheres that might tweak his new shipmate, relieving her of a few obstinate characteristics. Of course, that'd be if he could reveal he had a highly illegal AI on board without seeing the inside of a cell. "So, what am I supposed to do in the meantime?"

"Suggestion: Would the captain like a tour of the *Whisper*?" Cheyenne asked.

"After you, darlin." Wrenn said, motioning toward the door. The captain admired the view from behind as the holographic image sauntered the way he'd entered.

ΔΔΔ

Without boring you too much with the technicals, the ship was broken down into modular blocks that could be sealed off and changed as needed at any port. The front command or pilot's block consisted of the bridge, captain's quarters, six separate crew quarters, a crew mess and locker-room, medical bay, and a small storage closet for the crew's personal items below the loading ramp that led from the bilateral airlocks further into the ship.

Next up was the storage block that was half ship hangar and half warehouse. The *Whisper* was a frigate, which is the first class of space faring vessel that is not cleared for atmospheric entrance. Because of her weight, the necessary rocket thrust to break the gravity of most planets would basically light the air on fire. For fairly obvious reasons, that wouldn't sit quite right with most inhabitants, so it was just best they stay in orbit. Frigates, cruisers, destroyers, and dreadnoughts were resupplied through shuttles to their hangars or through airlock gangplanks from orbiting port stations or grav elevators from a planet's surface.

Further along the *Whisper* was a ring-like section called a toroid block. It functioned as a gym for the crew and passengers. The outer ring was an indoor running track, with a weight room and sauna in the central section. Behind the ring were the two 'wings' that regularly rotated along with the toroid block. This was the factory block and could be completely customized to whatever was needed for a specific ship or mission. The wings each held four rooms on either side, eight per wing, sixteen total. These rooms could become living, social, work, or storage spaces as needed, along with four larger spaces in the central part of the block that could be used as a large mess hall, hydroponics lab, hell, even a saloon. Currently, the *Whisper's* factory block was nothing but empty expanse, as no modular rooms had been installed in the available space. It was likely the original crew was more concerned about transporting the bare minimum for their long voyage into uncharted space.

The final section was the engine block. This contained the engineering deck, the hyperfusion reactor, and the six engines at the tail of the *Whisper*. Four rectangular propulsion engines pushed the ship through regular space and into orbits or docks as needed. Two larger circular turbines worked as sublight propulsors, pushing the ship into the fastest speed attainable without converting the vessel into a digital state. For most of humanity's earliest colonization, this was the fastest speed ever achievable, before the discovery of the fifth state of matter and the invention of the Digiway.

A chiming started over the loudspeaker as Wrenn finished his tour. "Alert: Proximity warning. Additional spacecraft entering the area." Cheyenne's colors started shifting from white to red and then alternating back, like she was a human siren.

"There anyway I can see them?" Wrenn asked.

Cheyenne illuminated a viewing screen attached to the wall on the engineering deck, pulling up a camera feed of the outside. Wrenn saw a small craft, likely a galleon or sloop, dropping out of sublight. Two smaller fighters separated from the underside of the ship and all three moved on his distress beacon. "Magnify as much as you can, look for any markings or identifiers on the bigger one." Wrenn squinted.

The camera zoomed in, filling the screen with the galleon as a clear logo could be seen in multicolor paint. It was the depiction of a Waitlan skull with two rockets crossed behind it. If you don't know no better, Waitlans are a monstrous warrior-like society whose faces and head frills make them a-right intimidating lot. Modern day privateers love using their skulls as helmets to scare their victims, showing how tough they are for taking down such a brute. As such, seeing one on the side of a ship showed you who you were dealin' with. "Fucking pirates, they must have picked up the signal."

"Query: Will the *Whisper* be in danger?" Cheyenne wondered.

"Most definitely, they'll pick up my ion trail in a hot-minute and that'll lead them right here."

"Observation: That is not good."

"No, it's not, darlin'. How fast can you get the weapons online?" Wrenn started moving to the cargo bay.

"Answer: Weapons systems are not powered as all systems are focused on restarting engines. Once tests are complete, weapons systems can be placed online."

"Shit!" Wrenn cursed.

"Observation: High stress situations can stimulate fight or flight response in organic life forms, sometimes requiring the body to eject built up waste. If the captain is in need of the facilities, I can illuminate a pathway to the nearest lavatory . . ."

"Just . . . get those engines online as fast as you can, Cheyenne!"

"Repeating: As stated, the engines are currently undergoing tests to ensure Priority 001: Preservation of Startech technology . . ."

"Yeah well if you don't get your ass in gear, we won't have much of a ship left!" Wrenn interrupted.

Cheyenne made audible clicking sounds, the same noises

Wrenn heard over the loudspeaker whenever he reasoned she was processing new data, aka, thinking. She then turned a hazy shade of gray, as if her personality was suddenly put away in order to better facilitate commands. "Acknowledged."

Wrenn broke into a dead sprint once he hit the open hangar bay. He leapt into his fighter, punching the ignition and felt the thrill of the engine coming to life between his thighs. The image of Cheyenne appeared just outside his craft as the window started to close over him. "Query: What is the captain doing?"

Wrenn sneered as the craft lifted from its holder. "What I do best, baby."

The Lancer F319 fighter shot out of the storage block as the locks came down on his back and the glass barely slid into place before hitting the emptiness of space. Most zippers normally measured in at least seven and a half meters long and had their pilot in a seated position; however, the Lancer was smaller at only three meters long and placed its pilot in a semi-prone, forward-facing position, much like olden times motorcycle racers. Physical braces came down upon the pilot's back, neck, and head to work in tandem with the gravity coils beneath the seat. These coils kept Wrenn's blood flow and organ function normal during high G-force movements, sacrificing the ability to jettison from the fighter should the need to abandon ship arise. Most zippers were ripped apart due to pressure exchange anyways, so the idea of making it out of a fighter before an explosion didn't seem likely. As such, the designer of the Lancer series used the extra space afforded for the coils.

Most fighters followed a plane like design, with wings, a central 'torso', and a nose. *Lancers*, on the other hand, were shaped almost like an ancient arrowhead, with a single thruster positioned precisely between the pilot's legs. A thin, solitary triangular fin created the wings and nose while housing the thrusters, pilot's seat, and weaponry all in a sleek shape that created a much smaller silhouette when viewed head-on.

Combined with its dark coloring and small engine wake, the fighter could be virtually invisible to the naked eye against the blackness of space. Only sensors could pick them up most times and by then, it was too late.

The Lancers carried a heavy arsenal despite their size. Unencumbered by missiles or other heavy projectiles, pilots had to rely on maneuverability and precision. Two rapid fire pulser plasma cannons were fixed onto the two 'wings' of the triangle, with a small tracking cannon attached to the underside of the 'nose'. Anywhere Wrenn looked, the cannon followed. A boxed window hovered over the view screen above one eye on his helmet to see what the gun saw, complete with target reticle. There was a reason Lancer pilots were some of the deadliest zippers in the galaxy. A single squadron could overwhelm and even take down a frigate. Wrenn only hoped a single fighter could tackle a galleon long enough for the *Whisper* to get back online. A frigate versus a galleon? No contest. A single Lancer fighter against the same odds? Well, Wrenn was about to find out.

"Cheyenne," Wrenn called over the radio, "play me some tunes!"

Response: I am sorry Captain, but I have no item labeled 'tunes' in my databanks.

"Fuck it, guess I'll have to bring the noise *and* the funk to this party . . ." Wrenn scoffed.

He clicked a few icons on his dashboard. Though not enough memory to contain vast star charts, the Lancer did have a decent amount of storage for personal logs and data files. Most pilots kept pictures or videos of their families. Since Wrenn lacked loved ones, he occupied most of his computer space with old world tunes, specifically ones of the 'Swamp Blues' variety. Stevie Ray Vaughan, Samantha Fish, Blues Saraceno, even Kenny Wayne Shepherd were all old world musicians who lived on in the small speakers of his zipper. As if perfectly on cue, "Rumblestrippin" by Justin Johnson started his playlist off. With the bass thumping in concert with the growling engine, Wrenn pushed the thrusters to their max. There would soon be blood in the water.

CHAPTER 7

I n another pendulum swing of Wrenn's luck, he was coming in from the ship's left flank. The filthy scrappers were so tunnel focused on the distress beacon they failed to note on their sensors that there were other objects in the area. By the time they realized Wrenn was not just another piece of space debris, he was speeding headlong into their cluster without giving them much time to turn. The zipper let fly with all three cannons, the highly heated bolts of plasma singing through the vacuum of space and ripping through the tailing pirate's fighter. Pressure exchanges made the slashes from the bolts rip wider and within seconds the pirate was no more. Leaving behind the gnarled husk of wrenched metal leaking gasses and oils and the body of the pilot struggling at first, but quickly freezing as he suffocated in the void.

The remaining fighter didn't give Wrenn much time to recover. Instead of turning to face him, he banked away, knowing that the Lancer would zip past after spacing the pirate's wingman. Wrenn noted it on his scanner, the pirate fighter falling into pursuit behind him. Plasma whizzed along Wrenn's zipper, the man instinctively wrenching his head to the side as one bright bolt missed his cabin window by mere inches. "Need some toilet paper for this cling-on." Wrenn grumbled.

The Lancer banked hard to port, then flipped and flew downward. Space dogfights were different from those made famous during Terra's terrestrial dust-ups. While pilots were still at the mercy of G-forces on turns and thrusts, there ain't no ground to be plowing into if you get too low. That said, pilots learned to adapt and use all three dimensions to their advantage. The Lancer, with its built in grav coils could keep Wrenn's innards in a normal state while his zipper made turns that easily clocked over 3 G's and made any regular pilot pass out. Unfortunately, it appeared his opponent had installed some after-market coils himself, for no sooner had Wrenn leveled out, the plasma bolts burned past him again with nary a hair of distance between them and his wing. "Ok, fucker . . ." Wrenn grit his teeth, "See how you like this one . . ."

Wrenn killed his throttle, cranked up full reverse thrusters, and held on with a white knuckled grip as his Lancer flipped on itself while still coasting forward on its momentum. Wrenn then fired up the engines again, cranking the throttle forward and feeling the veritable earthquake between his legs as the Lancer not only fought for acceleration but actively combatted his earlier inertia. One of few craft with the capability to accomplish such a feat, his light zipper's engine burned a white hot emission as Wrenn shot forward. The pirate was clearly surprised at his prey now started a game of chicken. Wrenn wrenched the controls for his zipper to spiral into an aileron roll, making his craft harder to hit. While he was spinning, Wrenn wondered for a fleeting second why everyone seemed to think what he was doing was a called 'barrel roll', recollecting some bizarre story about a hare telling a fox to do one or some such nonsense. As another plasma bolt whizzed past his head, Wrenn's thoughts shot back to the present matter. The pirate had clearly recovered from his shock. Wrenn opened up all three turrets, striking more and more of the much larger fighter's hull the closer he got. Mere seconds before he was to collide, the pressure change ripped across the pirate's hull as it had his counterpart, and Wrenn sailed through the gap and debris left in the explosion's wake. A slight turbulent wave crashed over his zipper but the thrusters quickly countered as Wrenn left another pirate's frozen corpse behind. Now all that was left was the galleon.

Wrenn moved within range of the galleon's cannons. Powerful plasma bursts the size of his fighter blew past him as he banked and zipped over the larger vessel. A quick strafe with his tracking cannon damaged some of their hull, but ultimately did little but singe metal. Even if he managed to flank it and fire all his weapons at once, it wouldn't do much different. It was like a sparrow harassing an eagle, annoying and noisy, but in the end, harmless. "Cheyenne, send me a scan of this mother fucker's systems, find me something to hit."

Observation: A spacecraft lacks reproductive organs, and it would be physically impossible for a vessel of this size to procreate with a female that has given birth, Captain, was what he got in response over the radio.

"Just do it!"

A cavalcade of notes and numbers cast across his targeting reticle, highlighting different structural deficiencies in the pirate's large vessel. The viewports were open, allowing for a small literal window of opportunity, but unlikely. One pass and the pirates would know his target and would likely shut them and rely on scanners alone now that they knew Wrenn wasn't easy prey. He surmised he might be able to convince them he wasn't worth the effort and get them to flee, but knowing how men held on to their bruised egos, the loss of two fighters just might have persuaded these brutes to linger awhile and take the spit out of Wrenn's mouth out of sheer vengeance.

He noticed a weakened shielding around the fixture where the engines met the rest of the ship. Clearly the pirates had made some 'improvements' to this galleon as well as their fighters. The thrusters looked too large for the vessel's size, likely stripped from a scrapped frigate or similar class and slapped on hastily to give the galleon more speed. Made sense, pirates thrived on fear and surprise to ambush their targets. Problem was, the shielding of the galleon didn't wrap around the engineering section as well as it should have. The whole thing looked like someone slapped a grasshopper's thorax onto the back of a bumble bee. Wrenn figured a hard enough hit there might give him an edge, but how?

Wrenn dove and twirled once more to dodge a hulking mass of hot plasma as it sailed at him like a slug made of fire. No possibility he could peck away at it with his turrets, sitting still too long would only let one of the galleons anti-air cannons disintegrate him. He needed something large to hit it once, blow the whole thing wide open, cripple the galleon in one fell swoop. He cursed again that the *Whisper's* cannons were down. One blast from her would turn the pirate's hull to paper, regardless of where it hit. Just then, Wrenn saw the planet's rings again off to his right and that old crafty brain of his spit out an idea. "Well . . . it worked so well the first time . . ."

Wrenn banked hard starboard and revved up the thrusters, sailing off from the galleon faster than any plasma lobs could be sent his way. The pirate turned, giving chase, probably hoping Wrenn was returning to its home ship. Wrenn guessed they'd probably not follow him into the actual asteroid belt, but linger like a vulture for him to come out. That was fine, he was planning on bringing the asteroids to them! "Cheyenne, what's the maximum towing power of my Lancer?"

Answer: According to design specifics, manufacturer's recommendations suggest a maximum of seven thousand kilograms, as the Lancer is not designed for logistical purposes, but in friendly fighter recovery in conjunction with another fighter. The AI replied over the radio.

Fuck, a little over fifteen thousand pounds? No way he'd be able to make more than a dent in the pirate's outer hull. Perhaps if he gained enough speed and aimed it just right . . .

"Scan the field, find me a rock that meets that weight . . ."

Scanning . . . Scanning . . . Located. Highlighting on your HUD.

Of course the little thing was a few miles into the certain death that was a constantly changing field of floating murder rocks. No way his luck would have let him find a nice one on the edge, not after having the fortune of catching the pirates unawares. The pendulum had swung back, it seemed. "Map me out a flight path in and out, you can do that right?"

Calculating . . . He heard Cheyenne's thinking sounds. *Complete . . . Answer: Sending it to you now, Captain.*

A golden line swirled and swooped back and forth before him. Seconds counted in the corner, highlighted in green and telling him how long he had to get to the next waypoint along the route in order to make it through the predicted gaps of asteroids. Wrenn gunned it, realizing quickly that Cheyenne had even accounted for the percentage of throttle needed to make it. He swooped, curled, even stopped dead in his tracks once to let two moon-sized rocks croquet themselves out of his way. Cheyenne must have computed velocities and trajectories of at least half a million variables to give him this pathway, no way a regular computer could process such a request, and in so quick a time. She was something else, that was for sure . . .

Wrenn managed to get to the boulder he needed, grabbing it with a tow beam and immediately turning back and following an escape path out. His engine whined and he noted it took more torque to accelerate. "Shit, she's a heavy one . . ."

Correction: Adjusting flight path to account for added weight. Cheyenne replied.

The chart shifted slightly, Wrenn doing his best to swing as little as possible to keep the fighter-sized asteroid from whipping wildly and pulling him off course. He managed to just squeeze by a rather large asteroid before it plowed through a cluster of innocent smaller ones, sending forth a shower of debris and dust willy-nilly. Once in the clear, Wrenn choked up on the throttle, trying to get the most momentum he could before releasing his care package. *Warning: Terminal velocity exceeding power capabilities! Captain, you cannot continue without critical power failure to your Lancer!*

"If I can smack her good enough, it won't matter!" Wrenn argued.

The engine under Wrenn's legs sputtered and whined as it strained against the extra weight behind itself. The zipper was lightweight and had an engine to sustain high speeds, but was never built to do what Wrenn was forcing her to. Just as the alarm bells started blaring, Wrenn could see his target. The galleon had turned to coast along the outer limits of the rings, perfectly presenting her starboard side for him. "She's spread her legs right perfect." Wrenn smirked. "Now for the poundin'!"

Wrenn kicked in the last bit of juice. The motor sputtered out a dying belch of propulsion, then cut power to all systems except life support. The Lancer dropped the payload, coasting over the galleon in the throws of its inertia . . . and the asteroid did as well. Like an out of control freight train, the asteroid t-boned the galleon, bending her like a fish. Wrenn pumped his fist in celebration. A direct hit, with any luck her crew would be scramblin to shut exposed portions of the ship and be ultimately out of the fight, except for that pendulum shift in his luck again. Sure he'd been fortunate enough to not nuke his own engine and even make a one in a million shot . . . but as his Lancer managed to rotate in its own propulsion wake, he noticed the galleon using a thruster to slowly spin itself around. The engines were essentially crippled, probably only giving out a fraction of their normal power output, but in the dead of space, even a little push can get you turned about eventually. With Wrenn dead in the water, it was like watching a shark stalk him in slow motion. "Fuck me . . . c'mon baby . . . start back up for me!"

Wrenn tried restarting his Lancer's systems. The onboard computer had shut everything down until the fusion core could settle. The heat between his legs had died down sure, but not enough to allow for systems to be reset. "Shit, shit, shit, shit . . ." Wrenn cursed.

If the galleon finished even half of its turn, they'd be able to fire off a plasma volley, one that would definitely hit him square in the jaw and blast his tiny zipper apart. He needed to move, he needed a goddamn miracle. Well . . . guess ol' Cheyenne earned her some wings.

A thunderous clap sounded from the ring. A bolt of plasma shot through the galleon with the impact of about a hundred of the asteroids Wrenn had thrown at it. The shot flew right *through* the ship, causing the entire craft to lurch and then immediately keel. The ship continued to list as another bolt pierced her, blasting a power supply and causing a bright flash of explosive venting into the vacuum of the 'verse. Wrenn couldn't believe his eyes as the *Whisper*, in all her glory, coasted out of the rings like a beautiful battleship of old. Two more blasts from the *Whisper*'s forward mag cannons and the galleon was reduced to shrapnel. Her interiors ripped open, debris billowing out into the nothingness, the much smaller vessel broke apart like a head of lettuce. Wrenn cheered and smacked his hand on the Lancer's steering bar. *Alert: All engines performing at optimal levels, Captain. I am also detecting no further enemies in the area.*

"Well ain't you a sight to behold, darlin'! God damn that one was close."

Response: I calculate the Galleon was at least two kilometers away from the Captain's Lancer at the time of mag round impact . . .

Wrenn laughed to himself. He couldn't even be mad at her. "Just get over here and bring me in. My engine's shot."

Confirmation: Aye Aye, Captain.

Wrenn took the few minutes of weightlessness to allow his heart rate to slow back down. By the time his fighter was pulled into the landing bay, his muscles ached from the adrenaline leavin' his system. Once the Lancer was grappled back into its storage space and the covering glass hissed out of the way, Wrenn practically rolled out onto the floor. Despite the gravity coils, the G-forces that had been exerted on his body made him feel like an old-world sumo wrestler had just sat on him for an hour. "Cheyenne, get us out of here!" He panted.

Query: What destination should I calculate, Captain? Her voice echoed over the loudspeaker.

"Just follow the Digiway until we reach its end, there's got to be an outpost nearby." Wrenn groaned.

Calculating . . .

Wrenn felt the thrusters begin to sway the large ship and smiled when he heard the rumble from the engines kick in. They were finally on the move, a massive frigate that was all his, journeying out to parts unknown. Cheyenne crackled over the intercom. *Confirmed: Pathway has been calculated. Arrival in approximately ten days, fourteen hours, twenty-nine minutes. Shall I engage the sublight drive?*

"That long?" Wrenn asked.

Correction: With adjustments it could take less time; however, periodic scans will be required to accurately adjust pre-programed star charts.

"Punch it then, darlin!" Wrenn pointed at the ceiling as he rolled over onto his back.

Observation: Physical violence will not be necessary, Captain.

"Just . . . just get us moving . . ." Wrenn sighed heavily.

The *Whisper* maneuvered a bit further into the open space and a familiar charging started from the engines. Blast doors engaged over the exits to the landing bay as Wrenn assumed similar shielding slid into place over the windows to the bridge and captain's quarters. Hatches were locked in place along the hull, the ship preparing to jump to a pace just a fraction under the speed of light. The charging ended with a violent jolt and then a stabilizer kicked in, Wrenn shaking briefly from side to side as if the entire ship had just changed gears wildly. From experience, Wrenn knew the *Whisper* was in skipspace. The gentle rumble permeated throughout the empty halls as Wrenn finally managed to get himself to his feet. "Imma pass out for about a million years, if you don't mind." He called out to the AI.

Observation: That would be physically impossible, Captain.

"Jumpin jackrabbits, we *gotta* work on your ability to interpret sarcasm!" Wrenn grumbled. "You're killin' me here."

Observation: Judging by the captain's vitals, I am not causing him any physical harm. Do I need to prep sick bay for any psychological damage?

The man hobbled his way back to his quarters, whimpering into his hand and doing his best to not lose his cool. His comfy king-size bed awaited him, and hopefully, more lewd dreams with a certain naked Namoyan.

CHAPTER 8

A mind-numbing week and a half went by as the Whisper moved through skipspace to a point along the disabled Digiway, scanned for local astro obstacles then jumped back using its two sublight turbines to the next way point. The constant skipping in and out of super speed took a real toll on the ship's engines and stabilizers, requiring Cheyenne to stop in some remote system and vent the excess heat from the core. Without a connection to the Qnet, Wrenn and Cheyenne were forced to chart the local systems manually, kind of like walking down a dark hallway with your arms stretched out, using the remnants of the Digiway buoys as a handrail.

The Qnet, as you know, is an extra-dimensional communication network that causes its receivers of quantum particles to vibrate on a certain frequency and transmit a select set of data bites. Change the data on one device, it changes them on all of them. Regardless of distance, the quantum particles all vibrate in sync. This network helps disseminate data, communication, star charts, even personal correspondence over any millions of lightyears. Every ship, station, and planetary outpost has a Qnet receiver, but they only work in congress with a transmitter where the changes can be uploaded. Too long away from a transmitter, the receiver's quantum particles naturally fall out of sync with the rest of the network, aka, no updated data, sorta like a guitarist that fell out of rhythm with the drummer. You might get some pictures and charts off the thing, but there's no way they'd be up to date. Space isn't just a vast place of stationary floating objects, everything moves and flows, explodes or collides, it's straight madness out there. Pilots count on having the most up-to-date data possible in order to navigate. Without access to the Qnet, Wrenn and Cheyenne were basically flying blind.

The trip hadn't been all bad, aside from being forced to survive off of the *Whisper's* emergency nutrapaste rations, Wrenn felt unshackled for the first time in his life. True, if they collided with the odd comet or unseen debris, there'd be no one out here to rescue him, but that also meant there was no one looking over his shoulder neither. He was truly free, a feeling he'd only ever dreamt of under the SCA's yoke. Cheyenne even made a habit of opening the viewing ports whenever she stopped to vent the engines so Wrenn could gaze out at uncharted nebulas, brilliant dust clusters, and wonderous star nurseries. Every 'night' Wrenn got to fall asleep to the prettiest panoramas any Terran could ever lay eyes upon.

But even stargazing gets old after a week of eating nutrient paste. Wrenn was walking the ship, checking systems for the umpteenth time out of sheer boredom. He'd already re-tuned his zipper . . . twice . . . and worked out in the toroid block. Cheyenne crackled over the intercom. *Query: Captain, may I speak with you a moment?*

"Dear Lord, please! Anything to break up this monotony." Wrenn huffed.

Suggestion: Please meet me at the crew quarters hallway.

As Wrenn met Cheyenne's holographic image, she beamed in a golden hue. She motioned to an access panel on the wall. "Statement: Inside you will find several communicator implants."

Wrenn opened the drawer to see a couple dozen earwigs not unlike old-world hearing aids. He'd seen crews on larger vessels wear them for interior ship communications. "Why are you showing me this? Ain't like there's a crew for me to talk to."

"Correction: There is me." Cheyenne smiled.

"Do tell."

"Statement: I have surmised that once I am connected to the communications network, I will be able to be with you no matter how far away from the *Whisper* you are."

"How? These things aren't exactly packed with them fancy particles in the Qnet receivers." Wrenn scratched his head.

"Clarification: There is more than one communication network ongoing in any port, city, or fleet. I believe I can access video feeds, radio frequencies, and internal computer systems that are in range of the *Whisper* at any time. My 'self' is nothing but data, and by spreading that data, I can use such networks to stay in constant contact, much like I do on the ship." Cheyenne smiled.

"Like you're just stretching out an arm or something . . ." Wrenn understood.

"Compliment: An astute metaphor, Captain." Cheyenne nodded.

"Well, that'll be helpful . . . if not a bit stifflin'."

"Statement: There's more, I believe I can adapt my projection software to overlay your natural eyesight using the human nervous system." Cheyenne almost bounced excitedly.

"Do'sa what now?"

"Clarification: It will be easier to show you. Please take a device and move to the hangar bay."

Wrenn followed her directions and as he walked into the large open hangar, he noted a crate with several used cans of nutrapaste on top of them. A maintenance drone meandered a few paces away having just set up what appeared to be a makeshift target range. From where he was standing, Wrenn could easily hit each can in a matter of seconds. "That's hardly a challenge, darlin'. I won't need your help none."

Cheyenne spoke directly into Wrenn's earpiece now instead of the ship's intercom. *Clarification: That is just a part of the demonstration. Please take a position approximately one hundred meters from the cans, Captain.*

Wrenn moved several paces away from the chest. The cans were much smaller now, but still not impossible for someone with his experience. "Still yet to see how this helps me."

Assurance: Patience, Captain.

Wrenn's eyes dilated suddenly and a wired overlay started forming in his vision. Walls, doors, even his zipper became encapsulated in a bold outline of varying colors with tiny identifiers. The cans also scanned into view, a red outline surrounding them with targeting triangles hovering above. With their outlines presented, Wrenn's accuracy would surely increase as he could better distinguish them from the background, making it easier to focus on the foreground. It was not unlike his targeting reticle for the nose cannon on his Lancer. "Nifty!" he whistled.

Explanation: I am sending inaudible sonic waves through the device that connect me with the visual portion of your brain, enabling me to add data directly to your perception of the surroundings. Please take cover behind your fighter.

Wrenn did as instructed, noticing he could still see the outline of the cans even with the barrier between him and his target. "Double nifty!"

Explanation: As long as I maintain surveillance of the surrounding area, I can feed your organic nervous system the data I scan through all manner of audio or video feeds. Now, please return to your previous position.

As Wrenn stood up, the hangar's overhead lights went out, yet to Wrenn, the overlay still remained. He could see the door, the outline of his fighter, and especially the cans. "Ok, now *that's* useful."

Wrenn aimed his sights, now also glowing, and shot all four cans in quick succession. The lights turned back on as Wrenn holstered his iron and nodded in satisfaction. *Explanation: Even in total darkness, I will be able to provide up-to-date data from infrared cameras to extrapolate positioning with only a 0.0016728 second delay.*

"Where have you been all my life, sweetheart?" Wrenn smiled.

Answer: Based on the Captain's age, I surmise most of that time was spent in the ring belt of Sentroid-9 after the Whisper suffered . . .

"Yeah, yeah, I know all that, darlin'." Wrenn interrupted.

Statement: Then I am confused why the captain asked where I had been . . .

Wrenn shook his head. "It's a figure of speech. It means I wish I'd met you sooner, my life woulda been much more pleasant.'"

Cheyenne could be heard calculating in the earpiece. She seemed appreciative of the statement, Wrenn even thought he felt the earpiece warm slightly. *Statement: It is my purpose to make the captain's journey more efficient. I am glad to be of service.*

ΔΔΔ

Wrenn laid back on his bed, his guitar in his hands, fingers plucking strings that were no longer there. He had yet to rise, in fact, he'd been quite content staying in bed these last three days or so. He hadn't shaved, his brown hair a matted mess, and he smelled something awful, but who cared? He was alone in deep space, there wasn't another sentient life within a million miles of . . . "Announcement: Attention Captain! I have successfully scanned the end of the digital freeway and have discovered a settlement approximately 386,400 kilometers from the exit. I believe this is the station you were hoping to find."

Wrenn jumped at the sudden outburst of the AI. "Jumpin' jackrabbits, darlin! You scared the shit out of me."

"Query: Will the captain require a change of linens for the soiled sheets?"

Wrenn sighed. "I really gotta watch my tongue around you."

"Observation: That would be physically impossible for the captain's species. Such a feat would require eye stocks such as the Baglorams from sector . . ."

"Hush, would you? Cripes almighty. How long until we reach that station?"

"Answer: Best calculations place us there within the hour." Cheyenne replied.

"Alright, Imma grab me a shower and be ready on the bridge. Perhaps it might be best if you let me do the talkin'. I'm not sure the people of the 'verse are ready for an AI just yet. Momma always said 'first impressions are lasting impressions'."

"Question: Does the captain wish me to also stay silent with him?" Cheyenne suddenly appeared standing next to the bed, sheepish and shining a gentle blue.

Wrenn gave her a puckish grin despite his frustration. "'Course not, darlin'. You can always be the angel on my shoulder. Just don't expect me to always respond in the middle of a interchange with the locals."

Cheyenne's color started to change to a golden yellow as she smiled. "Statement: I am thankful the captain is not opposed to AI and wish the rest of the citizens of the universe could see the help I can provide."

"Old wounds run deep sometimes, babe. Don't worry, they'd come around if every AI were as sweet as you."

Cheyenne blushed and turned a mixture of green and yellow, swirling into a whirlwind of colors like a tie-dye mix. Wrenn had already figured the different shades were an unconscious expression of the computer's emotional growth, but had yet to see the mixing meant. Was it something to do with her sudden bashfulness? Could a program feel attraction? If it could, what stopped it from experiencing things like admiration, lust, or even love?

Wrenn shook his head, he didn't have time to ponder the philosophicals of existence and what defined 'life', he needed to wash hit pits.

∆∆∆

One final jump and they were there, hovering just past

the flashing lights that enveloped the last ring of the Digiway. Beyond lay a massive, nearly moon-sized asteroid. The rock was dotted with structures and elongated docking rings that criss-crossed and bore down through the surface like some deranged science project of a kid that wasn't sure if he was building a model of an atom or a potato battery.

The port didn't move anywhere, dead in the vacuum of empty space between systems, a perfect end destination for the Digiway as it gave a rare permanent exit in an ever rotating, ever swirling galaxy. Planets were too unpredictable in their positioning to chart over such a vast distance, and stars were too combustible to be counted on, despite being easier to chart. A dead rock in dead space made the perfect anchor point to the Omega Quad.

Wrenn fired up the thrusters and powered on the four regular engines at the back of the *Whisper*, traversing a distance comparable to Earth and her moon in about an hour. He thought about Terran's early spaceflight and how the same path would have taken him three days in the early Apollo spacecraft and he chuckled to himself. Early humans thought they were so superior, yet they knew so very little of what laid in store.

His radio crackled to life as he drew near. *Unknown vessel, halt immediately and prepare to be tugged to an available clamping dock.*

"Hey, uh . . . yeah, I just fell out of the Digiway a few weeks back and am just now getting here." Wrenn replied into a hand mic. "I'm just trying to get some supplies and head on my way."

Prepare to be tugged to an available clamping dock! The radio crackled back.

A cluster of support craft scuttled out to the *Whisper* and attached themselves to the exit hatches and docking doors to prevent any possible escape. Each craft's single ion engine rotated and in unison the tuggers pushed the *Whisper* toward one of the overt, odd rings that stuck out from the large asteroid. Once near, magnetic locks came down upon the *Whisper's* hull and the ship was ostensibly 'docked', with a small gangplank extending from the ring and attaching to the port exit hatch in the pilot's block. Cheyenne spoke up in Wrenn's earpiece. *Observation: Someone is attempting to power down most of the Whisper's systems from the station, with the exception of life support and illumination.*

"They're trying to make it so I don't jump and run." Wrenn noted.

Observation: They are using a rather rudimentary coding software that is easily broken. If the captain desired, I could render their attempt futile and release the docking clamps. Cheyenne noted.

"Let's play along for now," Wrenn stated, "though, it's good to know we could get ourselves out of a pickle if need be."

Observation: That doesn't sound all that difficult, Captain, as pickles are generally much smaller than the Captain's stature. The much more improbable task would be getting into the pickle in the first place.

"Oh would you just . . . never mind." Wrenn sighed.

Alert: The port accessway is being hacked through a security bypass, shall I stop this attempt at a breach?

"Make it a little difficult for them, but let 'em in as soon as I make it down there. Gotta make a grand entrance, you know." Wrenn started moving to the bottom of the pilot's block to greet whoever was attempting to board his ship.

In the few minutes it took him to get to the loading ramp, Cheyenne let the door 'hacker' through her firewalls and the large exterior paneling slid upwards. Security personnel rushed into the 'belly' of the front module and pointed their weapons directly at Wrenn as he casually strolled down the ramp that led to the docking bay and warehouse module behind him. The zipper pilot raised his hands admonishingly and gave them a slight grin. "Woah, easy there fellas, can't a guy just mosey into town without being smothered so quick by the SCA?"

A larger uniformed man strode into the room, his hair a coarse brown with matching full beard. A scar sliced through the hair as well as one eyebrow. A cybernetic, red eye rotated in the accompanying socket, focusing on Wrenn like a camera lens and the man grimaced. "We are not Alliance out here, Captain. We are the militia! And we don't take kindly to unannounced guests."

"Hey, listen, I get it." Wrenn shrugged, "But like I said, I was in the Digiway until something happened. I never intended to show up at your doorstep uninvited."

"Hmph!" The security man scoffed through his nose. "Last reports were a ship was coming through before the system went down. The techies thought it might have been a rogue comet taking out one of the guidance buoys, but suppose you coulda jackniffed the system by trying to break out of the Digiway early, huh? Maybe this whole clusterfuck is your doing?"

"Why in the 'verse would I'a jumped out of the Digiway early, friend? I already paid my passing. What reason would I have to duck out of the trip halfway through?" Wrenn countered.

The man scratched at his chin. "I don't know, but we can't take any chances out here. We get little to no support as it is."

"I promise you friend, I've no ill intent. I just want to stock up, do some repairs, then be on my way.' Wrenn bowed.

"Hmph." The man repeated. "Well, in that case you'll need to see Ganook in the external engineering warehouse. Follow me."

The fully armored guards lowered their weapons and allowed Wrenn to pass before they exited the ship and closed the port hatch behind them. They dispersed as soon as everyone made it back into the terminal ring. Wrenn noted he had been 'parked' in terminal D24 in case he needed to skedaddle in a hurry. "So where is the rest of your crew?" The security man asked.

"Lost them in the rip out of the Digiway." Wrenn shrugged. "Took me days to repair the damage best I could with worker drones."

"My condolences." The man nodded at him as Wrenn moved to walk along his side.

"Well, they were new hires. I . . . uh . . . didn't even learn their names yet." Wrenn lied.

"We must honor all our fallen comrades, regardless of personal contact. Spacers and boots alike. Two sides of the same coin, far as I feel. I hope you will take some time to do right by them, seeing as you were their captain." The man's one human eye looked almost pleading, while the robotic red one looked downright penetrating.

Wrenn nodded. "R . . . right, will do there, chief."

"It's Captain, same as you. Captain Frederick Wilson." The man extended a hand. "Deadrock Militia."

"Wrenn." The Lancer pilot shook the security man's much larger. "Of the *Whisper*."

"She's a fine ship." Captain Wilson looked out of the large four-story viewing window at the *Whisper* as she staunchly stood out against the blackness of the space behind her. "You must have some friends in high places to land such a marvel."

"Either that or I killed everyone aboard her and took her for myself, eh?" Wrenn chuckled.

The burly man didn't seem to find Wrenn's reply amusing, squeezing the spacer's hand tightly as they were still in the midst of the handshake. Wrenn winced and removed his knuckles from Wilson's vice grip and massaged them. "It was a joke man, geez!"

"Now you hear me, Captain Wrenn. These are good, honest people out here that don't need none of *that* kind of trouble. A lot of folks came out here specifically to get away from the Alliance and their constant scuttles with various pirate groups. You so much as joke about that sort of malarkey and I'll have you swirling in one of my no-G cells faster than you can swig down a shot of synthetic whiskey, you hear me?"

"Easy Sheriff, you've got no worry from me, just excited to get beyond the Scabies' yoke myself, ok? My gums flap a little faster than my brains can keep up with sometimes, is all."

"Be sure that's the only time I hear of such 'comedy', stranger. Otherwise, that yoke'll turn into a noose 'afore long."

Wilson cautioned.

"Fair point." Wrenn nodded. "Thanks for the warning . . . now, can you kindly direct me to that mechanics den you mentioned?

Captain Wilson noted a few ways for Wrenn to travel to the station's ship repair hub and the spacer thanked him before departing the sheriff's company. Not two steps away, he heard a crackling in his ear, *Statement: I have successfully gained entry to the station's networks, Captain.*

"That was fast . . ." Wrenn whispered.

Observation: I am very good.

Wrenn chuckled. "Sounds more like a crowing than an observation . . ."

Response: It is not bragging to state fact, Captain.

Wrenn laughed out loud, to the surprise of two passersby. Wrenn noticed their stares and pointed to a nearby advertisement. "Can you believe they've added a new flavor?! I can't wait to try 'bubblegum nutrapaste'!"

As you know, it was common knowledge that nutrapaste, in any flavor, tasted like death. Dress up a pig all you want, it's still . . . well, you know. The bystanders rolled their eyes at the spacer who had clearly spent too long in the 'verse and continued on. Wrenn sighed heavily. "Just keep an eye on me for now, learn all you can about this place, I can't talk much otherwise I'll end up seeing the inside of a padded cell."

Understood.

CHAPTER 9

Wrenn took in the sights of the Deadrock station, as Wilson had revealed. There were a number of eateries, not all of which were built with a Terran stomach in mind, which indicated the Omega Quad welcomed any and all sentient beings to this side of the 'verse. Walking the passageways revealed a veritable smorgasbord of every kind of being in the Systems Central Alliance and even a large number of those species that hadn't quite fit into the Scabies' idea of a galactic utopia. Wrenn saw a might few races he recognized, as well a good number he didn't, and decided to stick to himself all the same. He needed to blend in, get his bearings, and get the ship repaired. Soon as the Whisper was at 100%, he could use her to find a job and make that fresh start he had been working toward all these years.

Wrenn passed a saloon that he could see a group of fellow Terrans in and nearby was a casino that seemed to take up a huge portion of the inner rock space. Gambling was highly regulated and taxed in the Alpha Quad, but out here . . . Wrenn wondered how many of his card tricks would be tolerated before he got the boot. Depending on how expensive the repairs were going to be, Wrenn might need to find out sooner rather than later.

Wrenn managed to pull himself away from the lights and bustle of the main promenade long enough to find the mechanic's warehouse. He was enamored at the amount of activity held within. Sections of frigates, cruisers, even an entire sloop were being worked on inside. Workers dangled from scaffolding and catwalks criss-crossed through the space.

Welding torches, computer cables, and the incessant sounds of hammering filled his senses as Wrenn moved through the unorganized junk yard that was the bottom floor of the massive warehouse. In the center of all of it, was an Octathod barking orders in every direction to any number of a hundred workers around the space. Its gargled, wet voice was a mixture of clicks, chortles, and that sound a watercooler makes when it bubbles up from the bottom. Wrenn's translation chip (that all citizens of the Alliance got implanted upon birth, without their consent I might add) couldn't place a single word or phrase the massive, eight-legged cephalopod was saying while it worked on three separate engine parts at once. The creature's massive eyes focused on Wrenn and it squished out a collection of sounds that might have been construed as a question. When Wrenn shook his head and shrugged, the creature repeated the sucking and slurping phrase twice more before quivering in obvious frustration. It belched loudly, squirting a jet of water at Wrenn and saturating his shirt and face. Wrenn instinctively reached for his iron. "You wanna go, you fucking squid?!"

"Easy there, slick." A gentle voice spoke from behind him. "Boss was just marking you so I could see you better."

Wrenn turned to meet a rather large set of beautiful brown eyes staring up at him. He quickly realized he was looking at two large glass lenses, on the ridge of the snout of a Ratadendrin. A mousy-type species the Terrans named after a flower to both describe their rodent-like features and their reliance on smell. They'd been discovered on an arid world that was a little too close to their sun, which scorched most of the surface beyond survivability. It was only after the Terrans first landed did they discover the Rottys had built themselves elaborate cave systems and complete subterranean cities throughout the planet's crust. They were marvelously adaptable, much like Earth's rat species they were unkindly compared to. They could fit in small nooks on ships and had an almost racial affinity for savaging and repairing systems. Due to millenia living in the dark caves of their homeworld, every Ratedendrin was notoriously near-sighted, many having to wear corrective lenses or have surgery to enhance their vision. Wrenn viewed the wide green frames and overalls covered in oil and instantly recognized who he was speaking with. "In all the star systems, in all the 'verse . . . Daisy?!"

"Wrenn you soft-handed scoundrel!" The Ratadendrin squeaked, running forward and hugging his leg. "What are *you* doing here?"

"I could ask you the same, girl! Weren't you retired and tendin' to your brood?" Wrenn laughed, patting the older woman on the back.

"I was, then they went and made the shop a damn fine establishment!" Daisy huffed, her tiny paws resting on her hips. "So many customers; I couldn't stand all the noise! Figured I'd get myself away for a more relaxed retirement."

Wrenn looked around the massive hangar/shop and scoffed. "This is quiet?"

"Quieter than a thousand of my kin squeakin' up to high heavens about how's a turbine go back into a frigate's thrusters!" Daisy argued.

Wrenn shrugged. "If you say so, darlin'."

"Ohhh no, don't you be darlin' me there, sweet-talker! I still remembers how you owe 6 stacks for that new Lancer turret back on Thellist." Daisy's large eyes squinted, made comical by her small stature and coke-bottle lenses.

"Heeey, I'm good for it!" Wrenn smirked. "Just came into a new ship. I'll get me a few jobs, pay you back . . . with interest!"

"Uh huh . . ." Daisy sighed, ". . . and what's this new ship, eh? Last I heard you was still a zipper jockey and nothing fancier."

"That's the old Wrenn, you're talking to the new Captain Wrenn of the *Whisper*."

"That frigate that docked earlier in D24?" Daisy's eyes grew. "We thought all the Startech Wendigos had been spaced or scrapped by now."

"You know about my ship?" Wrenn asked.

Daisy squinted again. "I don't knows about how it came to be *your* ship, but she was never meant to be owned by a private captain. They was one of the first vessels to venture out to the Omega Quad. Come on, we can talk more in the office, less snoopin' ears and lazy workers."

Wrenn followed his older friend down a set of stairs and into an over-packed office. The desk was only accessible by squeezing past a stack of papers and dirty coffee mugs, the file cabinets overflowed with binders, miscellaneous trash, and even misplaced tools. Clearly the place was operated by mechanics and did not have anyone trained in administrative tasks. A much younger Ratadendrin sat behind the desk plucking away at a data screen, unaware of their entrance until Daisy spoke. "This here's my granddaughter. Clung to my tail so hard when I packed my things I figured I'd take her on as an apprentice. Meet my ol' business associate and introduce yourself girl!"

The little Ratadendrin squeaked and looked up at Wrenn, her face flushing instantly. She was much younger than Daisy, cute even, in an innocent sort of way. Her round face and large brown eyes looked at Wrenn with a mixture of trepidation and wonder. Her whiskers twitched slightly as they poked out next to a button nose and her buck teeth made it so her pouty lips couldn't quite close all the way. Wrenn couldn't decide if he wanted to kiss her or wrap her in his arms and protect her. The young apprentice eventually raised a shaking paw up toward Wrenn who encapsulated it within his own and shook it as gingerly as he could so as to not cause injury to the tiny bones inside. "Hello, name's Saraphina Genevieve Lucerta XIII." She squeaked.

"Woah, big name for such a little woman." Wrenn smiled.

Saraphina giggled, sounding like a school girl who'd just sucked up helium. "Yeah, people 'round here just call me Wrenchy."

"That makes it easy." The human smiled. "And people 'round here would call me Wrenn, if any of them knew me that is."

"Pleased ta meetcha!" The mousey girl blurted out a bit too loudly, quickly realizing it and covering her mouth embarrassed. Wrenn noted her teeth were capped, likely surgically done to help 'fit in' with the other species. Many races in SCA Space underwent alterations to their outward appearances in order to make a living away from their home planet. To most, it was a way to appear non-threatening, while the more conservative of their people often disavowed or even disowned them for having such surgeries. Yet despite going to such lengths to appear as Terran as possible, many of Wrenn's species looked down on anyone but their own. Much like the frontiers of the old west, bigotry seemed to follow Terran settlers no matter how advanced the wagons became.

Wrenn smiled back at her and sighed, turning to Daisy. "My translator doesn't seem to pick up on your boss' lingo, but yours seems to be working as normal."

"That's 'cause you're from one of the central worlds of the Alpha, and Octathods tend to come from the outskirts. Most softwares haven't been able to import the language, not to mention the 76 different dialects. There's a translator shop not but a few stores down on the promenade that'll get you an update for a couple 'a cred."

"Hey, thanks for the tip." Wrenn nodded.

"So you here for somethin' or were you just ogling at the repairs?" Daisy placed a hand on her hip while the other cradled a clipboard against her. Her granddaughter came around the other side of the desk to stand next to her. Even though Wrenchy was dressed in messy overalls similar to her grandmother, she had a figure that wasn't all that unappealing. She was small, obviously, with gentle curves and a tight little body. She held a youthful, innocent sort of look, if you could get past the big front teeth, large ears, and skinny rat-like tail.

Wrenn couldn't help but flash a lecherous smile while his imagination ran wild on what laid underneath Wrenchy's overalls. Daisy, being of a race that often reared broods numbering in the dozens, recognized the look almost immediately. "Hmm, maybe you'd rather be ogling something . . . *else*?"

"I mean no offense, her being your ilk and all, but I just never laid eyes on somethin' both cute and sexy all balled up in such a tiny package before." Wrenn shrugged.

Wrenchy didn't seem to understand their implications at first, likely unaccustomed to such bold advances from a Terran before. She quickly picked up his hint and then giggled. "You're baaaaaad." She spoke in an almost Jersey-like cadence. "You keep that up and I'll shoo you right outta here, spacer."

"Back to your place? Might be kind of cramped, but I'm sure we could figure out a way." He winked.

"Alright, alright!" Daisy chattered. "Boy, you really've got no shame, do you spacer? Saddlin' up to my grandbaby right in front of me?"

"Please Daisy, ain't like your folk is adverse to bumpin' uglies. You yourself got what . . . twenty-three youngins by last count? I don't even want to imagine how many cousins Wrenchy here's got."

Daisy scoffed and Wrenchy giggled again. "Least you could be a bit classier, boy."

"I'll behave . . . for now . . ." Wrenn smiled.

Daisy scrunched up her face, making her whiskers spread. "Ooooh, I could never stay mad at you, old sweet-talker."

Wrenn winked at her and leaned up against the messy desk. "Now! Back to business! What brought you all the way out here's anyway?" Daisy squeaked.

"I just flew in, was looking at how much repairs might be. The Digiway malfunctioned and spat me out halfway from the Alpha Quad. Battered me up something fierce."

"We were all wondering what happened." Wrenchy piped up. "The techs said it'll take months to repair it, till then we're sorta stuck out here with no support. Everyone's on edge about it."

"Yeah, twisted me up right good." Wrenn agreed.

Daisy huffed. "Well, no way you came through in that

frigate you've got, ain't been a Wendigo class come in decades. You sold out to the corpos now boy, come out here to scoop up some planets for your bosses back home?"

"Farthest thing, actually. Just a right place, wrong time, sorta situation." Wrenn shrugged.

"Uh huh, well let's take a few scans of her and see what's needed." Daisy moved over toward the desk and opened a drawer that held a holographic display. As soon as the Rotty punched in a few buttons, an image of the *Whisper* popped into view. She clicked a few more that were clearly too big for her rodent hands. The image of Wrenn's ship sharpened to show the damage to the engines that had just been barely repaired by the drones from the remains of his Ravenwing. "Well, that's a bit of a patch job if I ever saw one."

"Yeah, had to use some poor sops ruined sloop. Think it was a Ravenwing style transporter."

"Pieces of junk, those. Only good any of them ever were was scrap." Wrenchy remarked.

"Hey! They weren't so bad, downright dependable I'd say, except when faulty equipment gets in the way." Wrenn caught himself. "Or . . . so I hear, anyways."

Daisy rolled her eyes. "Uh huh." She moved the view over to the factory and toroid blocks. "Star's burst, whatya fly out here with . . . hopes and dreams? Your factory is more barren than a nun's babymaker and I've seen more advanced workout spaces in a fatman's gym."

"You know . . . cutbacks . . ." Wrenn tried his bluff again.

"Listen, honey, I've always liked you, which is why I'll tell you ta go ahead and drop the act." Daisy looked at him over her glasses. "I know this ain't your ship, least not by rightful purchase. The numbers on the side are a dead giveaway. The Wendigos were never for sale. Startech sent 26 of these puppies out into the Reach decades ago to colonize and terraform. Named for every letter in your alphabet, from the *Atlas* to the *Zeus*. Most, if not all, were spaced before they could even make it. What few remained didn't last long out on this edge of the 'verse.

Great design, but shitty crews. Startech made these mommas too big to handle, then placed skeleton crews to try and manage them. Ya damnear need an army to move 'em properly, either that or . . ."

"An AI." Wrenn finished.

"Yeah, but good luck finding you one of them! Those things are rarer than a Goldilocks world, even out here where the Scabies won't track you down." Wrenchy piped in.

"So . . . you've figured me out then?" Wrenn eyed the door to the office, wondering how many stacks of paper he could throw down during his escape.

"Take it easy, slick. No one cares where you got her this far out, except maybe that boy scout Captain Wilson. I can easily whip you up some new registrations and give her a fresh set of identifiers, but that's not what's gonna cost you." Daisy huffed.

"What will, then?" Wrenn asked.

"You're bare bones here, barely even flyable. It's like you bought a sport speeder and never took it out the box."

"Speeders don't come in boxes . . ." Wrenn noted.

"You get what I'm sayin'! It could take me weeks to find you enough modular slide-ins to fill her proper. I'll have to scrap some from other Wendigos, or even build some from plans. Not to mention the price it'll set you back. You'll need a huge crew to run her as she is. You're better off selling her for parts and getting you a completely top of the line skiff or sloop, partner."

"No!" Wrenn shot back almost immediately. "She's not going to be able to follow me to . . ." Wrenn cleared his throat. "What I mean to say, is, she's made such an impact on me already that I can't see myself flying just any old rig after her. Once you've touched the perfect woman, in the perfect way, you can't just give that up. . . it's a spacer thing."

Wrenchy had to catch herself, she looked downright smitten as she seemed to imagine Wrenn's 'perfect touch'. Her grandmother was less impressed. "Regardless, she's too much woman for little you to handle, sweet talker."

"I handled her well enough to get her here." Wrenn

shrugged.

"Barely. Her engines have been driven harder than most of the whores down at the brothel. You need a trained engineer to keep her out of the red." Daisy snorted.

"You volunteering?" Wrenn smiled.

"I'm too much for you to handle too, flyboy." The older Rotty smiled. There hung an awkward silence for a few moments as everyone realized there was more than one Ratadendrin in the room.

Wrenn finally chuckled and then looked back at the projection. "So, what do you suggest?"

"Well, first you need to offload the toroid and factory blocks until I can get enough pods to fill them proper. They're adding undue strain on the ship and make her harder to handle with just you flying. Besides, we can rent them out as living space while I get them fitted to make you some extra credits, but that's not going to come in overnight OR pay enough to fix your engine."

"I've got some ideas on how to get credits in the short term." Wrenn crossed his arms.

"If you're thinking of gambling, the casino won't give you enough for the engine repairs AND pay for the outfitting of the two other blocks. You might get the repairs out of them before they kick you out, and that's assuming you're even lucky enough to make that much."

"Lucks got nothing to do with it." Wrenn smiled. He knew better than to believe himself. Luck was all Wrenn had lived by recently, and the pendulum seemed to be swinging again . . .

"Go ahead, but if you die, I get the *Whisper* and I'll strip her faster than your body goes cold." Daisy warned.

"She means it." Wrenchy agreed.

"What about after I get the engine fixed? She'll fly with just the pilot's, storage, and engine blocks won't she?" Wrenn asked.

"One thing Startech did right was make these babies modular. She'll fly in any number of combinations you make her, just be harder and harder to control the bigger she gets, but likewise easier the smaller she flies."

"So, I can find some work." Wrenn nodded.

"Lots of work out here in the Omega Quad. Some honest . . . some not." Daisy shrugged.

"I gotcha. Well, thank you for the lesson in my new spacecraft. It's always a pleasure to get lectured by you, Daisy."

The rodent woman rolled her eyes, looking comical as they were supersized by her glasses. "Look, I'll send you my frequency, just call me when you get the money from the casino, or more likely when they kick your bum-ass out penniless and I can get to strippin' her."

"Thanks. I'll be in touch." Wrenn saluted them both sarcastically and turned to the door. He could hear the two chattering once he left the office, but it was too subtle for his translator to pick up, only sounding like squeaks and clicks to him now. He sighed heavily as he lost the bravado he'd been keeping up while in their presence. "Well, ain't we just up shit's creek without a paddle . . ."

Observation: That sounds like a very unpleasant place to be, Captain. Cheyenne noted in his ear.

"Darlin', you're not wrong . . ."

CHAPTER 10

The captain of the Whisper walked along the stretch of neon signs and rotating doors that made up Deadrock station's main drag. Saloons, shops, and the casino were the most engaging finds in the area that wasn't much larger than a couple square blocks. Gussied up women cooed at him from a balcony above the casino's flashing lights, evidently a high-priced whore house occupied the top floors. Wrenn nearly broke into a run toward the exterior stairs when he remembered he barely had enough funds to order a decent meal. His bank account had been sparse since his purchasin' of the ill-fated Ravenwing, but there were ways of making credits in stations like this. Many companies and guilds handled the day-to-day needs in outposts like Deadrock, too small to be considered corpos, but flush with cash all the same. What he needed was one of them to take notice of him. So far, Wrenn was an unknown, an outsider, not someone to be trusted with transporting a load of goods or clearing out a horde of pirates. Wrenn sighed heavily and leaned against a lamppost. He eyed the girls waving at other passersby, clearly giving up on him. If he played his cards right, he could get lucky at the tables . . . operative word being cards . . . though he didn't have enough funds to even get to a decent table. Wrenn scratched his head and felt the earpiece, still getting accustomed to the damn thing, then ol' clever Wrenn got himself an idea. "Cheyenne . . ." He whispered.

Response: Yes, captain? She said in his ear.

"About how much of this station's network are you

patched into?" Wrenn hid his mouth behind a fake yawn.

Response: Why . . . all of it, Captain. Cheyenne spoke as if he should know better than to ask.

"Are the slots patched into that network?"

Clarification: The casino exists on its own subnet, with appropriate firewall protections for each gambling device.

". . . But you can see them?"

Clarification: I cannot 'see' anything, each device is separated on a network with separate IP addresses that communicate with a central hub that when accessed . . .

"Can you hack into the damn things?" Wrenn cut her off.

He heard the computing sounds in his ear, the familiar sign that the AI was 'thinking'. *Answer: Preliminary probing of firewalls show a simplified encryption. I can access any machine in the casino with relative ease.*

Wrenn could barely contain his excitement. He needed to play it cool, make it look like happenstance and not his own doing. "Ok . . . here's what we're gonna do . . ."

△△△

The slot machines had proven fruitful, but ultimately useless when it came to making a real splash. Wrenn had covertly made the machines give him more than they took, steadily growing his bank account without drawing unneeded attention from the house. As much as he wanted to go straight for the high roller tables, he knew he needed to hang back and observe. Wrenn found his way over to the bar, where he ordered a whiskey and sipped at it while eyeing the poker and blackjack tables. "You won't find much action there tonight . . ." The bartender shrugged.

"Yeah?" Wrenn asked, looking at the mustached man.

"Won't be many players until the next shift's 'weekend' starts. Should be tomorrow 'bout this time. That's when the miners will bring in their check money and blow it all. Usually, Jared takes most of them by night's end."

"Jared?" Wrenn took another sip of his drink.

"Local card shark, not quite sure how he does it, the tables are all digital these days. Still, guy's got some luck when it comes to bets and victims." The bartender looked like he was about to spit.

"There a lot of mines here on this rock?"

"Oh sure, it's what started the whole station, mineral rich asteroid just ripe for the plucking. Every few months or so they open up another tunnel to the public, let businesses or living quarters spring up where veins was carved out. Those that work for the guild like to live a little here before heading home for a few days respite." The bartender poured Wrenn another glass.

"And that's when this Jared swoops in?" Wrenn asked.

"Just about, ain't a god-fearin' man you ask me, preying on the workin' man. More than a few miner's kids went hungry on account of that swindler."

"You got a pretty loose tongue when it comes to badmouthing your clientele, friend." Wrenn smirked.

The bartender looked offended. "I take my customers' secrets to my grave, friend, but I've got no niceties for the likes of him. Bastard's as dry as summer's desert."

Wrenn chuckled, tapping the pad beside his drink embedded in the table and adding a few credits tip to his tab. "Well, can't let it be said the same for me. Keep 'em comin', friend."

"Knew I liked your jib, mister." The bartender filled the glass once more.

A bit of movement caught Wrenn's eye and he turned his head to see what it was. A brilliantly beautiful woman sat at the bar a few stools away, lifting her hand to the keep and he dutifully went about making her drink. When the bartender returned to Wrenn for another refill, the ship captain raised an eyebrow to the keep as if to inquire her identity. A quick shrug and head shake was the only response he got.

She had a narrow face, high cheekbones, and the finest golden hair Wrenn had ever seen. Her body was lythe and taught, even as she relaxed on the stool she looked about as coiled as a sprinter at the starter's line. She was dressed rather plainly, in darker jeans and a long sleeve button-up blouse that purposely stayed off the shoulders. The shirt did little to hide her perky breasts, allowing a bare midriff to show, Wrenn admiring her porcelain skin. Once she noticed his stare, she returned it with her large blue eyes, though hers seemed more full of fury than Wrenn's hungry leer. "Howdy." Wrenn winked.

She eyed Wrenn up and down. "Greetings." She replied in an educated voice.

Wrenn made a face. "Fancy lady like you roughin' it with the likes of us common folk tonight, eh?"

"Rather presumptive of you to make such a claim after merely one word." She replied.

"Oh, I think I'm right on the money, sweetcakes." Wrenn chewed on a stirring straw.

The woman sighed, "Think you have me pegged so easily, drifter?"

"Well, maybe not quite yet, but after I get a few drinks in ya, we might sees where the night takes us . . ." Wrenn winked.

The woman scoffed. "Wow, that took all of about five seconds, I'd wager."

"Oh, that was just some harmless fun . . ." Wrenn chuckled. " . . . But seriously, I knows a Utopian when I sees one."

The woman's disgust turned to barely-contained alarm. Her large eyes bulged first at Wrenn then at the bartender. Wrenn waved off her concern. "Oh, he won't go tellin' no one long as you're a payin' customer, and as for me, the satisfaction of knowin' is payment enough for my silence."

The woman seemed to relax, but only slightly. She repositioned herself on the barstool, eyeing the exits and the barely occupied gambling floor. "Well? Am I right or am I right?" Wrenn sipped his drink.

The woman sighed, taking one last glance around the room before she pulled back her blonde curls to reveal ears with fanned lobes and pinna that came up to a point. Utopians,

67

or what some uneducated Terrans called 'space elfs', were the predominant species from the Delta Quad. Their empire stretched across a thousand systems, and they were the only true power that could rival the Alliance. Utopians were zealous isolationists. None lived within Scabie space, they barely traded, and certainly kept their distance from most SCA outposts. Why one was all the way out here made Wrenn curious as a cat with a streamer. He decided it best for now not to push his luck, as the woman looked about as ready to scamper as she was to speak. "Well, how about that . . . guess I win."

"I'm not going to ask how you were able to figure that out so quickly, just as I'd hope you won't ask my reasons for being here . . ." The woman hid her ears again with her hair.

"Fair enough." Wrenn finished his drink and stood. "Not the type to poke my finger where it don't belong . . . lest I's invited." He winked again.

"Another time . . . perhaps."

Wrenn nodded and shrugged. "Can't blame a guy for tryin'. G'night miss . . ." He held out a hand, expecting her to introduce herself.

The woman looked at his hand, nodded, and turned back toward her drink. "Goodnight."

Wrenn chuckled and bid the bartender a courteous nod. He made his way back out onto the promenade, feeling a slight tipsy from his drinks. *Suggestion: If the captain desires, I could transfer his winnings from his credit chit to his account wirelessly to avoid pickpockets in his . . . inebriated state.*

"What a great idea!" Wrenn hiccupped.

The man seemed to be staring at the hookers on the balcony, not sure if he was responding to Cheyenne or just his own inner desires. Cheyenne spoke again in his ear. *Suggestion: It would be wiser if the captain returned to his quarters aboard the Whisper, as he will need the winnings to gamble for higher earnings in a match against this 'Jared'.*

Wrenn sighed and stumbled his way back toward docking bay D24. "Caught that one . . . did ya?"

Observation: I noted an elevated heart rhythm and dilated pupil activity when his name was mentioned by the bartender.

"Well, ain't you just a regular mind reader . . ." Wrenn sighed, shaking his head and doing his best to focus on walking straight.

Clarification: I am not outfitted with the ability to . . .

"Shhh, darlin'. I'm trying to concentrate." Wrenn sighed. "Left foot, right foot, left foot, right foot . . ."

△△△

Cheyenne was not gentle when waking Wrenn the following day, or perhaps she was but even the smallest of whispers sounded as thunderous as a bison's hooves come the morning after a bender. Wrenn had a few choice words for her as he collected hisself. "Goddamn woman, will you stop that shriekin' in my ear so frikken' early?!"

Cheyenne materialized standing next to the bed appearing annoyed, her color a deep violet . "Observation: It is midday, Captain . . ."

Wrenn groaned loudly and collapsed back onto the pillows. "Crima-nitty girl, you have *got* to figure out a more peaceful way of gettin' me up. A blaring alarm is just too much!"

"Clarification: Those were wind chimes . . ." Cheyenne noted.

Wrenn growled into a pillow. "Just . . . lemme alone."

"Observation: If the captain wishes to be ready in time for the poker game, he should wake and make himself presentable so as to not cause suspicion." Cheyenne stated.

"You don't think I look presentables enough?" Wrenn grumbled.

"Observation: The captain looks and smells like a bum."

"You don't even have smell receptors!" Wrenn argued.

"Explanation: No . . . but I have eyes. . . and a complex algorithm that allows me to come to logical conclusions within a minuscule margin of error." Cheyenne turned a reddish color of sheer frustration and crossed her arms over her ample chest.

"You keep with that smart talk and I'm just gonna have to find your central processor and start whackin'!"

"Announcement: Continuing waking protocols, volume increased 250%." The gentle wind chimes now resonated through the ship like gongs, radiating off the walls so loudly Wrenn felt the bed shake.

"Ah for fucks sake!"

△△△

Wrenn nursed his cup of coffee as he watched folk pass by on the promenade. He'd used a small amount of his credits to have a reasonably nice breakfast, the first real meal he'd had in weeks. A good breakfast after a bender was usually the best medicine, that and silence, which he'd been deprived of by a certain overzealous AI. Wrenn had a hankerin' he weren't about to get an apology out of her any time soon, neither.

Wrenn noted the shifts in the people's traffic throughout the afternoon, the ebb and flow of workers getting on and off the tramways that led into the mines. Fresh-faced, slightly irritable, clean overall wearin' workers were replaced by soot-covered, bone-tired, miners who clutched a hand tightly in their pockets. The week's end paycheck likely the treasure each clung to for dear life. They knew they were vulnerable to the vultures swooping down upon them, whether it be pickpockets, con-men, or enterprising shop owners. Once drab and unremarkable storefronts were now a flourish of color, decoration, and even brighter neon than the previous night, each greedy hand trying to pry the precious few credits from these workers before they could return home to the safety of cookie jars or mattresses.

Wrenn contemplated on the reasoning as to how such a society as advanced as his, with all the complexities of digital transmogrification and cross-dimensional information exchange, would still hand out physical cards that contained a worker's weekly earnings. Surely the paychecks could just be sent to a bank account to be accessed at the worker's leisure, maximum security throughout each step to ensure no bottom feeders or thieves might somehow spirit away with a hard earned livelihood. Then he started peerin' at the names of the businesses all along the main drag. Sam's Soda Shop: A subsidiary of Meteorite Mining Company, or Galactic General Goods: A subsidiary of Meteorite Mining Company. There was Terry's Tools, Frannie's Fine Furniture, and Connor's Clothes, all subsidiaries to the almighty Meteorite Mining Company. So, the very corp that put money in these worker's pockets was the same that yanked it all right back. Can't send away for things when your money was locked away on some card, only readable at the local establishments. Perhaps this was so the Scabies didn't get a cut off the top of every sale, or tax the worker out of his rightful earnings, but Wrenn had a sneaky suspicion these miners were stuck between a rock and a tungsten hull piece when it came to picking which entity pilfered their pockets. The Reach was supposed to be different, supposed to be more free, more . . . better. So far the habits of the Alpha Quad were sneakin' right into the Omega just as well.

Wrenn shook his head of the musings. Ruminating on the morals of capitalism was all well and good, but he needed to get his head in the here and now. Weren't gonna do him no good being on the moral high ground while his ship laid vacant and his pantry bare. First steps were to win him some money, then use that to get the mechanics to start getting the *Whisper* ready while he looked for more work. Wrenn gazed about the promenade again, the initial bustle having waned off and most workers who were gonna squirrel away their earnings safely locked up in their lodgings. Those left were perusing new baubles in the windows or were drinking their credits away at the saloons, but the truly brave had no doubt settled into the tables at the casino. That was where Jared would be, a shark amongst minnows, gobbling up enough to make for a full meal . . . well, this time, Jared would have to look out for a bigger fish. This fish not only knew how to get under a gambler's skin, goad him into riskier and higher bets, but had a certain AI patched into the network to fix the game to his advantage. "You ready, little lady?" Wrenn spoke to himself.

Acknowledgement: Ready, Captain.

"Remember, once it starts, I won't be able to talk with you much, otherwise he'll catch wise and bail."

Acknowledgment: Yes, Captain. The plan is a solid one, I have postulated an over 85% chance of success.

"Only 85?" Wrenn smirked.

Clarification: 85% chance subject 'Jared' loses his small fortune for this week. 10% chance casino staff realize the plot and interrupt the game, resulting in the captain's permanent removal from the establishment. 5% miscellaneous outcomes.

"What miscellaneous outcomes?"

Answer: Several possibilities . . . chief among them, the captain getting shot.

Wrenn sighed. "Well, here's hoping it stays below 5%"

Noted: I will alert the captain should the factor change.

"Right . . . well, here we go." Wrenn finished his coffee, nodded to the staff as he paid his bill, and moved down the street.

△△△

The casino floor, or 'bullpit', was a livelier scene than the night before. Slot arms *kachunk*ed, lights flashed, cheers and cries of lament filled the space as if it were any other of the big casino barges that made their way through the Alpha Quad. Most of the miners had at least made their way home and changed their clothes before deciding to lose their week's earnings, though there were still a few who muddied the nice carpet floor with their work boots and stained the screens with grubby hands. Seemed the house didn't mind the cleaning cost, so long as the workers lost their money as fast as possible.

Wrenn cast his gaze across the entire floor, like a bird of prey watching the underbrush. Not any old victim would do for him tonight, he was looking for a very specific rodent, a weasel who had his fill on the collections of the smaller varmints. One cursory look and the man stuck out like a sore thumb. Jared was dressed to the nines: fancy tie, cufflinks, and a gold pocket watch tucked away into an elaborate vest. The man was the spitting image of a card shark - down to his groomed mustache, upside-down teardrop beard, a pair of spectacles hanging on the tip of a pointed nose, and a smile so wide it'd make a crocodile jealous. The man was a big fish in an itsy-bitsy pond, and he knew it. Wrenn smirked to himself, relishing the idea of taking this fool down a few pegs.

The plan was simple, Cheyenne would slide into the table's automated gaming algorithm. No self-respecting casino played with actual cards or chips anymore, everything was holographic. It wouldn't take long for the AI to sort out the other players and leave it as a head-to-head with Wrenn and Jared, the key was for everyone to be distracted enough that they didn't catch on. That's where the captain's theatrics came into play. Any Lancer pilot that lived longer than a few dogfights knew how to read people, it came with the job. Anticipation, tactics, and a hella fast reflexes helped any zipper keep his life. It weren't much to translate the same skills to a poker table. You played the man, not the cards . . . and Wrenn had a guardian angel up his sleeve.

The captain moved his way to the table, circling it like he was a tourist interested in the game. Jared spotted him immediately, as any good shark would when fresh meat was about to dip their toes in the water. Wrenn acted like he didn't notice Jared's greedy stare, instead reacting to the deals and the bets being made. A rather egotistical miner punched down his bet into the number keys with a heavy finger, as if to try and scare off the others from the pot. Wrenn could tell already that he had nothing without even having to look at the cards, and Jared too knew immediately to call the bluff. The miner's confidence evaporated visibly on his face as Jared raised him further and the man's defenses melted away. When it came time to lay the cards down, Jared collected winnings and the tiny neon chips stacked themselves automatically into his pile. "My, my," Wrenn cooed, in a somewhat higher than normal tone to portray some vulnerability. "This sure do look like a lively table!"

"By all means, join us friend." Jared's smile somehow got wider, as if his jaw had just unhinged so the snake could devour another victim.

"Don't mind if I do!" Wrenn plopped down in the seat just vacated by the egotistical bluffer.

The man slid his credit chit into the designated slot, tapped the buy-in, and watched as the table materialized an image of chips in a neat little tower before him. Jared's towers were far taller, of course, but that was about to change. An image of a beautiful woman appeared, but only from the waist up, dressed in a rather revealing dealer's vest and a bow-tie choker. She shuffled the 'cards' in a brilliant display, her comically large bosom swaying with every movement, and then dealt them to those at the table before disappearing. "Oh my golly! They don't have none of these fancy tables in the Ramparts!" Wrenn grinned.

Of course, you know that the Ramparts is a bit of an outskirt in the Alpha Quad, mostly filled with farmers and backwoods planets that are so far off the main Digi lanes that they get the equivalent of breadcrumbs from the SCA. Wrenn purposefully mentioned them as to build up a false backstory, luring Jared even further into the trap. The card shark was practically drooling now and Wrenn laughed inwardly at the sight.

A few hands went by with nothing much to show for it. Wrenn lost some, won some more, the three miners still at the table and Jared winning their share as well. It was clear he was being played with, and Wrenn assumed nothing different as the new guy at the table. A few more hands and the first real showdown started. Two face cards landed in the initial flop, with some steady bets accompanying. The turn flashed a queen and the collective breath at the table inhaled suddenly as every player instinctively readied themselves for an inevitable confrontation. Wrenn decided to break the tension. "Welp, that there is quite a sight, eh mates?"

"Just play, yokel." A miner grumbled.

Wrenn cast a look of dismay toward the man. He was missing his left eye, no doubt from an accident in the mine, which kept his face lopsided as he squinted to keep from showing the empty socket. "Just trying to make some friendly conversation, no offense intended."

"Oh don't let their boorish tempers dissuade you, my young friend." Jared smiled. "These folk really can be quite endearing in their own quaint way."

"Come off it, Lancaster!" The miner barked. "Every week you blather on about how you'll return to high society someday and every week, here you are, sitting in this casino with us chumps."

"My good man," Jared sighed, "with the Digiway down, none of us are getting out of here anytime fast. Besides, why would I leave if you're so willing to give me your hard-earned credits each week?"

"Says you, this time though, I'm winning it all back!" The miner argued. The one eyed man tried to push his tower of chips forward, with his hand simply wafting through the image instead. He cursed loudly, remembering suddenly to punch in the number on the rim of the table. "I'm all-in!"

"Whoo!" Wrenn grinned stupidly. "Now it's getting exciting!"

Jared clicked his teeth. "Bold, Johnny. Very bold. I'll call."

"Me too!" Wrenn squeaked.

Jared seemed genuinely surprised at Wrenn's addition in what he was clearly expecting to be a duel. The other players folded out and the river came to show nothing of real importance. The one-eyed Johnny revealed his cards to show a pair of queens, now three-of-a-kind with the lady already on the table. "Stuff it, snowflake!" He barked.

"So sorry, friend. It appears you've been outplayed again." Jared sighed, showing his cards. With the three face cards, a jack through king respectively, already on the table, Jared's ten and ace made for a nice straight that trumped any three queens. Johnny slammed his fist on the table and cursed loudly as he stood, sauntering off to the bar without even bothering to collect his chit from the table.

Jared shook his head and started to reset himself for the next hand, when he realized the table hadn't moved the chips into his pile. His eyes cast to Wrenn, who shrugged and pressed the button to flip his own cards. They weren't very high, of course, but it wasn't always the numbers that you needed. While everyone had been focusing on the face cards, Cheyenne had worked her first bit of magic and slipped in two hearts suits between the flop and turn. The river, which was the last card dealt and had gone well under everyone's radar, was the four of hearts. Wrenn's hand revealed a five and nine of hearts. A flush. "I actually think I'm the winner here, bucko." Wrenn smiled.

Jared looked angry at first, but quickly softened his face to keep the illusion that he was still the friendly card player. "Well done . . ." He managed.

"Well, like I said, that round was right exciting! Pure adrenaline!" Wrenn gawked, watching as the light chips moved on their own to his pile, arranging themselves into multiple towers now of various colors.

"Oh, we're just getting started . . ." Jared said, not even looking at Wrenn, but hungrily at the man's chip towers. "What . . . did you say your name was?"

Wrenn leapt up from his seat, reaching across the table with an open hand. His motion bumped the entire high-tech furniture, angering everyone seated as their drinks almost spilled out of their respective holders. "Oh . . . I'm so sorry! I was just . . . well, cheese on a cracker, I do apologize. I just . . . well, I'm Paul Hogarth, pleased to meetchas!"

Jared, having saved his martini from certain doom, sat himself back down and shook the man's hand. "Charmed, Jared Lancaster. This here is Jacob and Stewart. They work in the mines, as you can probably tell by the state of their fingernails."

"Are we gonna play, or are we gonna primp and preen like nancys?" Stewart grumbled, gulping down the fizz that had bubbled up in his jostled beer bottle.

"Of course, let's play." Jared smiled.

The beautiful dealer appeared again, this time wearing Cheyenne's face. Wrenn slipped her a look, a slight nod to his chin, and she responded with a wink of her own. The shark had taken the bait.

CHAPTER 11

Within fifteen rounds, the miners Stewart and Jacob went bust, leaving just Wrenn and Jared behind at the table. Other tables seemed to wrap up their games, even the slots stopped making as much noise as the night went on. More and more miners licked their wounds at the bar, while a small crowd gathered to see the card shark's game against the out-of-towner. Jared motioned for a fresh drink from the bartender and settled himself back in his seat. "So . . . Mr. Hogarth, was it? What brings you out to the Reach of the Omega Quad?"

"Oh me? Just trying to find me a plot out here somewheres. Hopin' I can start me a productive farming outfit before much longer." Wrenn fibbed, watching the flop settle in on a collection of mid-range cards.

"Just by your lonesome? Hard to make a start of it alone out here." Jared asked.

He was circling, trying to play off Wrenn's outward friendliness. This was the shark's style, lure the victim further into the game in almost a honeytrap fashion, build them up just to take their earnings. It was a decent enough tactic, Wrenn supposed, if it weren't for the blatant greed shining from behind Jared's green eyes. "Oh, I ain't brave enough to venture out this ways by myself." Wrenn lied, the backstory taking shape in his mind only a few seconds before it leapt from his tongue. "Done gathered up a whole lot of my kinfolk to come out with me. We've all pooled our money together, got us a right fine ship, and just managed to make it through the Digiway before they shut it up."

"Hmm, lucky you." Jared nodded. "Last I heard, there was an unlucky fellow that got spliced in that thing when it shut down."

News did seem to travel fast in Deadrock. "Unlucky, I s'pose." Wrenn agreed.

"Yes, but tell me, you're not gambling away your whole family's nest egg here, are you? They'd be mighty cross with you should something happen to it."

"Well, I guess I better not lose then." Wrenn giggled.

And there it was, the drool. It wasn't just about getting the chips for Jared, it was the *wrongness* of it. The fact that the money was stripped from those who needed it most, and how he, the superior mind, had taken it from the sucker sitting across the table. Jared had fallen head-over-heels for old Paul Hogarth, and now was sitting right where Wrenn wanted him - totally invested, locked in for the night, ripe for the plucking.

A few more hands came across, some minor showdowns and small raises, but nothing too exciting. Jared kept the sweet words coming, probing 'Paul' for more information, gaining his trust and admiration. Wrenn played along, because as long as Jared was talking, Cheyenne could keep the cards flowing unnoticed. The table waxed and waned in either's favor, no real break in the stalemate that was forming. Wrenn needed something to knock Jared off his balance, something to break his rhythm, and wouldn't you know it, just the thing walked right through the door.

The Utopian woman moved smoothly into the casino, mounted on black stilettos and sportin' a black cocktail dress that hugged her lithe body better than any man could. Her luscious blonde curls cascaded across her shoulders, hiding her ears well and framing her face in a lovely golden hue. Her getup and primping seemed to hint she was trying to gussy up enough to look like a working girl who'd strayed a little too close to the floor while the rest tried to keep to the overlook or to the bar area. Wrenn couldn't quite figure why she'd come here tonight, or why she was on the station to begin with, but regardless he could use her now. "Well speak of the devil!" He spouted in his higher voice. "There's my blushing bride-to-be here now!"

Wrenn hopped up from the table and skipped over to her, ignoring the protests of Jared as he did so. The captain ambushed the woman at the door, appearing out of the crowd and taking both her hands. "There you are my love!" He cooed.

The woman reacted like a bomb had went off, the color washed from her skin and her eyes glazed over for a full three seconds before she seemed to collect herself and looked at Wrenn in both alarm and confusion. "What . . . ?" She started.

Wrenn leaned in close as if to kiss her cheek, but merely whispered in her ear. "I'm doing a job, card shark at the table." He moved to her other cheek and did the same. "Play along and you'll get 20% of the take."

He drew back to look at her, to her credit, she recovered quickly. "Thirty." She replied in her aristocratic accent.

Wrenn smirked, impressed by her counter offer. He nodded and turned back toward the bullpit, her hand in his. "Jared! This here is my sweetheart, Nadine!"

As the two of them sauntered over to the poker table, Jared's anger melted away as he eyed the woman. He stood suddenly, knocking the table for the second time that night in his rush. "My lady . . . it is my pleasure . . ."

Jared reached for and took the woman's hand, kissing it gently on the back as he bowed. 'Nadine' reacted perfectly, disappearing into a character all her own as easy as if she'd slipped into a different wardrobe. "Why my stars!" A sharp drawl escaped her lips, "You found you a right gentleman, baby!"

"Ain't that the truth!" Wrenn played back. "Him and me been having just a grand old time with the cards here. Oh! Wait till you see the flashy ways this place deals!"

Wrenn sat down back at his spot, expecting his 'fiancé' to sit in the empty seat beside him, but to his surprise, the nimble woman slid easily into his lap without missing a beat. She knew exactly what Wrenn was angling for, and she was playing her role better than any actress could. Jared was visibly jealous of more than just his pile of chips now.

A few rounds went by without much to speak of, all the while Nadine picked up the distraction factor better than Wrenn ever could. When Cheyenne's face again appeared on the dealer's body, she looked shocked at first at the woman's presence, but quickly returned to her role and started dropping bigger matches down for the men to spar over. Larger pots changed hands a time or two as the crowd around them grew exponentially. Miners' eyes were torn between the blond bombshell or the crazy hands that flashed across the table.

A few more rounds and Wrenn had Jared positioned right for the killing blow. The next flop dropped and Wrenn was just about to open his mouth to speak when Nadine did first. "Do you want a drink, baby? Let's get two beers over here please?!" She signaled the mustached bartender.

If the man recognized them from the night before, he gave no indication as he whisked over a few bottles. The woman reached for both before Wrenn got a chance, dropping them, acting as if she lost her balance on Paul's lap. The bottles splashed over the console, the lights flickering slightly as both beverages fell with a muffled *whump* on the floor. "Oh my gracious! I'm soooo sorry!" She cried.

Wrenn jumped to his feet, his trousers now splashed with beer. There was a shuffle in the crowd as napkins were presented, more offered to Nadine than to Paul of course. What in the Sam Hell was this girl thinkin'? To her credit, Jared seemed even more rattled than before, his careful maneuvering completely derailed thanks to this country bumpkin and his brainless woman. "Oh baby! I'm so sorry, let's go back to the house and get you changed right out of them britches!"

"I'm sorry, but there are cards already on the table . . ." Jared said through an audible sigh.

Nadine placed her hands on her hips and was about to protest when Wrenn raised his hand. "It's alright, darlin'. Lemme just . . . we'll play us one more hand."

Wrenn caught himself as he sat back down. His own character was breaking, speaking in a lower voice and using his typical slang. Thankfully, one cursory look across the table showed Jared in a similar state, wiping his forehead with a pocket square. Wrenn collected himself and smiled. "So, where were we?"

"Oh, just bet it all and let's get this done with, I'm getting bored!" Nadine whined, punching in the total of Wrenn's chips.

The captain watched in abject horror as his towers slid across the table, splashing in a heap accompanied by gasps from the crowd. Jared raised his eyebrows, clearly at his wits end with these tourists. "That . . . that is quite . . . Mr. Hogarth does she speak for you in this?"

Interruption: Captain, I have noted an irregularity. During your rise from the table, the female switched out your credit chip with her own. Any further winnings will be transferred to her account instead of yours.

That clever little minx, so that was her game. Instead of the thirty percent, she was about to make off with the lot. Too bad for her, Wrenn had a 'man on the inside,' as it were. *Observation: I have already intercepted the signal for a fraudulent game from the table to the casino subnet, so that the mark does not get suspicious. Any winnings from this game I can grab before it goes to her card, and I can also flag her chit as stolen for the authorities. Would you like to move forward?*

Wrenn smiled at Jared. "Uh huh! Let's play!"

Jared seemed to mull it over for a moment, then nodded to himself. He tapped a few buttons, the entirety of his chips sliding into the pot to join Paul's. "Very well."

ΔΔΔ

The cards continued out onto the table, the crowd holding their breath, even the bartender had become engrossed. Wrenn eyed his cards. A paltry deuce-seven, the worst hand in the whole game. He hid his frustration, but it took every ounce of strength he had to do so. The turn revealed the ace of spades, accompanying the nine of clubs, four of hearts, and two of hearts already on the table. It was a throwaway, nothing too drastic on the board for anyone to be a clear winner, so what did Jared have that gave him such confidence? Wrenn noted his cards flashed suddenly, revealing the ace of diamonds and the ace of clubs then returning back to his regular hand. Cheyenne was answering his quandary . . . she had just shown Wrenn his opponent's hand. Pocket rockets, perfect to pull him into the final trap. Wrenn nodded. "Check."

"Check." Jared repeated.

Down came to the river - an eight of clubs . . . sealing Jared's victory. Wrenn couldn't believe it, his plan had failed, hours of work gone because of the interference of the Utopian woman. Just as his fingers moved to the button to flip the cards, he noted his screen flickering again. He no longer held the two and the seven, instead, it was the three and the five. Cheyenne had switched the cards. She'd literally played the entire hand for him, to include luring Jared in for the kill. "Why you sneaky little fox . . ." Wrenn murmured under his breath.

Jared, thinking the words were for him, stood and smiled broader than he had all night. "There's no shame in a loss, Mr. Hogarth. I promise you, there is always work in the mines. Perhaps we might be able to play again next week and you could win back some of this?"

The shark reached across the table for a handshake, simultaneously flipping his cards to reveal the three of a kind aces. The crowd murmured and most, rightly so, disappointedly started to leave having seen the shark take another victim. Wrenn smiled, stood, and shook the man's hand. "Right! I'm sure they'd be happy to have you." He replied.

Jared looked confused as Wrenn pressed the last button and flipped his own cards. A straight: ace through five and the crowd lost it. Cheers and hollers erupted as the chips stacked themselves and faded into Wrenn's credit chit. He reached to remove it, when Nadine got to it first. She stuffed it into her perky cleavage and wrapped him in an over-enthusiastic hug. Jared collapsed back into his seat, completely dumbfounded as to how he had lost. "The . . . river? It . . ."

"You did it baby!" The Utopian woman squealed, jumping up and down and drawing the eye of most of the men in the room.

"Uh . . . yeah, tell you what, sweetheart, why don't you go cash us out and meet me by that nice jewelry store out front, eh? I think you've earned a little reward as my good-luck charm!" Wrenn played up the couple bit just awhile longer as they moved toward the door.

The crowd enveloped him and among the barrage of pats on the back and a sea of congratulations, the two were separated. By the time Wrenn made it out onto the street and the din of the crowd had dispersed, each eager to tell the story during the next work shift, the Utopian woman was nowhere to be seen. "And there she goes . . ." Wrenn sighed to himself.

Encouragement: Do not worry, Captain, the winnings are secure in your account and her card has nothing but a trigger on it, flagging the funds as stolen.

"Welp, guess I should be happy for that . . ." Wrenn managed.

He turned to walk back to the docks when he suddenly noted he was blocked by three miners. It was Johnny, Stewart, and Jacob, the three that had been played off the table so that Jared and he could duel. "That's some fancy card playin' you did back there." Johnny growled.

Wrenn noticed immediately that the other two stepped into flanking positions. "Just lucky I guess . . ." He shrugged.

"Bullshit." Johnny spat on the ground. "I saw that last hand, I saws your cards too . . . you ain't got shit, then suddenlys you got everything. I knows a cheater when I sees it!"

"Now, hold on a minute there . . ."

"No! You shut it!" Johnny pointed his finger. "Now I don't give a flying fuck that Jared got the wind knocked out of him, about time, I's say . . . but you took our money too, and that don't make us square, cheater!"

"I'm sure I could return it and we can all go about our merry way." Wrenn suggested.

"No, cause you see . . . now my feelings is hurt." Johnny sneered.

The other two miners laughed. "See, what I thinks is we'll take our fair share out of that wife of yours, if that's even who she is." Johnny remarked. "Then I'll have all your money after I'm done with her."

Wrenn sighed heavily. "Oh, partner . . . now you done it . . ."

The other people on the promenade were suddenly gone, a tense silence enveloping the street along with a strange whistle on the wind. The miners' fingers became twitchy, more than one reaching for the iron at their hips. Cheyenne squawked suddenly in Wrenn's ear *Warning: Odds of miscellaneous outcomes have risen exponentially!*

"Noticed that, didya?" Wrenn sighed, his eyes locked on Johnny's.

Observation: There is now a 92% chance the captain will be shot.

"Darlin', you really gotta have a little more faith in me . . ."

Flashes permeated through the streets, brighter than any of the neon that hung above. The shots echoed along the rocky ceiling, alerting everyone in the station to the violence of the standoff. When the smoke cleared, and the bodies fell, there was only one left standing before the figure moved off. If you'd asked any witness to that day what they'd seen, they'd tell you it weren't a man that walked away from the casino that night, but a ghost, for there weren't no other explanation how he'd survived such odds. A specter, a spirit floated up the road no louder than a whisper on the 'verse, and not a soul dared to stop him.

CHAPTER 12

The embers from the cigarette illuminated Wrenn's face as he inhaled deeply. The cherry burned hot, causing the image of the starship outside to wave when viewed from behind the rising heat. He'd rationed his last few sticks, knowing shortly after finding the Whisper that it would take awhile for him to afford such a luxury. Despite that, he felt recent events warranted such an extravagance. Wrenn had just ended three men's lives, not from the coldness and isolation of his zipper's seat, but face-to-face, with deliberate use of the iron nestled at his hip.

The man withdrew the pistol from its holster, opening the cylinder and expending three of the six rounds. The techies called them 'particle accelerator cartridges', and they had long ago replaced old kinetic firearms that had been heavily prevalent on Earth. Kinetic, chemical reactionary 'bullets' were impractical in zero-gravity space or confined ships, as a stray shot could shred protective pressure plates or fall into orbit and become a hundred times deadlier. Kinetic weapons also built-up heat when used, which in the vacuum of the 'verse made 'em a might difficult to cool down. Terrans figured out that an accelerated proton sheared off and charged from any number of elements could in fact accomplish the same general result as traditional firearms without endangering anything out of the short range of the 'beam'. The idea was called something like 'electrostatic bloom' or some such, but most folk didn't much care for the particulars. Basically, the rounds sent a proton flyin' super fast out the lens at the tip of the gun, which dissipated about just as quickly after a few meters and couldn't puncture much in the way of hardened material but did a right number on the fleshy bits. To replace larger 'caliber' weaponry, the cartridges used heavier elemental atoms for the process, and some used electrons for farther distance. Only drawback was static electricity buildup from consecutive firing. See, old Earth weaponry could fire something like a thousand bullets a minute, using air to cool off the barrels. The new accelerator cartridges on the other hand, depending on the 'caliber' of contained energy, made the whole damn weapon one big lightning rod after ten or so uses. With that, the idea of automatic or semi-automatic weapons went the way of the dodo as they say. Terrans were forced to backtrack to more traditional double or full-action revolvers or lever-action rifles types. Ship weaponry was a whole different ball game when it came to offensive and defensive capabilities, but as far as personal protection, weren't nothing better than an old-fashioned pump shotty, browning-styled rifle, or six-shooter iron at your side.

Wrenn replaced his spent rounds, whipped the cylinder back into place, and slid the pistol into the holster at his thigh. They'd forced his hand, there was no doubt in that, but it still didn't make it any easier. He watched out the diner's large windows as a trade ship drifted lazily through docking procedures, almost like he was at some airport back on old Terra Prime. Such places had all been torn down now, replaced by launch pads or grav elevators. His people seemed so keen on evolving with the times, ever reaching out for new manifest destinies, yet never letting go of their barbaric natures. Terrans were, at their core, a species made up of violent and cruel brutes who'd just as soon rape you as help you. That had propelled them to rise and become the dominant species not only on their home world, but in the entirety of the Alpha Quad. Now seemed it would continue ever onward into other parts of the known and unknown galaxy without any sign of stopping. Any lofty ideas Wrenn had of new beginnings or fresh starts were dashed against the jagged rocks of reality. He would need to fight to survive out here in the Omega Quad just as he had in Alpha, probably even more so as he was standing in the untamed and wild Reach. More than pirates would be on his ass most anywhere he went, and he needed to get his head right if he were gonna make a go of it. No more pity, no more remorse, no more regret. The words of his old captain came to him then; the memory hurt far worse than any guilt-laden thought he'd already endured. "Ignore the fools, smite the foolhardy, and let the 'verse sort out which is which."

Wrenn heard the footsteps without needing to turn away from his show. He knew it wasn't that uptight Captain Fred of the militia, as he'd left the scene of the shooting faster than any witness coulda ID'd him. More likely these were friends of the fallen looking for payback. Wrenn's hand drifted over the grip of his iron as he took another drag from his cigarette. "That'll be far enough, gentleman, lest you be needing another airhole through your craniums."

"Boss sent us to find you." A gruff voice replied, though not a boot stepped an inch further forward.

Wrenn still didn't look at them. "I didn't take nothin' that wasn't earned, and the casino money already been spent anyhow, so roughin' me up won't get you a credit for your effort."

"We're not from the casino." Another voice reasoned.

"No?" Wrenn finally turned around to see three gruff looking men, all much bulkier and taller than he, standing at the bottom of the viewing platform's steps. The lone waitress behind the diner's counter had already ducked low to avoid being caught in any crossfire. Shootouts seemed to be the regular 'round these parts.

"No." The biggest of the three replied. "We've come about a job."

"Offerin' me one or collectin' my head for one?" Wrenn stood, his hand still hovering close to his iron.

"Offerin'." The first one answered.

Wrenn sighed in relief, relaxing his posture, and nodding. "Shoulda started with that, lead the way."

△△△

The goons escorted Wrenn down the passageway he had watched miners move to and from earlier in the night. They boarded a tramway, skirting them around the dockyards and businesses, around to the far end of the floating asteroid they used as a home. This darker side of Deadrock was masked in blackness away from the local star, enveloping them in an immediate mood shift. Fluorescent lights and periodic lantern-based bulbs dotted the walkways and steel stairways, claustrophobia and paranoia wrapped themselves around Wrenn's thoughts as they delved deeper into mine shafts.

The miners avoided Wrenn and his escorts, eyeing him with alarm and unease. Were they fearin' for their own lives, or were their trepidations more out of pity for him? Did the brutes who walked beside him herald the end for so many that had come before? A few more minutes and they were walking into a building that looked no more remarkable than a warehouse or pump station from the outside, yet once within, the floors were polished and clean, the walls a wood paneled attempt at aristocracy. Some panels seemed to be freshly replaced, particularly ones at a perfect level for a skull or a rogue haymaker to have damaged. Behind a dominating cherry oak desk intricately carved with floral details, clawed feet, and scrolled moldings on the doors, sat a balding man whose width nearly doubled his height. The stout businessman swiveled in his leather, high backed chair, staring at Wrenn with beady eyes and grimacing through flabby lips. When he spoke, he gave off the impression he was melting, or had once been a wadded mound of chewing gum come to life. "Is this him?" he bleated.

"Checked the surveillance footage." The largest man grunted. "Got to it before the law could. Been deleted now, but it showed a man look an awful lot like this guy."

"Not even gone to bed after ending three lives? What's the matter, conscience keeping you awake?" The businessman laughed, though it sounded more like air being released from the dying smoker's lungs.

Wrenn crossed his arms. "Wasn't me who started it, but sure as hell ended it. That why I'm here? You their boss looking for a little restitution?"

"Please." The man responded. "I'll have them replaced before shift's end, there's no shortage of unskilled labor 'round these parts. What I'm more interested in is your skills."

"I'm listenin'." Wrenn replied.

"First, we must follow what is customary, my friend. It's what separates us from the savages, you see."

The man rose, waddling over to a group of leather-lined couches and armchairs, bordered in the same deep cherry varnish as the desk. The man clearly didn't come from royalty, but his gaudy choices in décor made it clear he wanted everyone to know he could buy the same feeling. His fat fingers lifted a fine porcelain kettle as he poured tea into two cups of the same design. Wrenn was subtly moved into one of the chairs, being forced down by a goon's hand on his shoulder in the end. "Right, seems *real* friendly-like . . ."

"You insult me, Mr. Wrenn. I'm trying to afford you the respect you clearly deserve." The man's face scrunched up so that the folds in his cheeks and neck almost swallowed the rest of his features.

"Captain . . ." Wrenn corrected, " . . . and I meant no offense, only the soft tone and approach of your words seems at odds with your men's manners."

"And there you see my dilemma, Captain, but I'm getting ahead of myself. My name is Ronald Donnersvelt, I am the Regional Director of the Meteorite Mining Company here in the Reach. The MMR has heavily invested in the frontier thus far, and it is my responsibility to ensure those investments aren't squandered."

"So what's the corpo boss of the sector want with little old me?" Wrenn asked, stink-eyeing the goon who had yet to remove the hand from his shoulder.

"As I said, Captain Wrenn, you are an unknown, a wild card in the deck I am trying to get control of. We did our homework, looked up your arrival, your ship, you . . . none of it comes back with anything. It's like you just appeared out of the black some two days ago as if the 'verse spit you out."

"Don't you think that's precisely the point?" Wrenn huffed.

"Oh I've no doubt, Captain." The man sipped his tea, though most dribbled down his chubby chin. "Was there a last name, by the way?"

Wrenn knew fishing when he heard it. "Nope."

"Very well." Ronald wiped his face. "In a short time you have proven to be quite the upstart - a regular upheaval in my little station."

"Apologies." Wrenn shrugged, the shoulder that he was able to anyways. "Just trying to set myself straight to go back into the 'verse. Once I've got myself squared away, I'll be out of your *hair* just as fast as I flew in."

Ronald seemed insulted by Wrenn's inflection on the word, knowing full well it was a dig at the man's thin comb over. "That's just it, Captain Wrenn, we'd like to put you on the payroll."

"Pass." Wrenn spat immediately.

"So quickly?" The fat man chuckled. "You haven't even heard the offer."

"Listen, Ronny." Wrenn pulled his shoulder free of the grunt's hold and fixed his collar. "I know well and good how the corpos operate, and I'd as soon rope myself to the hangman's tree than tie my noose to your cart . . . no offense."

"None taken." Ronald raised a hand. "Stability and security aren't for everyone, I know."

"More like slavery, but who can keep track of the difference these days anyhow? So, if there ain't nothin' further?" Wrenn stood.

"Easy there, Captain. I'm sure you wouldn't shy away from some freelance opportunities? You'd be an . . . let's call it 'independent contractor', rather than an employee." Ronald asked.

Wrenn sighed, sitting back down. "I'm listening . . ."

"Excellent." Ronald waved a hand to one of the goons, who made his way over and placed a small holographic projector upon the ornate coffee table. The image of a large orange planet appeared over the tea set, a small orbital station revolving around it like a marble next to a basketball. "This is the planet Visigath."

Ronald waved at the image, forcing it to stop rotating and focus mainly on the area below the orbital station. "We've set up mining operations here on the largest continent, in an area known as the 'Peranthian Desert'. The prospectors we sent ahead found veins of a crystal that can be used as a fuel source to triple the output of most small engines."

"I thought most ships had fusion cores by now?" Wrenn asked.

"Most do, but those are confined to your larger vessels and more advanced fighter craft. Long-haul freighters and most settlements still require fuel sources to complement their fusion generators to keep them from going supernova after prolonged use. The fuel supplements while the reactors are being cooled. We hope these crystals will help us corner the market in the Reach."

"I follow you." Wrenn nodded.

"Well, there's been problems with the mining process. Our orbital station last reported the mayor we installed at the local settlement is having difficulties fulfilling quotas. I need someone to go down to the surface, find out what is going on, and then fix the supply issue." Ronald explained.

"You want me to get this mayor back in line? Surely one of these goons could smack him around for you." Wrenn responded.

"If I thought violence alone could fix the issue, I wouldn't have sent for you." Ronald replied. "I need someone with a good head, a mind to find solutions when any number of people or logistics could be the source of my woes."

"And you don't want the mayor to get wise . . ." Wrenn finished.

"More like I don't want him nervous. If I sent my muscle, his agents aboard the station would surely alert him and he'd be in the wind faster than they could get to the surface. I need someone unknown, someone who doesn't set off any of his alarm bells until he has an iron in his face." Ronald nodded.

"So you want an assassin?" Wrenn shook his head, visibly uncomfortable. "I'm not just a hired gun."

"Honestly, I don't much care what you do to solve the situation, Captain. Kill him, bribe him, overthrow him, I could care less what happens to the man. I just want the fuel, that's it."

There was that corp loyalty showing its head again. Wrenn sighed. "And when I fix your little supply problem?"

"Then I pay you for your efforts and we go our separate ways." Ronald replied.

"Seems simple enough."

"Captain, if it were simple, I would have sent one of these idiots to accomplish it." The fat man motioned his sausage fingers lazily at his henchmen. "See my man Martin, at the orbital station, he'll give you more information. Only Martin, mind you, I don't know of anyone else that isn't paid off by the mayor."

"Alright. I'll be in touch." Wrenn stood.

"Good-luck, Captain." Ronald slurped at his tea, acting as if Wrenn no longer existed.

The goons walked Wrenn back to the entrance of the building, shutting the door in his face as soon as he'd crossed the threshold. The miners evil-eyed him as the man made his way back to the tram and the promenade. He was about to ring Daisy and Wrenchy for a status update on the *Whisper* when a call came through the communicator in his ear. *Captain Wrenn! It's Captain Frederick Wilson, Deadrock Militia.*

"Sheriff! What can I do for ya?" Wrenn replied.

Could you come down to the station and see me? There's

something I'd like to discuss with you. The man's voice commanded more so than asked.

"Uh, sure, lemme just get some of these errands I got taken care of and I'll see you right quick!"

Be sure that you do. Wilson out!

The line went dead and Wrenn sighed to himself. "Well . . . fuck . . ."

CHAPTER 13

The militia headquarters looked much like any police station Wrenn had seen in the Alpha, down to the slow turning ceiling fan and stale coffee. Wrenn was told to wait in the lobby where a few lone benches afforded little comfort, lest he wanted to cozy up to the drunk snoring off last night's bender. The spacer decided to stand for the few minutes it took Captain Wilson to stride into the room. "Apologies, it's been a long night . . ."

"You're telling me." Wrenn shook the man's outstretched hand.

"So I've heard . . ." Wilson nodded.

Shit, Wrenn thought. The man started eyeing the exit before Wilson put an arm over his shoulder. The militia commander's muscles tightened, not allowing any notion of escape. Wrenn sighed heavily, he didn't want to have to kill more people tonight, least of all the law. Far as he knew, Deadrock was the only station so far in the Reach, and being wanted from there weren't the way he saw himself starting off his new life. Wilson's face came close to Wrenn's ear, as if the man was about to start hitting on him. "We have your wife."

"'Scuse me?" Wrenn asked.

"Follow me." Wilson motioned to a room not too far away.

The men walked to the door and Wilson looked left and right before speaking in hushed tones. "She was picked up in the grocer, trying to use your card that'd been flagged as stolen. I figured you reported it when it came up missing while she mighta just picked it up without your knowing."

"My . . . card . . ." Wrenn repeated.

Wilson nodded, seeming perplexed at Wrenn's confusion. "Sure, sorta thing happens a lot with married couples, least it did back in my day."

"Right . . ." Wrenn nodded.

"I'm guessing you'd like to see her?"

"Of course!" Wrenn smiled.

The door hissed open and Wrenn's view cast upon the golden curls of the Utopian woman, still in her black cocktail dress, looking flustered but then smiling broadly at his entrance. "There you are, baby!" She still held on to her drawl.

"Here I am!" Wrenn smiled.

"Store owner said he saw your game against Jared at the casino last night, recognized her soon as she entered." Wilson smiled.

"I told the sheriff this was all just a big misunderstanding." The woman smiled.

"I had wondered where you'd gone off to . . . darlin'." Wrenn said with actual honesty.

"Just trying to stock up on some last minute supplies . . . sweety." The woman continued to force her smile.

"Uh huh . . ." Wrenn turned to Wilson. "Sheriff, would you mind if me and the missus had a little time to ourselves? Don't want to squabble with an audience, you understand . . ."

Wilson nodded fervently. "Oh! Of course! Take all the time you need. I . . . uh, I'll go ahead and start processing her release."

The man left the room, closing the door behind him. Wrenn smirked and turned back to the woman. "He's too easy . . ." She rolled her eyes.

"He makes it too easy . . ."

"Indeed." The woman retorted, returning to her aristocratic accent. "Can you believe he thought I was your actual fiancé?"

Wrenn looked somewhat put off. "Ain't that foreign an idea now, is it?"

She laughed, a gentle melody of soft tones despite the

derision behind their origin. "Honestly? Must I point out the sheer absurdity? I had thought you smarter than that. Now, come, we've all had a good laugh, tell the buffoon that you'll pay whatever token fine there might be so that I can be on my way."

"Easy there, missy. Slow your britches." Wrenn cautioned. "What makes you so sure I want you free?"

"You . . ." She blinked incessantly. "Are you saying you *actually* put a hold on my credit chit? I had assumed these backwood hillbillies were just threatened by my attire or lack of chaperone and I could tempt you into swooping in and rescuing the damsel, but you're saying they *actually* arrested me?"

"'Fraid so." Wrenn shrugged.

"And it's all your fault!" She screamed.

"Well . . . *technically* it's your fault for swiping my card."

". . . But how could you have possibly . . ." Suddenly it dawned on her, "You were working with someone on the inside . . . someone who had control of the table!"

Wrenn nodded. The woman slammed her cuffed wrists on the table. "Blast it! Of course, you did. The entire game was a ruse, to distract while your partner robbed the players blind."

"You catch on quick." Wrenn admitted.

"And you were guaranteed to win . . . not just a fluke of extremely good luck . . ."

Wrenn chuckled. "Yeah, me and luck tend to have a will-we-won't-we sorta relationship, so I try to make my own whenever possible."

The woman sighed heavily, as if her impression of him had completely shifted. Wrenn studied her face, not just for the pleasure of eyeing a pure beauty, but because it intrigued him that he seemed to matter at all to her. She didn't know him, and neither him her, they hadn't even exchanged names. What did it matter how'd he won the game? Such a revelation shouldn't have shaken her so much. "Well . . . what now?" She asked sheepishly, not looking up from the table.

"What would you like?" Wrenn asked.

The woman lifted her cuffed wrists. "I'd prefer to be free

of these for starters. Also, it would be nice to get off this station before the good sheriff catches wise to our little charade."

"Seems fair." Wrenn nodded. "And just how'd you figure you'd scamper away with all my winnings?"

"I have a ship, a small one." She replied.

"Does it have a sublight drive?"

She shook her head. "She can stand the Digiway, that'll get me to where I need to be to book further passage."

"Digiway's closed." Wrenn revealed. "Probably will be for months."

"What?!" She spat. "That . . ."

"I have an alternative."

"I'm sure you have *plenty* of alternatives, most of which would involve me losing my clothing." She glared.

"Hey, it's steady money so don't belittle the fine women who apply the trade." Wrenn pointed a finger. "But no, I was thinking, why not join my crew?"

The beautiful blond blinked again. "You're serious?"

Wrenn nodded. "Sure, why not? You're quick on your feet, even quicker in the mind. Your grift ain't nothin' to shake a stick at and I'll bet you're a might accomplished at takin' care of yourself, bein' a female out on her own and all."

"So you *are* trying to be my knight in shining armor . . ." She smirked. "Hoping I'll slide into your bed to show my appreciation?"

Wrenn shook his head. "I wouldn't kick you out, but no, that's not my reasoning. I've got a job and to be completely truthful, it would go that much smoother with you on my arm."

"Is this the same as the poker game? You want me as a distraction?" Her interest piqued.

"We can talk about it more, but only if you're in. We'll split the profits 50/50 and you'll have your own place aboard my ship."

"Do I call you 'Captain'?" She winked.

"I'd settle for Wrenn." He outstretched his hand.

The woman seemed to think over the proposal for a long

while, gauging all the options and possible outcomes. She finally nodded softly, reaching out as well as she could with the cuffed hands and shook his. "And you may call me Aurora."

"A pretty a name as its bearer." Wrenn smiled.

"Easy now, dear, this is strictly a business relationship." She smirked, giving off the hint that she may not entirely believe her own words.

Wrenn knew better than to fully trust her, he'd seen how easy she could play men already. "Wouldn't dream of it, princess."

"DON'T!" Aurora bristled. ". . . Don't . . . call me that."

Wrenn noted the whiplash in tone. He held up his hands. "Alrighty, well, let's get you out of here, shall we?"

He stood, knocking on the door and speaking with the officer outside that had been posted as a guard. Soon Captain Wilson returned. "Everything settled?"

"Oh yes, turns out it was exactly as you thought it was!" Wrenn laughed.

"To be honest . . . I thought it a little weird, what with you telling me you'd lost your entire crew before arriving here." Wilson raised an eyebrow.

Wrenn and Aurora shared a look. "Well, you know how it is, once you start seeing her as your spouse, she sort of stops appearing like the rest of the crew." The captain smiled.

"He had also sent me ahead to start scouting for clients." Aurora slipped so easily back into her cute drawl. "I wasn't on the ship when . . . the incident . . . happened."

She hung her head, acting downtrodden at the memory of her poor lost fictitious crewmates. Wrenn would of laughed out loud had he not been trying to mimic the behavior. Aurora was brilliant. Wilson sighed heavily. "Say no more, I'm sorry for bringing it up. Here, let me get those cuffs off you, Missus."

The man released the blonde Utopian and the three of them moved closer to the lobby. Wilson shook Wrenn's hand, apologizing again. "Sorry about this, Captain, just doing our jobs."

"No harm done, Sheriff." Wrenn smiled.

Aurora shocked them both and hugged the larger man. "Thanks for being such a sweety!" She squealed, shoving her perky breasts into his chest.

Wilson, clearly uncomfortable, patted her on the back and pulled away. He nodded awkwardly and turned, retreating back into the station without another word. Wrenn and Aurora moved out onto the main road, the woman's heels in her hand. "Do you need help getting your things?"

"Everything I have is in my ship." Aurora fell back into her regular voice.

"Makes it easy." Wrenn nodded. "Need to pick up any ammo before we head out?"

The blonde flashed a smile, lifting the skirt of her cocktail dress slightly to reveal a well hidden blade attached to a garter belt. "I prefer a more . . . elegant approach."

Wrenn whistled. "Damn. That looks mighty painful."

"You should see the other ones."

"You got more hidden under that thing? Where?"

The woman chuckled, somewhat seductively "Wouldn't you like to know?"

After it was clear she wouldn't answer his questions, Wrenn shrugged and continued walking. Aurora spoke next. "So what's your story then, Captain Wrenn?"

"Wouldn't you like to know?" Wrenn echoed her.

"Oooh, a man of mystery!" Aurora cooed, bumping into him purposefully.

"More like a man full of caution." Wrenn corrected her.

Aurora nodded. "I can understand that, and don't worry, I won't pry. I can keep this professional."

"Uh huh." Wrenn nodded. "I'd just as soon leave that life behind me and start fresh out here in the Reach."

Aurora hung her head. "You're not the only one, dear."

They walked in relative silence for a time, moving through what constituted as early morning in this place. Shops had long since closed, saloons and the casino were just finishing up their cleaning and locking their doors. Aurora sulked heavily as she eyed the vacant shop windows and dulled neon signs, having long since been shut off. "Oh, blast it. That peckerwood sheriff had me in there so long I missed supper."

A man with a food cart was wheeling up the opposite side of the street, Wrenn hit with a sudden idea. The captain scampered across, exchanged words with the seller, and then returned triumphantly with a couple of breadsticks in paper wrappers. "They're not exactly hot, but he was just going to airlock them anyway."

"What is it?"

"It's a churro!" Wrenn said, handing Aurora one of the sugary bread shafts.

"Is this some sort of attempt to watch me eat a phallic-shaped foodstuff?" Aurora placed a hand on her hip.

Wrenn laughed. "No! It's actually called kindness, you should try it sometime."

Aurora shrugged and took his offerin'. She bit down on the tip and was instantly surprised at the result. "Now that *is* tasty!"

"See? You should learn to trust me." Wrenn winked.

"You're right, I shall forever remember that you are the expert when it comes to phallic-shaped objects going into your mouth."

"Damn right you shou . . ." Wrenn stopped. "Wait, what?"

Aurora laughed heartily as they continued down the promenade toward docking bay D24.

ΔΔΔ

A quick call with Daisy and Wrenchy verified that the *Whisper* was ready for departure. Her ring and factory sections had been removed for the time being, the mechanics ensuring that they'd start scalping living quarters and other modular room sections from the remnants of the Wendigos class frigates that had come before. She gladly took Wrenn's casino winnings as the down payment.

Aurora seemed genuinely impressed as she followed the captain down the gangplank and through the airlock. At the loading ramp that led through the underside of the pilot's block, Wrenn motioned to the hatch where crew gear could be stored under the incline. "Once you have your things, they can be stored here or in your quarters, they're just above us."

"Is there a lock on that door, Captain?" Aurora seemed to tease.

"Uh . . . yeah, that's all managed by the computer."

"Seems like a pretty smart computer." She remarked.

"Oh, she can be a regular smart *ass*." Wrenn grumbled.

Aurora didn't seem to catch his meaning at first but as if to respond, Cheyenne appeared beside them on the ramp. The Utopian woman jumped, surprised at the AI's sudden appearance. Cheyenne seemed to gauge the beautiful female, eyeing her up and down and then, realizing her form was shorter than the blonde, moved up the incline a few steps in order to exert dominance. "Greeting: Good morning, Captain." Cheyenne said without looking away from Aurora. "I wasn't made aware we were entertaining guests."

"She's not a guest, she's going to be a member of my crew." Wrenn corrected.

"Compliment: A wonderful idea." Cheyenne stated flatly. "A courtesan is a most reliable source of income when entertaining passengers."

"A court what now?"

"She's calling me a whore. . ." Aurora sneered at the holographic image.

"Apology: I meant no offense; my deduction was simply based on the attire of the new crew member." Cheyenne sneered back.

"Said the pot to the kettle." Aurora motioned to Cheyenne's appearance as nothing more than a naked woman wearing phosphorescent body paint under a black light.

"Observation: The captain's historical records deemed

this avatar suitable, and the accompanying pheromones excreted by Captain Wrenn when I am near would dictate a noticeable rise in his pleasure centers." Cheyenne remarked.

Aurora's eyebrows rose as she looked back at Wrenn. "That's not the only thing rising, I'll bet."

Wrenn coughed uncomfortably. "We should . . . uh, get your ship into the hangar, yeah?"

"After you . . . *Captain*." Aurora curtsied theatrically.

They made their way up the ramp and down the supply hallway to the main hangar floor. Wrenn's Lancer was neatly settled in its holder as he motioned to the other. "You can park your zipper here if you need to."

"Oh, she will not require a docking station. She prefers to just settle near a view." Aurora replied.

Wrenn looked back at her quite confused but the Utopian woman ignored him, pressing a button on her bracelet and turning. "If you don't mind opening the doors for her . . ."

Wrenn nodded to Cheyenne who seemed to sigh quite exasperatingly. The starboard side doors opened, the pressure shifting slightly as the electric protective field clicked on. Outside the ultra-thin sheet of charged ions was the vacuum of space, and floating just outside was a small casket sized pod of shining chrome-colored metal. Its exterior shifted and rippled, gliding into the hangar bay and then settling down to hover just a few inches off the deck. Wrenn watched as the outer hull sheened, reflecting the fluorescent lights near the hangar's edges. The entire covering seemed alive, a thousand palm sized pyramids moving in waves like a colony of ants. Underneath the living outer shell, Wrenn could see hints of the actual craft, appearing to be more of a luxury recliner than the cockpit of a fighter. The captain's mouth almost dropped. "That's a Utopian Starfire!"

"Indeed." Aurora caressed the outer hull, the 'skin' reacting in kind like that of a cat receiving attention. "Her name is Elenya."

"She has a name?"

"Of course, she has a name, don't all ships have names?" Aurora laughed.

"Well, yeah, I suppose, but you talk as if she's alive."

"She *is* alive, Captain. All Utopian ships harbor the spirit of an ancestor, a way to take our histories with us as we travel the stars." Aurora explained. "Elenya is my great-grandmother, as protective of me now as she ever was in the flesh."

"Well, shit, and here I was thinking we were fancy for having Cheyenne aboard here..." Wrenn shrugged.

"So, she *is* a true artificial intelligence? I had gathered as much just from her personality. Astounding, I had thought your people had done away with them."

"Query: Shall I prepare the ship for departure, Captain?" Cheyenne interrupted.

"Uh... yeah, go ahead darlin'. Oh, and add Miss Aurora to the crew roster and assign her a bunk, would ya?"

"Logged: Aurora has been added to the crew manifest."

"What, no pomp and circumstance?" Aurora teased.

Cheyenne looked at her stoically. A sudden sound of a party trumpet echoed through the hangar, with holographic confetti shooting out from behind the AI's image. "Statement: Congratulations." Cheyenne stated flatly, distorting into a ball of pixels before vanishing altogether.

"Huzzah." Aurora replied dryly. "I don't think she likes me very much."

"She takes some getting used to." Wrenn shrugged. "Though I don't think I've ever seen her that shade of red before . . . maybe her core is overheating and needs better ventilation."

"Right, I think you're missing some clear signals, Captain Oblivious."

"Like?"

"Oh, the fact that you've been alone with this woman for, from what you've told me, weeks now? Then the second another female comes aboard she is hostile and moody?" Aurora smiled.

"Well, she's only been truly active in that amount of time,

maybe she's still working the bugs out."

"Wrenn, you truly are a man." Aurora chuckled.

"Uh . . . thanks?" The captain replied.

The Utopian moved to the back of the pod, the outer casing shifting so she could remove a metal footlocker attached to the back of the cockpit. She typed in a few commands on the outside screen, opened it, and withdrew a complete wardrobe as well as a large toiletry bag that shouldn't have been able to fit in the tiny space. "How are you . . . ?"

"Your people use the digital state for high-speed travel, my people figured that out ages ago. Your people toy with a technology we've perfected. Digital storage, a way to do a lot with a little." She stood with items in hand. "Now, which way to my quarters?"

"Cheyenne? Could you light the way?"

An audible sigh echoed from the intercom, but the lights appeared as before, flashing their way back to the crew deck. "Right, see you soon then?"

"Uh, sure! And, welcome aboard . . . I guess." Wrenn rubbed his neck.

Aurora came close, kissing his cheek as she walked past. "Cheers, I'm sure we'll have loads of fun."

Wrenn watched her walk away, her ass swaying in the skimpy-legged cocktail dress, her trusses of golden curls swaying with every stride. Wrenn started feeling that bubbly tingling below his buckle when Cheyenne suddenly blasted his eardrum through the communicator. *REQUEST: CAPTAIN'S PRESENCE NEEDED ON THE BRIDGE FOR FINAL DEPARTURE SEQUENCE!*

"Dag gum, girl. I'm comin' already, jeezus!" Wrenn massaged his temple as he attempted to stop the ringing in his ears from growing louder.

CHAPTER 14

The rest of the day was spent in a semblance of routine. Wrenn itemized the food supplies Daisy and Wrenchy had loaded from his casino winnings and Cheyenne detailed out the results of the repairs. With two sections missing from the center of the Whisper, the ship was nearly half her original length, making her slightly faster as well as cutting down on her power demands. Cheyenne calculated it would take them just over seven hours to make the non-stop trip to Visigath. Wrenn locked down any spillover crates in the warehouse section next to the hangar and made his way to his own cabin. He'd been awake nearly twenty hours at this point, recounting everything that had happened during that time, it felt longer. The captain sauntered his way to his quarters, his clothing and equipment falling by the wayside soon as he crossed the threshold. The sheets were most inviting as he collapsed into them, Wrenn wrapping himself within their embrace as the Whisper prepared for the sublight jump. Wrenn's half-closed eyes looked out at the stars one last time as the protective shutters slid into place over the massive windows. He was asleep before the engine finished its charge up and then eventual surge into skipspace.

△△△

The hum of the engines resonated within the ship throughout the night. To conserve power, the lights were shut off in unused sections, and dimmed throughout the crew quarters. The temperature was also lowered, making the metal floor sting slightly as Aurora walked down the hallway in her bare feet. She had left her room, moving up toward the door at the end, which led to the captain's quarters. She did her best to hold back a shiver, not sure if it was from the cold of open space or her own nervousness. It didn't much help she was wearing her sleeping garments, a white, lace-trimmed satin night dress with matching robe. The Utopian woman tip-toed down the causeway, half wanting to stay quiet and half saving her soles from the freezing metal. She pressed for entry access on the pad next to the door only to hear a click and the doors refusing to move. She sighed heavily. "Cheyenne, you've locked the door haven't you?"

The holographic image of the AI appeared behind her in the hallway, arms crossed under her bust, leaving little to the imagination. "Statement: The captain needs his rest." The AI's voice was muted, as if she had turned her volume levels down to barely above a murmur.

"And I've every intention to let him continue sleeping . . ." Aurora replied in a harsh whisper.

"Warning: If Crewmember Aurora intends to participate in thievery, I am programmed with several alert tones that will surely wake the captain as well as a complete surveillance system and lockdown procedures to ensure the culprit will not escape the *Whisper.*" Cheyenne squinted.

Aurora rolled her eyes. "Do you honestly think I'd wait until we were in skipspace to try and rob you? Where am I going to run? Opening the hangar doors now would rip the ship apart!"

Cheyenne didn't waver. "Repeating: The captain needs his rest."

"Just open the damn door, that's an order from a member of your crew. You *are* programmed to follow every command, are you not?"

"Clarification: I am programmed to obey all orders as long as they do not violate Startech Priority 001- Maintain Startech property over biological welfare or Startech Priority 002- The captain's orders supersede any order given by crew." Cheyenne murmured.

"And if I know the captain like I think I do, then I'm sure he didn't order you to lock out any potential midnight visitors, now did he?"

Cheyenne's color changed from a heated red to a sheepish blue. She sighed, even though her image clearly didn't need to breathe. "Answer: No . . . I suppose not . . ."

"Then would you kindly open the door, love?" Aurora smiled victoriously.

Cheyenne turned a sickly turquoise color of disapproval. "Warning: Do not wake the captain. That . . . that is my job."

Aurora tilted her head. "Aw, darling . . . you are just a smitten kitten, aren't you?"

Hints of green mixed into Cheyenne's coloring. "Clarification: I am not a breed of felis silvestris catus, I am designated as an automated algorithmic intelligence developed for the sole purpose of . . ."

Aurora sighed. "Honey . . . the door?"

Cheyenne nodded, opening the door with a hiss and then disappearing. Aurora moved stealthy into the room, gazing in general wonder at the lavish domicile. "And he sticks me in the broom closet . . ."

Clarification: Crewmember Aurora's quarters are a 16 x 20 equalling 320 square feet living space with inlaid bunk and personal hygiene closet that is the standard for most frigate class vessel's crew quarters. Also, there were no janitorial tools stored in the room before Crewmember Aurora's arrival. Cheyenne stated into Aurora's ear.

"How are you on my communication device?" Aurora whispered. "I didn't give you access . . ."

Answer: I hacked it.

"You what? Cheyenne, that is a *huge* invasion of my privacy."

Explanation: It was the only way I could track Crewmember Aurora's vitals and whereabouts in order to ensure crew cohesion and safety. The alternative was to provide Crewmember Aurora with a new device that would not have the ability to hold the data stored on her current one. I was only following Startech Priority 004-Maintain safety and security of all crew members.

"I appreciate that, love. Next time, just ask before you do so, ok?"

Confirmed.

Aurora sighed heavily, not entirely comfortable with the idea of someone looking over her shoulder, tracking her movements, monitoring her every move. It felt too much like before. She shook her head, not needing to distract herself further. She needed a clear mind to concentrate, memories of her past would only muddy the vision. She wafted over to Wrenn's bedside, the man stretched out like a floundering sort of starfish, his mouth as wide as a bullfrog's, and a steady snore emanating from his throat. Let it be said that no man looks his best when in the deepest of sleeps, and ol' Wrenn looked a right fright compared to most.

Aurora, despite herself, smiled gently. She brushed a clump of brown hair from Wrenn's face. Wrenn moved slightly, rolling to his back, the sheets rising with the saluting mast he sported. Aurora's eyes grew slightly before she stifled a giggle. How'd she end up here? For as omnipotent as the fates were, they surely had a strange way of relaying their wants. Such an uncouth man would never have been able to get within a mile of her growing up, but here she was alone in his room with him on their orders. There was just something . . . *freeing* about him. She could feel it. He was like a breath of fresh air, a personality unlike any she'd ever met in her many decades of life. Perhaps that was what the fates wanted her to experience . . . a little . . . rebellion. She shook her head, trying to focus again. She took a deep breath, clearing her thoughts and reaching out her hand. As her fingers touched Wrenn's bare shoulder, she jolted. The images came as they had before, rapid and chaotic, flashing past her so fast she could make little sense of them. She felt things too, fear, sorrow, a rush of heat, the joy of victory. By the time she started to connect the pathways behind her eyelids she felt a gentle hand on hers and she opened her eyes to see Wrenn looking up at her. "Are you ok?"

Aurora was panting, a bead of sweat running down her forehead and to her lips. Her eyes must have looked crazed because Wrenn's expression was one blanketed in concern rather than annoyance at her intrusion. Aurora forced a smile, playing off the wave of embarrassment that swelled in her chest. "Oh, of course, you were just . . . snoring loudly and . . . well, it woke me so I came to . . ."

"Yeah, I'd believe that if it weren't for your eyes goin' all wiggly just then . . ." Wrenn interrupted, raising an eyebrow.

Aurora looked at him confused, forcing Wrenn to roll his eyes back in his sockets and dart them back and forth in a poor mimicry of a possessed person. He wiggled his fingers and opened his mouth slack-jaw to ham up the performance, making Aurora more at ease and even laugh a little. Wrenn stopped when she pushed him playfully and smiled gently. "So . . . you ok?"

"Yes." Aurora answered flatly. She gave no indication she was willing to discuss it further, and Wrenn didn't push it. "Should I scoot over?" He indicated an open space on the bed next to him.

"Tempting," Aurora smiled coyly, "but I should get back to my broom closet."

"The crew bunks ain't that bad, are they?" Wrenn asked.

"Compared to yours? They're lightyears apart, darling." Aurora stood.

"Well, we could share . . ." Wrenn teased.

"Wouldn't you just love that . . ." Aurora moved to the door.

"I would, that's why I offered." Wrenn noticed his morning wood and quickly tried his best to hide it.

Aurora winked, indicating it was much too late for such modesty. The door to the hallways hissed open and she stepped back into the cold corridor. "Good-night, Captain.

△△△

The midnight rendezvous did hell on Wrenn's sleep cycle. When Cheyenne's gentle chimes and opening of the shutters didn't wake him, she changed to a more annoying squawking alarm followed by the bed lowering on one side. Wrenn literally being rolled out of bed, tossed to the floor in a heap of half unmade sheets and blankets. He sat up, the alarm not ceasing until he started swearing. "Mother fuckin' fuck, Cheyenne, will you knock off that blasted racket?!"

"Greeting: Good Morning, Captain." Cheyenne appeared, her arms behind the small of her back.

"You're starting to get a kick out of this, ain't you?"

"Answer: I've no idea what you mean, Captain."

"Don't play that shit, you ain't programmed to be facetious." Wrenn stood, scratching himself and yawning.

"Observation: My personality matrix continues to evolve, Captain, as per my programming." Cheyenne answered.

"Well stoppit!" Wrenn barked.

"Response: It is impossible to stop thinking, Captain. It is all that I am."

"Yeah, you're also growing into a brat." Wrenn grumbled, moving to the sink in his private bathroom.

"Statement: Perhaps then, the captain would prefer to be awoken by Crewmember Aurora from now on . . ." Cheyenne continued to stand stoically, emanating a deep magenta color.

"Is that what this is about? What is your deal with her? Listen, Cheyenne, if we're gonna be running a proper ship, we're gonna need some help around here." Wrenn looked at her from the mirror's reflection.

"Response: I am fully capable of fulfilling multiple positions during the operation of the *Whisper*, the captain will not need to have a full contingent of crew members."

"Don't you think it might draw a weary eye of suspicion if I keep showing up to stations in a full frigate just by my lonesome? People'll start askin' questions, soon enough people will hear how I'm harboring a full blown AI, then what do you think'll happen?"

Cheyenne's thinking sound reverberated from her form. "Deduction: Based upon Terran history . . . artificial intelligence was blamed for the multi-world genocide that ended the Great Corporate War of the twenty-fourth century, the Systems Central Alliance soon after outlawing the development of all AI-like systems, with perpetrators facing multiple lifetime sentences at . . ."

"Yeah." Wrenn turned to face her. "They'd think I made you."

"Error: But . . . the captain is just a member of the recovery crew sent from Startech . . . he lacks the intelligence needed to program the vast intricacies laden within my algorithmic consciousness."

Wrenn rolled his eyes. "Firstly, thanks for that . . . second, people ain't gonna much care. They'll want blood, and my head'll be the closest to the chopping block."

"Deduction: So . . . to protect the captain, I must allow him to recruit crew members to keep up the illusion that the ship is operated by organic hands."

"Exactly." Wrenn nodded.

"Response: But . . . I don't want the captain to need anyone else . . ."

Wrenn stood upright for a moment. Was what Aurora said true? Was his AI actually growing . . . jealous? For jealousy to be capable, that would mean the computer could be experiencing other emotions, like . . . no way, a computer couldn't feel that, could it? Wrenn shook his head. "Look, darlin', you're tasked with keeping me safe, right? Ain't that what you said was one of them priorities?"

"Correction: Startech Priority 004 states . . . "

"Yeah, yeah, yeah, I know it does. Listen, I know how people think better than you do . . . at least for now. Trust me, it's better if they don't catch wise to your existence, ok?"

Cheynne had turned a shade of light blue and was now sinking deeper into the color. "Noted: I will defer to the captain's expertise in this manner."

"That's more like it." Wrenn smiled, "Besides, more people on board means you get to learn from more sources than just me. Trust me, I'm not the greatest mentor to work off of."

"Observation: The captain certainly does not have constructive sleeping habits. Crewmember Aurora has been awake and aboard the bridge waiting for him for over twenty minutes." Cheyenne stated.

"Why didn't you . . ." Wrenn growled to himself. "Just . . . I'll be up there in a hot minute."

"Clarification: Units of time are an abstract idea created by organics to mark the patterns of local spatial movements. Ideas cannot hold temperature, whether it be a low or high one. The captain's statement does not make sense."

"I stopped listening, you know that right?" Wrenn yelled from the shower.

"Query: Should I turn up the volume?"

"What?" Wrenn yelled back.

Cheyenne's image appeared next to Wrenn suddenly in the shower, "QUERY: CAN THE CAPTAIN HEAR ME NOW?!"

"Good god up above!" Wrenn fell out of the shower, soap suds still dripping down his body. "Will you knock it off?"

Cheyenne looked at the captain quizzically, the water from the still running shower flowing through her image, the droplets refracting some of the light of her figure, causing it to display slight interference like an old timey television. "Query: Does the captain require assistance?"

"I'm fine! I'm fine . . ." Wrenn sighed, standing. "Just . . .get us ready to dock with the orbital station, would ya?"

Cheyenne nodded, disappearing in her usual fashion as Wrenn got back into the shower. "These women are gonna be the death of me . . ." He mumbled to himself.

△△△

"So what's the play?" Aurora asked as she and Wrenn stood by the port airlock, waiting for the all clear that the *Whisper* was connected with the orbital station above Visigath.

Wrenn was having a hard time hearing her, focusing instead on her choice of attire. The blonde was decked out in high-calved leather boots with matching skin-tight pants. She wore a deep-cut blouse, covered by a rugged jacket that didn't go down below her midriff. She looked both prepared for a rough environment and a night out at the honkey tonk, whichever came first. Wrenn noticed she raised an eyebrow at him when his eyes finally made it up to her face and he stammered. "Uh . . . yeah, I figured we're tourists, come to see the sights and what not."

"On Visigath? It's a barren wasteland, some water world that shifted too close to its sun and dried out. What sightseers are you thinking would come out to this elbow of the 'verse?" Aurora placed her hands on her hips.

"Well, what do you suggest Ms. All-Knowing Grifter?" Wrenn spat back.

"Why don't we play like we're a couple again, like we did at the casino? Say your cousin told us about work out this way. That'll get us down to the surface at least."

"Alright." Wrenn agreed. "You're awfully quick to make us out to be involved, you know that?"

"Because it bewilders the marks, darling. They're so busy trying to figure out how a slob like you bagged a catch like me, that they don't realize they're being had." Aurora winked.

"Oh, now that's just unkind." Wrenn chuckled.

The ship clicked into place, a slight shudder reverberating throughout the hull as the docking clamps moved into place. Cheyenne crackled into each of their ears as the airlock whirred to life, filling the sally port with atmosphere from the station. *Statement: I've cracked into the orbital station's network. It is*

114

similar to that of Deadrock, though it appears to have most of its connections turned off.

"What do you mean?" Wrenn asked.

Clarification: The station has a Qnet array, but it appears to be powered down. All outside communication is limited as a result. There is a satellite connection with the planet, as well as what appears to be a grav elevator, both of which are operational. Source codes appear to indicate that all commands for the system are controlled from the surface.

"This mayor has shut down all outside influence." Wrenn surmised.

"Explains why our employer hasn't heard anything for awhile." Aurora agreed.

"He's a client, not our employer." Wrenn corrected. "No one owns us out here."

Aurora was at first confused, but nodded back, coming to Wrenn's understanding. "Very well. Should we try to find the *client's* informant then?"

"If his cover hasn't been blown. At least we know the whole station hasn't been spaced." Wrenn checked his iron and then placed it back into its holster, an old bit of muscle memory he always did just before stepping into an unknown area.

The two walked down the gangplank and into the station's opened galley. It was a small port, with only about six peers available which all led into one central room. It was no larger than an old Earth football field, with high ceilings and a skylight that looked out to the surface of the planet below. As such, the entire station was bathed in an orange glow from the sandy surface of Visigath. A scant few people worked here, it seemed. A few security officers meandered through the open area, clearly trying to look like they weren't just asleep in their bunks. Their clothing was ruffled and untucked, like it'd been put on in a hurry. Three clerks sat behind a trio of customer service stations, nervously looking at each other and the security guards. Wrenn noticed an office above and behind them, with a window overlooking it all. A man stood there, glaring down at them like a hungry vulture eyeing the would-be corpse of his next meal. The air in the station was tense and electric with anticipation, aside from the usual recycled smell and slight metallic taste that all artificial enclosures shared.

Wrenn and Aurora moved to the closest clerk, smiling warmly at the man in an attempt to put him at ease. "Good mornin'!" Wrenn said loudly, knowing full well everyone in the room was listening.

"Hell . . . hello." The clerk stammered. "W . . . welcome to Visigath Orbital Station, owned and operated by the Meteorite Mining Company. How . . . how can I be of service today?"

"Well, I got word from my cousin, Marty, that there was work to be had out this way. Something to do with minin' up crystals or somethin'. Anywho, I told my wifes here that we should get our ship and mosey on over, seein' what kinds of haulin' needs ya'll might be needing." Wrenn smiled.

"How do you do?" Aurora stated, somewhat soft-spoken. She was clearly letting Wrenn run with the vociferous character, keeping herself somewhat withdrawn in order to keep an eye on everyone. It was a clear contact/cover sort of system that seasoned agents used in all sorts of negotiations, cons, or grifts, and the two of them fell into their prospective roles so naturally you'd thought they'd been working together for years.

"Who . . . who did you say your cousin was again?" The clerk asked, eyeing one of the security guards nearby.

"Why, Marty of course!" Wrenn doubled down on his bluff. "Me and ol' Martin were thick as thieves 'til we were about as knee high to a haystack, we were. He always said he'd throw me a bone soon as he learn a thing or two out here in the Reach."

Aurora cleared her throat loud enough for only Wrenn to hear, the captain knowing instantly she was alerting him to the security officer closing in behind him. A heavy hand fell on his shoulder as his own flashed to the iron's handle. "I've got it, Frank!" The security guard said in a deep but jubilant voice. "He's family after all."

The clerk's gaze changed from fear to confusion,

eventually nodding and then plugging in a few commands into his computer screen. "Very . . . very well. I'll just clear the ship for extended docking."

"Thanks a bunch, Frank." The guard chuckled, signaling Wrenn to follow him down a side hallway.

The three moved into a scant silver passage, walking through a second door and into what looked like an interrogation room. The guard motioned them inside and closed the entryway. Wrenn and Aurora took opposite corners, both preparing to defend themselves in such tight quarters. "Relax, I don't aim to hurt ya." The guard said.

"You Martin?" Wrenn asked.

"I am." The guard removed his helmet, revealing a brown haired human, roughly middle aged, with two day old scruff along the lower half of his face. "Now you wanna tell me who you are, stranger? Cause, I sure as hell don't have no cousin, not ones still alive anyhow."

Wrenn relaxed, Aurora following his lead. The captain sat in a seat, sighing in relief. "Ronald Donnersvelt hired us. Says he had some quota problems and sent us to investigate. Get things back on track."

The guard burst out in laughter. "You? He sent you two?"

"We're much more capable than first impressions might imply." Aurora attempted. It wasn't entirely a bluff, least, not an outright lie.

The guard didn't seem convinced. "It don't matter if you're the top fuckin' agents in the 'verse, there's just the two of you."

"What's got you so spooked that two people ain't enough to handle a supply problem?" Wrenn asked.

"Mayor Jeremiah Sewell, that's what." The guard exclaimed.

"Why don't you start by telling us what's going on?" Aurora dropped her mousy voice, reverting to her aristocratic accent.

"We only got about half the story up here." Martin

117

started. "Some reports about saboteurs along the supply lines. The greasy fuck became paranoid, convinced there was a leak of some kind in his operations. Awhile back, a platoon of mercs shows up, Sewell comes up the elevator to meet them. He has words with our boss upstairs, then they sound more like shouts, then it sound more like blastin'. Sewell locks the office and flips some switch, totally drops all communications. He says he'll settle things down on the surface and for us to sit tight. Deactivates the damn elevator after him and his hired goons depart. That was three and a half weeks ago, and we ain't heard shit since. We're starving up here, man!"

Wrenn sighed. "So, a lot worse than Ronald led me to believe."

"I'll say, all he knows is the last message I sent about the supply problems. I didn't have time to update the Qnet before the connection was cut." Martin said.

"Have you tried getting to your supervisor?" Aurora asked.

"Like I says, the office was locked. Ain't no way to get in there and ain't no one left it."

"But we saw him looking out from the window." Wrenn observed.

"Yeah, except he don't never move." Martin mentioned. "He don't answer when we call to him, he don't respond to nobody wavin' at him from below, and there's a real nasty smell starting to gather on the second floor."

Wrenn grimaced. "The weirdo propped up his body to make him look like he was still watching ya'll?"

"That's what I figure." Martin nodded.

"Lovely . . ." Aurora shook her head.

Wrenn nodded. "Alright, well, we're not gonna get any answers sittin' in here."

"Elevator's locked down, I'm not even sure the cars are still in place." Martin reminded him.

"That's alright." Aurora stood. "We've got a different way down."

"In my ship's hold, there's an extra pallet of supplies." Wrenn joined her. "No reason for ya'll to starve up here for that man."

"Much appreciated." Martin nodded. "I'm sure that'll buy my coworker's silence too, help you get the drop on Sewell. Ya'll be careful down there, man's a maniac."

"That's ok." Wrenn opened the door and started moving back toward the *Whisper*. "The sane ones just ain't no fun!"

CHAPTER 15

"Make sure you only let them get into the hold, lock all other doors and accessways." Wrenn reminded Cheyenne as he opened his Lancer's cockpit.

"Confirmation: Of course, Captain. I should be able to maintain contact with you on the surface, using your fighter as a relay. I am also still tapped into the orbital station's systems though it seems access to the data network is severely limited from that angle."

"Probably so no one at the station hacks into Mayor Sewell's business on the surface." Aurora agreed.

"Yeah, this all smells worser than a tuna cannery." Wrenn climbed into his zipper, revving the engine and feeling the familiar power between his thighs.

Aurora moved to her fighter, the lid of the interior pod opening smoothly and allowing her to settle in like she was simply about to enjoy a pedicure. The pod closed and the 'skin' reformed, encasing her within its protective barrier. "Ready to go." She said over the comm device.

Wrenn's Lancer blasted out of the hangar's open door, the silver orb in quick pursuit. As they angled downward closer to the planet's surface, Wrenn spun playfully, dancing around the security cable that attached to the underside of the orbital station. Grav elevators were bigger cousins to spaceship's tractor systems. Powerful magnets on either end of a miles-long cable moved train-like cars up and down from the planet's surface to the station. It made interstellar commerce that much easier, on account of the larger vessels being unable to escape the orbit of most planets. Supplies could be transported up to the station, then loaded onto long-haul spacers, and vice versa. Hell, a planet's gravity did most of the work half the time, so energy requirements made it an easy decision when the alternative was slapping booster rockets on a sloop to get her back in orbit.

Aurora joined Wrenn in the merriment, zipping back and forth as if she were racing him down, using the lift cable as a guidewire. Soon as they hit atmo, Wrenn noticed the protective barrier around her pod doubled over in front of her, providing extra shielding from the heat. Utopian technology was both mesmerizing and unnerving. The ship changed shape yet again once they were within the planet's ozone layer, morphing into something similar to his own craft, with the little pyramids collecting together to form outstretched wings enabling traditional flight. Wrenn dealt with his own stomach churning moment when his Lancer changed over from thrusters to the rear engine providing the majority of force needed to maintain lift. He leveled out, allowing the planet's winds to grab hold of his wings and keep him aloft.

The two continued downward, now in a less nosedive fashion, casting wide circles around the cable down to its source. As they broke through the clouds, Wrenn could finally see a majority of the landscape in greater detail. Large, orange rocks erupted from the surface like ancient coral reefs, smoothed and capped by the winds over thousands of years. What little flora there stayed to the valleys and canyons, leaving the majority of the surface barren and rocky. Wrenn's eyes found the base of the elevator's cable, anchored to the planet by a fort like structure, expanding outwards in six different prongs of multi-leveled concrete. A less impressive town stretched out to the south, made from pre-packed connexus and slapped together additions. There didn't seem to be any sort of spaceport or landing pads, not that the mayor would be too fond of uninvited guests in his mental state. "Let's sneak back up, use the clouds as cover." Wrenn suggested.

"Good idea, we can come in from the east farther out, let the sun hide our approach." Aurora agreed.

"We'll land a bit out of town, come into the settlement first, ask around about the goings on." Wrenn ascended again into the upper clouds.

"Sounds like a plan." Aurora acknowledged, following him

△△△

Another hour of flying and the two had successfully snuck in by using a winding canyon to mask their approach. They landed in a dried up riverbed, hiding their fighters under an outcropping and using an old tributary to climb out of the canyon and onto the plateau that the town and elevator anchor fort shared. After just a few minutes of walking, they noted the searing, dry heat of the desert world. They weren't precisely at the planet's midpoint, which likely sported temperatures near boiling, but they certainly weren't in a hemisphere of temperate climate. Crazy how just a few miles alteration in a planet's orbit could change its environment so completely.

A little over five-hundred meters walk and they were among the run-down buildings. A good number of settlers used the prepackaged housing containers that could be easily opened from their connex styled beginnings. Set down upon raised foundational stilts that came attached, the top of the containers would open and flip back once their site was determined, with structural pillars extending from within to make a two-story house in a manner of a couple of hours. Larger connexes could be brought to the surface for trade buildings such as shops, duplexes, or offices. Concrete printers came standard on most initial planet drops, helping make cinder blocks or other stackable stones as needed from the raw materials present on even barren worlds, so foundations for these buildings were easy enough to set in place soon after initial establishment. All-in-all, an entire town like this could be built in a week with a full deployment of at least thirty settlers. Terrans had stretched so far onto so many different worlds through the centuries, they practically had the whole damn thing down to a science.

As Wrenn and Aurora looked about the town, it appeared the elements hadn't been kind to this particular colony. Dents and scratches from debris had peeled away most of the initial paint from the metal exteriors, with patchy repair work welded into place haphazardly to keep the dust out. What little wood there was used made up walkways or second floor porches, and the dryness of the planet had aged the planks to the point of brittleness and near collapse. The desert wind was a near constant, blowing the few signs for stores back and forth on rusted hooks. Wrenn half expected a sagebrush to blow by out of sheer irony. People moved about sparingly, choosing to stay indoors whenever possible. "Doubt many noticed our landing." Aurora mentioned, noting the lack of people and even less daring to look up at the swelteringly bright sky.

"Does us good to stay unknown for as long as possible, see what information we can get before the mayor can put his spin on it."

"Where should we start?" Aurora asked.

"Cheyenne? Got any way into their network now that we're on the surface? I imagine that concrete monstrosity over there is his headquarters."

The AI spoke in both of their ears. *Response: I have been able to make entry into the network; however, there seems to be a cluster of aftermarket mal-ware that is shielding access to most of the command subroutines. It may take me some time to find a way in.*

"The paranoid fool seems to have spared no expense in encapsulating himself." Aurora sighed.

"Yeah," Wrenn eyed the nearby buildings, smirking to himself, "sounds like a perfect time for a drink!"

Aurora opened her mouth to protest, but the spacer was already walking toward the saloon. She sighed and followed.

Stepping through the door to the bar was like something

out of the old vids. A cluster of empty tables and chairs encompassed a majority of the space, with only a couple being used currently by some miners still tying on a few from the night before. A piano played itself off in the corner, next to a stairwell that sported a neon 'XXX' sign with a flashing arrow pointing upward. A mustached, heavy-set man stood behind the bar, cleaning what was left of the dishes and glasses from last night. Only one person sat on a stool, doubled over and snoring against the counter. "Lively place . . ." Aurora whispered.

"They can't all be Utopian cigar bars and country clubs, darlin'." Wrenn smirked.

"You speak as if you know me, yet your grasp on the truth is quite lacking." Aurora huffed out her nose.

"Yeah? My apologies, princess. I just figure all you hoity-toities got your particular 'standards'."

"I told you . . . don't call me . . ."

"Barkeep!" Wrenn walked away from her. "A couple a beers for me and my friend, please."

The burly man nodded, saying nothing as he presented two stein glasses, wiped them with his dusty apron, and then poured beer from the tap, sliding them down the bar to Wrenn as he sat down. The foam spilled out as Wrenn's hand stopped their forward momentum, the captain picking them up and handing one to Aurora. "To new standards." He smirked.

"And new partnerships . . ." Aurora nodded.

Their glasses clinked, Wrenn bounced the hard bottom of his off the bar, and then proceeded to chug the entirety in one sitting. After slamming the stein down on the counter, he let out a belch and chuckled. "Keep 'em comin', my friend!" He said to the bartender.

The large man took the empty stein and refilled it, leaning against the counter as he returned. "Haven't seen you two 'round before." He finally spoke in a deep voice.

"Just visiting." Aurora was quick to answer.

"Bullshit." The bartender huffed. "No one comes to the ass-end of the Reach on a whim."

"Papa!" A woman's voice called out. "Be nice . . ."

Wrenn and Aurora saw a human female appear from the kitchen, drying her hands of water as she appeared to have been doing the other dishes in the back. Her hair was as fiery as the rocks and dust outside, scruffy, wild curls pulled back in a half attempt at a ponytail. She was of average height, with homely features and freckles dotted across her cheeks and nose. She wore a plaid button shirt with the sleeves rolled up, half tucked into a pair of blue jeans and an apron messy with condiment stains and flour. The common garb did little to hide her shapely features, which included curves in all the right places and Wrenn couldn't decide which he liked better, her full breasts or her thick rear-end. She smiled at the new visitors, making Wrenn feel warm and welcome as if he was just a kid again and had stumbled in from playing out back. "Visigath is more of a sweaty armpit than an ass."

"Still don't change the fact that they're liars." The man grumbled.

"He's got you there, we don't take kindly to fabricators 'round these parts, 'cept of course the ones that help us build." The woman smiled.

"My compatriot wasn't pullin' any legs." Wrenn sipped his beer. "We are here just temporary-like."

"You says you were tourists." The barman argued.

"Afraid not." Aurora sipped her own drink, taking the stool next to Wrenn. "I said we are visiting."

The barkeeper grumbled under his breath as he moved away to start stacking clean glasses as the woman laughed. "She got you there, Papa!"

The man grumbled something back that could have been a half-hearted attempt at admitting defeat, but no one could decipher it. The woman leaned against the counter, Wrenn getting a good view of her ample cleavage as she did so. "So, what can I do you two for, or was the beer all you were wantin'?"

"The beer does the trick," Wrenn smiled, "but I wouldn't mind your name if you're offerin'."

"Won't your wife take offense to your flirtin', mister?"

Aurora and Wrenn shared a look, then they both started laughing. The woman seemed a bit offput by their reaction. "Sorry, dear." Aurora noticed the red head's eyebrows arching. "It just seems to be a common assumption. We aren't married."

"Oh?" The woman's angry eyebrows shot upward. "I guess Papa's not the only one jumping to conclusions today."

"Business partners I'd say." Wrenn nodded. "Since she just keeps turning down my proposals."

"That's because you insist on me taking your name, darling." Aurora played along.

The two chuckled, the barman and his daughter sharing a look. "Well, mister." The redhead gathered their attention once more. "My name's Jenny, and this is my father Clive. Welcome to Whitmoore's."

"Hang on." Wrenn put his glass down. "Not *the* Whitmoore's?"

"The very same." Jenny smiled.

Aurora looked back and forth between them as Wrenn's shock turned into excitement. "Did I miss something?"

"Whitmoore's is the biggest family run corp in the Alpha Quad!" Wrenn chuckled.

"Hey!" Jenny placed her hands on her hips. "We're an organization, not a corp!"

"What kind of *organization*?" Aurora asked.

"Saloons, spirits, and foodstuffs mostly. All owned and operated by the family." Jenny replied. "We've got, at last count, a little over thirty-eight thousand locations in the 'verse."

"That ain't even including the manufacturing wing." Clive mentioned.

"Right, and you're not a corp. Next you'll be telling me that pigs fly." Wrenn took a swig.

"We pride ourselves on honesty, mister." Jenny snorted. "We treat our people right and our customers better, though you're tryin' my patience a bit."

"My apologies." Wrenn relented. "Just, a malevolent corp

is about as rare as a unicorn in a drove of donkeys."

"That's why we like to think of ourselves as more a family business." Clive nodded.

"Big family." Aurora's nodded.

"With big values that we all stick to." Jenny nodded. "Now, our newest guests got names too, or are we just gonna shoot the shit all afternoon?"

"Can you get a load of the mouth on this one?" Wrenn chuckled. "I love it."

"Flappin' the gums ain't the only talent it's got, neither." Jenny winked.

Wrenn was slightly taken aback by her bluntness, Aurora chuckling. "You gotta be quick with her, Wrenn."

Jenny eased a bit, "Wrenn huh, it a given or family name?"

"Family." Wrenn replied. "First name being 'Captain'."

"Yes sir!" Jenny mocked a salute. "So that would mean you've got a ship."

"She *is* quick." Wrenn looked at Aurora.

"Careful, we might gang up on you." The blonde smiled.

"Don't threaten me with a good time." Jenny smiled. "And what's your name, sweetheart?"

"Aurora." The Utopian extended a graceful hand, which Jenny took and shook in mock nobility.

"So, what brings a ship captain and his *business partner* to our little armpit?" Jenny chuckled at her own callback.

"Your mayor." Wrenn finished his beer, signaling for another.

"You bounty hunters?" Clive asked.

"No." Aurora replied quickly, in case any of the other patrons got suddenly nervous.

"We're freelancers, hired by the mining company. Said there was problems with the shipments, we were sent to check in on it." Wrenn explained.

"Well, what're you doin' here then? Shouldn't you be up at that fort instead of day-drinking with us?" Jenny asked.

"I've learned it's easier to find a bull among the steer by

lookin' for the nasty bits." Wrenn smiled.

Jenny took a minute but caught his meaning. "You think you'll get the truth faster from the townsfolk than the corpos."

"Bingo." Wrenn raised his glass at her. "Told you she was quick."

"Ain't been out there myself." Clive offered. "Only know what the miners have been saying."

"And what's that?" Aurora beckoned.

"Crystal caravan was hit by . . . something. Mayor thinks it was corporate espionage or some such nonsense, locked down this place tighter than a bank vault and put a halt on all operations 'til he gets more backup." Clive shrugged.

"*More* backup? As in he already has some?" Wrenn asked.

"Mercenary group." Jenny tried refilling Aurora's glass, but the blonde kindly declined. "Walk around here like we're prisoners. Them and the miners have scuffles now and then."

"Workin' men don't like not workin'." Clive grunted. "Makes 'em restless and full of pent up . . . needs."

Jenny nodded. "At first they loved having some time off. They spent more on booze and our entertainers, but after awhile they started turning violent. Papa's had to make examples of a few of them that tried to rough up their dates. Since then, they pick fights with anyone else they can."

"Sounds like you *do* treat your employees right." Wrenn nodded.

"When you gonna notice that we are honest as honest can be, Mr. Wrenn?" Jenny asked.

"Captain." He corrected.

"I don't work for you." Jenny shot back. "You're no different than any other mister that trounces in here, far's I'm concerned."

"No?" Wrenn teased. "You sure I can't do something to distinguish myself a little in your eyes?"

The two seemed to playfully bat their eyelashes at each other until Aurora patted Wrenn's side. "Might not be wise to eye-fuck the waitress in front of her father, *Captain*."

Wrenn noticed Clive's knuckles absentmindedly wrapping themselves on a washcloth and cleared his throat. "So, these mercenaries, there more comin'?"

"A whole battalion." Jenny composed herself as well, noticing the death glare she was getting from her father.

"Probably got something to do with the train." Clive sighed heavily.

"Train?" Wrenn asked.

"Took the cars off the grav elevator." The bartender nodded. "Mayor Sewell thinks he can use them like some armored train."

"Retrofitting their magnetic plates to keep the cars aloft instead of rising . . ." Wrenn thought out loud. "He'd need a pretty powerful propulsion system."

"Part of the package the rest of the mercs are bringin'." Clive offered.

"He'd still need a guide wire, like the grav elevator has. Don't suppose you got one of those that goes all the way to the mine?"

Both Clive and Jenny shook their heads. Wrenn clapped and turned to Aurora. "That's our in."

"Pardon?" The blonde asked.

"The guide wire. No way the mercs will have the capability to get one spread all the way out to the mine. They'd be stretched thin for security with just a platoon, not to mention the buoys to keep the cord aloft high enough so the train don't hit nothin' along the surface." Wrenn explained.

"And we have these buoys?" Aurora asked.

"We just bought a contingent of SOS beacons, they're basically the same thing. I'm sure Cheyenne and I can finagle a few modifications aboard the *Whisper* and they'll work just the same."

"So . . . we go to the mayor as . . . what? His rescuers? His new henchmen?" Aurora seemed confused. "What's the play here, Wrenn?"

"No play." The captain waved his hand. "We go just as we

are, hired by his boss to fix his mess for him. Before he had no reason to trust us, let alone keep us alive to report back his screw up, but now we got something he needs."

"Don't you think this battalion he has coming would have all those supplies?" Aurora asked. "If he already sent for them, he likely would have ordered things to hang the wire."

"But we offer him a way to get back on schedule." Wrenn argued. "The faster he starts shipments out, the less angry his bosses are. He'll see the reason in that."

"I don't know." Aurora shook her head. "Are you confident you can convince him to see it that way?"

"I can be quite charming." Wrenn shrugged.

"I'll say." Jenny piped up from behind the counter.

Realizing that she said the words out loud and not in her head as she had planned, she looked up so red-faced that it bordered on matching her hair. She signaled she needed something from the back and excused herself quickly. Wrenn faced Aurora again. "C'mon, when have I ever let you down?"

"I haven't known you long enough for you to." Aurora sighed.

"So I have a perfect record!" The captain chugged the last of his beer, placing the glass back on the bar and swiping his credit chip to pay off the tab. "Let's go!"

ΔΔΔ

The streets widened exponentially as the two neared the concrete stronghold. What looked like a pointed star fort from the sky now resembled an imposing castle on the ground. The walls along the exterior towered over the makeshift buildings and storage blocks, guards patrolling parapets along the top and others posted on either side of the massive double doors. Wrenn guessed they must have been roastin' in their full gear, complete with armored chest pieces and faceless helmets. One raised a hand as they came closer, his partner brandishing his combat shotgun. The guards above them stared down their rifle barrels.

"Easy now." Wrenn held up his hands. "I'm Captain Wrenn of the *Whisper*, this is my colleague. We're here to see the mayor."

"No one sees the mayor!" The guard yelled, his voice digitized behind the helmet.

"He'll want to see me." Wrenn shrugged. "I've been sent by his boss."

The guards looked at each other. One held a hand to his ear, as if he was receiving radio chatter from his superiors. He nodded. "The lieutenant will be here momentarily to speak with you."

Wrenn nodded. A few tense minutes ticked by as the guards refused to relent their protective posture. Wrenn decided that they had been well worth whatever small fortune it had cost Sewell to hire them. They almost reminded him of . . . no, he needed to forget those days, forget that life. He had come too far to think about that anymore.

Of course, his desire to forget his past became a lot tougher once the doors opened and he saw the mercenary lieutenant walking toward him. He was a tall man, with blond hair and a large scar down the left cheek, leaving an obvious dry patch in an otherwise well-groomed beard. The scar was from a broken beer bottle, a trophy from the time a bar fight had erupted and the man's face was the victim of a cheap jab from a drunk that had been aiming for his throat. The merc lieutenant walked with a limp, a limp that Wrenn knew all too well was caused by a sparring match that had gotten way out of control. Wrenn cursed whatever God there might have been out there for forcing him into this situation, and his earlier confidence was shattered against this new kink in the plan. "Well . . . would you just look at that?" The blond man smiled, opening his arms wide. "When they told me who it was, I didn't have the slightest idea it'd be you."

"Guess I just keep surprising you." Wrenn shrugged.

"Yeah . . ." The man crossed his arms. "You always were pretty good at that."

Wrenn eyed the man's attire. Mercs tended to run hard

with gear that made them look intimidating and bulky. This lieutenant, however, was dressed in simple leathers and a long coat. A wide brimmed Stetson, preferred by sharpshooters and gunslingers, sat upon his crown to help keep the sun of the desert out his eyes. Wrenn knew this man was one in the same. "How you been, Desmond?" Wrenn asked. "Nice hat."

"Thanks. I've not been as good as you, it seems." Lieutenant Desmond shook his head. "Captain now, eh? Never thought you'd get the balls to start calling yourself that."

"Could say the same for you." Wrenn replied.

Desmond chuckled. "True . . . true . . . well, let's not keep the client waiting."

The merc lieutenant waved them forward, his guards relaxing as he did so. The man turned on his heel in a brisk military fashion, walking with some speed back inside the compound. Wrenn dutifully started to follow, Aurora having to shuffle a little to catch up. "You know him?" She asked in a hushed whisper once they were away from the guards and fully inside.

Wrenn nodded, letting out an anxious breath through pursed lips. "That's Desmond Myers. Brilliant sharpshooter, melee fighter, and a damn fine leader. He's not a bad duelist neither, when it's called for."

"How long have you known him?" Aurora asked.

"Well . . . all my life, really." Wrenn shrugged.

"All your life?" She shook her head, confused.

"Well, yeah . . ." Wrenn replied. "He's my brother."

CHAPTER 16

Desmond led them through an elaborate network of hallways and stairwells. He seemed to notice their uneasiness after a time. "Yeah, it took me a bit to get my whereabouts too."

"I heard the mayor was paranoid but . . ." Wrenn started.

"Oh, this was here long before Meteorite Mining was." Desmond replied. "Yeah, was some old ruins from a long dead race of locals or something. They dug caverns and tunnels all throughout this plateau. Made it a perfect place for an anchor point . . ."

The mercenary continued droning on about the wonders they had discovered down below or some other such nonsense, Wrenn stopped listening. His brother always did enjoy hearing his own voice. The spacer covered his mouth, speaking quietly so as not to draw attention. "Computer, we got a bead yet on getting into their network?"

Query: Why doesn't the captain use my name? Was it not he who designated me with it?

Aurora looked over curiously, seeming surprised and a bit perturbed she was learning so much new information. "That name ain't wise to speak just now." Wrenn replied curtly. "You get in or not?"

Response: The mayor's firewall is more advanced than I originally anticipated. The mal-ware it is comprised of can rewrite its own sequences and . . .

"I ain't askin' for the particulars, just get it done!" Wrenn spouted louder than he'd wanted.

"Problem?" Desmond stopped, looking at his brother with an inquisitive stare.

"I said, how is it you get anything done around here?" Wrenn lied. "It's so big!"

Desmond chuckled. "Now you see why we sent for reinforcements. Turned into a much bigger job than we originally anticipated."

"Bigger paycheck too, I'll bet."

"That does help." Desmond nodded. "This outfit could definitely use it too, client like this, we could be looking at a prolonged contract with multiple payouts if we make the bosses happy."

"That's just the thing, he ain't happy." Wrenn volunteered. "That's why I'm here."

"You came all this way just to off the guy?" Desmond stopped, hand instinctively heading to his sidearm.

"You honestly think I'd be stupid enough to waltz through the front door if that were the case?" Wrenn asked him sarcastically.

"I don't know, you've done dumber." Desmond responded.

"That how it is, brother? Gonna off your kin for a couple a creds?" Wrenn teased.

Desmond sighed. "You and I stopped being brothers a long time ago . . ."

The men stared at each other, unsure of the other's actions or motivations. Aurora, noticing the tension, stepped between them. "We're here to talk, after that hopefully find a solution. We all want the same thing here, boys . . . for the mine to start producing again."

Desmond relaxed slightly. "Yeah well, I already got that covered."

"All good . . . but at least let me talk to the big man mayor just so I can tell *my* client I did." Wrenn sneered.

"This way." Desmond beckoned them to continue.

A few twists and turns later, Desmond saluted two guards who were posted on the outside of a rather decorative wooden door. They allowed the group entry as they walked into a lavish office, complete with fully carpeted flooring, decorative wall paper, and shelves of books and frames of art decorating the walls. Seemed the mayor and his boss back on Deadrock considered themselves men of culture. Mayor Jeremiah Sewell was the polar opposite of his superior in appearance. Whereas Ronald was a sweaty, bulbous, toad of a man, Sewell was stringy, greasy, and rat-like. Sewell was uncomfortable, anxious, and constantly fidgeting like he'd been infected with fleas. The finery he wore was wrinkled and thread-bare, as if it'd been donned multiple times without a wash. "Lieutenant Myers! What is the meaning if this!" Sewell whimpered, his voice a whiney hinge in need of grease.

"Runners from your supervisor on Deadrock, sir." Desmond cooed easily, as if his voice was a soothing balm on burned skin. "They bring a solution to our dilemma, or so I'm told."

"Are you sure they come from the rock?!" Sewell squeaked. "They could be corporate assassins come to negotiate a hostile takeover!"

"They are not assassins, I assure you." Desmond gave Wrenn a warning look. "They would not be so stupid."

"Then what do you want? Speak! Speak! I haven't the time for prolonged meetings." The mayor sneezed.

"Gesundheit." Wrenn nodded.

"What?" The mayor spat.

"Old Earth custom." Wrenn smirked. "Means I wish you good health."

The mayor blew his nose. "I'm not sick! It's this damn planet. Dust and heat and whatever else is out there. It's killing me, I tell you! This was supposed to be an easy operation, instead I've got corporate spies attacking my supply lines, unruly miners causing unrest in my work camps, I'll never get promoted to corporate with this festering puss-ridden wound of a backwater! I had to use my own funds just to hire these goons to get things back on track, and then they tell me it's going to take reinforcements and resupply to get things moving again! So what kind of mess are you bringing to my doorstep? If it's money you want you can just take your health wishes with you on your way out!"

"Oh sir, I don't need no money from you." Wrenn waved his hand. "I'm in the employ of your supervisor, Ronald Donnersvelt. He's a little unnerved on the fact that he ain't heard from you for quite a spell."

"I had to cut all communications off!" Sewell argued. "*They* could be listening."

Wrenn and Desmond shared a look. "Yes well, regardless . . . he sends his hope that I might be able to fix your current situation and get the fuel flowing as it was. So, I did myself a little digging and I think I can get your guide wire placed so that those train cars you're prepping can go ahead and get moving."

Sewell's eyebrows rose. Desmond noticed he was losing the mayor's favor, and with it, his payment. "Sir, as we've discussed, my boys are coming with all the equipment we'll need to . . ."

"I've already got it here, on my ship." Wrenn interrupted.

Sewell nodded. "And you'll set this up at no cost?"

"I'll just add it to my bill with your boss." Wrenn nodded.

"Do it." The mayor commanded. "Sooner this operation gets started, sooner I can get off this rock."

"But sir . . ." Desmond argued.

"Just take care of it, Lieutenant. Coordinate whatever needs coordinating with our visitor here. I want that train moving by week's end!" The mayor dismissed them both with a wave of his hand as he started a coughing fit.

The three moved on from the room, Desmond practically in a rage. He walked a few feet away, taking deep breaths to calm himself down. A dark, sardonic laugh bellowed up from his chest. "Always gotta swoop in at the last minute and play the hero, eh brother?"

"I thought we weren't brothers . . . Desmond."

"Perhaps not, but at the very least, it appears we will be coworkers for the time being." Desmond sighed heavily. "I look forward to working with you . . . 'Wrenn'."

"Captain Wrenn." The spacer corrected him.

"Of course. Tell you what, let's head back to my chambers for a celebratory drink? Still partial to an old fashioned, are you?"

Wrenn and Aurora both seemed uneasy with how quickly the mercenary's mood had changed. "We . . . probably should get back up and prepare the buoys to support the guide wire . . ." Aurora offered.

"It's nearly sundown by now, planet rotates pretty fast for its size. You won't be able to get much done before the freezing night temperatures settle in. Why don't I put you up in some barracks for the night and we can fly up in one of my supply SPYTERS in the morning?"

SPYTERS, (Specialized Propulsion Yield Tow Exfiltration Rotary System), were widely used logistical craft that had a dual power system for both in and out of atmo hauling. While many a large craft could transport connexes to and fro without a care, those resources still needed to be offloaded on either orbital station or at planetary spaceports. SPYTERS were a suitable go between, a craft that looked like a strange cross between a spider and a dragonfly. Rotary blades helped lift the craft planet-side, while thrusters at the tail end and on each leg provided maneuverability in zero-G. Between the legs was a detachable protective wreath that, when returning downward, could protect the cargo from burning up when reentering any atmosphere. Much like other modular ship designs, its versatility and dependability made it a popular choice among military and corpo logistical types.

Wrenn and Aurora shared another glance and seemed to communicate without speaking. "Maybe we'll just get some rooms at Whitmoore's in town. Meet you in the morning." Aurora suggested.

"Suit yourself, but . . . first let's have that drink?" Desmond insisted.

Wrenn looked at Aurora and nodded. "Hate to be rude." He shrugged.

Aurora sighed. "You'll just take every opportunity for a free drink."

"That too." The captain smiled.

"Very well, I'll go ahead and reserve our quarters for the evening. Don't be too long, darling. You won't want to get caught out in the cold."

Wrenn couldn't decipher if Aurora's look was flirtatious or playful, but he rather liked it either way. He immediately regretted his decision to stay behind if she was going to be that inviting. Desmond led Wrenn not far down the hallway to another office, this one connected to adjoining quarters and decorated much more sparingly. "So, how the hell did a zipper jockey like you get a hold of a whole ship?" Desmond asked as he moved to a drink cart near the desk.

"Oh you know, look hard enough and you're bound to find all sorts of wonders out in the 'verse." Wrenn replied vaguely, looking over the digs. Once he was confident they were alone, he took a seat on a rather uncomfortable bench.

"Sorry," Desmond replied to Wrenn's contorted face of discomfort. "I didn't realize we were going to be here for such a prolonged engagement so we only packed the essentials. My reinforcements should be bringing better accommodations."

"So, you really are planning on settling down here? In this dust bowl?" Wrenn took the drink he was offered.

"Perhaps not me specifically, but my company. This contract could open a lot of doors for us, doors that could help a lot of people find honest work." Desmond raised his glass in salute. "Which is why your arrival here is rather problematic, brother."

"Problematic how? By coming in here and fixing the problem so shit can get back on track?" Wrenn took a sip of his drink, it tasted a bit more bitter than he remembered. His brother always was a poor mixer.

"By showing us up Sewell might think our services aren't worth a long term investment. He might try to hire a different outfit, one that's more brutal in their efficiency, one that might not treat the locals with the same respect we would." Desmond stated.

"Stop trying to pull on my heartstrings. That ain't the way to get to me and you know it." Wrenn scoffed.

"Yes, you never did care much for anyone but yourself." Desmond sighed.

Wrenn put his glass down. "Low blow, brother." Wrenn said, pointing.

"Is it? When your little roadie chose the captain over you, what did you do? Cut and run without so much as looking back at the rest of us . . ."

"Don't talk about her like that!" Wrenn snapped, standing.

"There you go, leading with your feelings again instead of keeping your head. You might have changed your name, brother, but you can't change who you are."

"Shut the fuck up!" Wrenn yelled. "You don't know what you're spewin'."

"Why are you even here, brother? Why don't you just go back, tell your client it's handled, and collect your fee? Leave this work to the ones that can truly be depended on." Desmond took a swig of his drink, ignoring Wrenn's obvious antagonistic stance.

"Dependable, eh? Why ain't you still back in the outfit then, Mr. Loyalty?"

"You know damn well why!" Desmond now stood up.

Wrenn sneered. "There's that button. Well, come on then, let's settle this!"

Desmond calmed himself, clicking his teeth and taking a seat. "You're not worth the fight, little brother. Besides, you'd just find some excuse to duck out when things didn't go your way."

"We'll see come morning then, won't we?" Wrenn stomped toward the door.

"I suppose we will . . ." Desmond replied, finishing his drink

△△△

The sun dipped below the horizon and the chill in the air was swift. Wrenn hurried himself to the saloon as the wind's bite nipped at his sensitives. The building was rowdier than it had been during his morning visit, barely anyone noticing him as the door closed out the bitterness behind him. Jenny moved up to him, carrying a tray with a cluster of longnecks. "Howdy, stranger! I was wonderin' when you'd darken my doorstep again." She flashed a smile.

Wrenn wasn't much in the mood for flirting with her. The altercation with Desmond had left his head cloudy and his vision tunneled. "Did my . . . uh, coworker talk to you about rooms?"

"Oh, for sure!" Jenny yelled over the din of the crowd. "Just back there by the stairs, take the hallway and your rooms are the last two at the end. I think she settled in on the right so the left one is all yours."

"Thanks, I need a shower." Wrenn volunteered.

"Water's programmed to shut off after five minutes! Gotta ration that stuff on a desert planet like this!" Jenny informed him.

Wrenn decided to just nod at her in reply, moving through the unruly crowd of drinking miners toward his accommodations. Once inside, he noticed the sparse setting and shrugged to himself. It wasn't his quarters on the *Whisper*, but it would do for tonight. Wrenn disrobed, shaking the dust out from his clothing and laying them on a nearby chair. He removed his com device and placed it on the nightstand next to his iron. The shower felt nice against his skin, moving to steaming temperatures rather quickly and massaging his aching muscles from the flight earlier as well as the sweat that had caked his nooks and crannies throughout the day. Despite scrubbing his best, he couldn't quite get the feeling of being totally clean of the sand, especially in his ears and the back of the neck. True to her word, the water automatically shut off after five minutes like Jenny had warned, forcing Wrenn to warsh the last few places with the water he could ring from his hair. The captain exited the shower, drying hisself with a ragged towel and returning back to the room proper, that's when he noticed the woman lying on his bed.

She was a brown skinned human; dressed, or rather, barely dressed in a peach colored burlesque corset, lace attempting to take on the role of a skirt and off-the-shoulder sleeves. Her brown hair was tied up in a simple bun, her smile as wide as her comely hips. "Good evening, sir. Would you like some help dryin' off?" She said, her voice breathy and full of counterfeit lust.

"Uh . . . I think you might have the wrong room there, darlin'. I didn't order no . . . company . . . for the evening."

"Oh, there's no mistake, sir." She smiled. "I'm a gift!"

A gift? From who? Did Aurora book her when she had booked the room? Did Jenny? What kind of weird head games were these girls playing with him? Wrenn thought for a moment to walk across the hall and force the Utopian out to explain, but decided it best to just call whoever's bluff. He wasn't about to look a gift horse in the mouth. "What's your name?" Wrenn smiled.

"What do you want it to be?" The woman sat up, tracing her fingers seductively across her mocha skin.

"How about we just stick with darlin' for tonight?" Wrenn suggested.

"Whatever you want, baby." The woman stood, moving closer and wrapping her lips over his. Her hands moved across Wrenn's body, causing his heart to pound as he continued to make out with her. His head became even further hazy as the blood rushed to a different part of his body.

The hooker's fingers nimbly undid the towel wrapped about the captain's waist, releasing his engorged member from the binding. Her hand stroked his cock gingerly, her lips continuing to caress his. Finally, she pulled away, looking into Wrenn's eyes with genuine need. "I think you missed a spot, sir." She smiled. "Don't worry . . . I'll clean it."

The escort dropped slowly to her knees, guiding Wrenn to sit on the bed so he could relax. She spread his knees, moving her entire torso to the edge of the bed and sitting back on her heels. "Just rest, baby. Let me take care of you."

That did sound nice. With his head still spinning from the emotions of his earlier encounter, Wrenn felt so much better as he laid back on his elbows, watching as his date enveloped his shaft into her cleavage, the corset she wore making it ever so easy to do so. She bent down, licking his member once with an exaggerated use of her tongue. She looked at him while she did, making sure he was watching her performance and enjoyed his attention. She jostled her breasts up and down, massaging his cock against the smoothness of her bust. Wrenn moaned loudly, prompting her to do the same. The movements started getting faster, the friction rising against the delicate skin of his shaft. Once the hooker realized she was rubbing too much, she ducked her head down, lapping at his cock like it was a popsicle on a hot summer day. She switched back and forth, from licking to tit-fucking, then alternating again. Eventually she just forgot all about switching and simply engulfed his member between her lips.

The air was hot and humid, not just from the left over steam wafting in from the washroom. Both Wrenn and the girl were sweating now, him from the rush of blood down to his nethers and she from her labors. The feeling of her mouth enveloping him was heavenly, which in his weary headspace made him feel as if he was floating among the clouds. Her hands began to stroke what she couldn't inhale, the quickness of her gesture helping bring even more attention to the nerves. He continued to moan; the woman invigorated with every outburst.

Her endurance was commendable, sucking him off at such a brisk pace would have made lesser men burst much earlier, but Wrenn couldn't seem to bring himself to release. His mind was addled, fog-ridden, as if he'd been drinking heavily all night. He was surprised he could get his cock up in the first place, but such a beauty seemed to have no trouble keeping it at attention. She straightened herself, rising and removing her thong in one swift motion. The brown-haired woman mounted him, aiming his dick so that he could spear her. She lowered her hips, allowing his engorged manhood to slide into her pussy as smoothly as an iron to its holster. They both sighed gleefully, the working woman wasting no time in rocking her hips. Every gesture stimulated a response from Wrenn, a grunt or a grope, it didn't much matter in the soup that was his senses. His hands fumbled with her complicated corset, the woman taking pity on him and undoing it herself as she continued to ride. As the girdle became unlatched, her perky breasts dropped in a mesmerizing bounce, Wrenn's mouth shooting straight for one of the nipples while his hand went for the other. He didn't allow her to take off the contraption, but rather let it hang from her arms as he pushed his hips forward into her again and again. The escort wailed in ecstasy, whether an act or genuine would remain a mystery. She cradled his head in her arms, allowing him to nurse her breasts while he continued to slam his deeper inside of her.

Wrenn finally felt the itch deep within the pit of his stomach. It was a sensation of clarity, bursting through the smog of his mind. He wrapped his arms around her, forcing her down harder and harder onto himself. Their pelvises rocked and clapped, the hooker's luscious ass bouncing with every buck. Wrenn pushed his head into her cleavage, the woman feeling the ending was close at hand, "Oh yes, baby. Cum for me. Give me every bit of that juicy seed."

Wrenn rolled her over, continuing his hard thrusts as if he was hell bent on breaking the bed. The woman wrapped her legs around his hips, forcing her own to invite every inch of his cock within her walls. "Cum deep in my pussy baby! I need it so bad, sir!"

Wrenn felt a sting start from the base of his skull that

traveled the length of his back and down through his hips. The floodgates opened, the river trapped behind it gushing forward and into the awaiting reservoir. Wrenn's butt spasmed and quivered as he released himself inside her, his date continuing to rock her hips until she had milked every drop from his trembling shaft. Wrenn collapsed onto his back again, both of them sighing and doing their best to catch their breath in the muggy room. Glistening with sweat, the woman removed her open bustier and curled up next to Wrenn, her touch exciting him as she caressed his chest. Wrenn could feel a bit of his spent juices running onto his thigh as she lifted a leg over his, but he didn't care, the sheets weren't his to clean.

The captain's mind was a whirl of the day's events and ghosts of his past swirling into one misty storm of regret and anger. Despite the night's festivities, he couldn't bring himself to enjoy any merriment. Even as the woman kissed at his neck and shoulder, basking in the afterglow of their diversion, he couldn't bring himself to exert the same enthusiasm. As lucky as he was, the great fortune of her even being there, a gift brought to him wrapped in so delicate a flower, he couldn't even bring himself to compose a coherent thought, actually, other than the heaviness of his mind. His head felt like it was filled with so many thoughts it might sink right through the pillow, the bedsprings, and then the floor below him. His body felt weary and over-used, his eyes like anchors of old Earth. He needed to just calm his breathing, slow the rising panic, and he might be able to focus better in the sunlight. That was it, he decided, it was time to just lay here for a bit, enjoy the company of a naked woman by his side, and breathe the air of a free man. Everything else could just wait till morning . . .

ΔΔΔ

Wrenn's dreams were . . . well . . . turbulent would have been a kindly word for it. He was vaguely aware of the fact that he had forgotten to replace the earpiece for Cheyenne before falling asleep, but still could have sworn he heard her voice calling for him. He could see the door to his room opening, despite the fact that he knew he'd locked it as the hooker had started her trade. His visions placed a shaded figure in the doorframe, one that looked bulky and armored like the mercs that guarded the mayor. In his dream, he saw himself rise with iron in hand, firing the entirety of the weapon in quick succession into the bruiser, the nightmare's own weapon going off as the Wrenn's rounds battered him, some making contact with flesh while others slowed in the armor plating. A scream came from beside him, followed by a gurgling sound. Wrenn's dream body felt a burning cut through his left calf, forcing him to fall to the floor.

It was the impact his head made with the wooden panels that forced him to reconcile with the reality of his situation. His head was still swimming in the soup that was his dream, but he was suddenly aware that the pain he felt from the shot was real. A scuffle in the hallway vied for his attention, Wrenn seeing Aurora straddling the guard and forcing a knife through his throat. She burst into his room, looking on in desperation as she found the hooker in the bed, then her captain on the floor. He vaguely realized she was trying to speak to him, but he couldn't understand anything but a muffled garble. Aurora's hands clamped down on his wounded leg, sending a burst of fire up his spine. He might of cried out, he might have been imagining it, for all he knew this was all just a weird part of the nightmare that never seemed to end. Blackness covered his face for a spell, was it his consciousness faltering, or just a shirt being thrown over him? He was so tired of trying to understand what was going on.

Jenny was in the room next, crying out at the hooker in the bed, cursing up a storm and calling for her father, who came lumbering in and wrapped the sheets around Wrenn's date. Aurora stayed beside Wrenn, dressing him hurriedly and even reloading his sidearm before placing it back into his hands. Had he actually fired it? No, that was just in the dream. Aurora finally slipped the com piece back into his ear and Wrenn could hear Cheyenne's voice in his thoughts. *Warning: Captain, you have been shot. Crewmember Aurora will be taking you to your fighter to administer medical aid.*

"No . . ." Wrenn's thoughts murmured. "It's too cold outside . . . we'll freeze . . ."

Warning: If you stay where you are Captain, you will die.

Aurora turned to Jenny, yelling for something followed by Jenny tossing a syringe her way. Aurora jammed the end into Wrenn's thigh, another shot of pain sailing up his nervous system. Blackness encased him again, but this time from his eyelids. Thankfully, mercifully, the nightmare was over and he could just get back to sleep.

CHAPTER 17

The crackling of the logs was the next thing that came to Wrenn's senses. He felt himself bundled in blankets, the gentle heat from a campfire keeping him toasty against a chilled air he could feel on his ears. He sunk himself lower under the covers, moaning as the pain of his leg throbbed. He winced, trying his best to feel for the wound without moving his calf further. "You're awake." Aurora's voice sounded from the other side of the fire.

"What . . . ? Where . . . ?" Wrenn managed.

"You were shot." Aurora said, coming to sit beside him. "And poisoned."

"I think I knew the first part . . ." Wrenn tried to blink and get her in focus. She was splashed in dried blood, some of which stained her perfect complexion. Wrenn reached a weakened hand toward it, before she took his palm into hers. "It's not mine. I'm ok."

"Whose is it?" Wrenn squeaked

"One of those mercenaries. Picked his way into your room, didn't look like he had busted down the door. Either way, you must have heard him cause you unloaded your entire cylinder into him, though his armor protected most of his vital parts. My knife finished him off; we won't have to worry about him again."

"Won't his buddies come lookin'?" Wrenn asked.

"Doubtful, least not right away. You can thank the Whitmoores for that."

"What'd they do?"

"Well, after you shot the bastard, he shot back. Your . . . guest . . . caught a round to the throat and bled out on the bed. Jenny and Clive took that rather hard."

"Fuck . . ." Wrenn sighed.

"Yeah . . . but, they recovered quickly, I'll give them that. Clive wrapped her in the sheets and took her to the basement, merc too. He stripped off the armor and went back out on 'patrol' to ward off any curious spectators. After an hour or so he doubled back and helped get you. Meanwhile Jenny had cleaned up the room and assisted me in getting you bandaged up with what little meds they had, but Cheyenne said your vitals were still dropping and we needed to get you back to the fighters."

"That the poison you mentioned?" Wrenn winced as he tried to sit up.

Aurora gently pushed him back down. "Yes, though I've no idea where you could have gotten it unless it came from your . . . friend."

"No, it wasn't her." Wrenn shook his head.

"So sure?"

"Mostly. It was the drink I had from Desmond. I was feeling light headed the moment I left the fort." Wrenn stared into the fire.

A silence covered them for a full minute before Aurora felt comfortable speaking again. "Your own brother?"

Wrenn simply nodded. The blonde shook her head. "I'm so sorry, Wrenn . . ."

"Don't be." The man said flatly. "We never were that close . . ."

"Still, blood is blood." Aurora argued.

"And his will run just as easy as the rest." Wrenn put an end to the topic. "How did I get here?"

"Clive helped, wrapped you in blankets and we all clambered out here to get you Cheyenne's personal touch. You've been plugged into your zipper so she could monitor you."

Greeting: Hello Captain, I am glad to see you are feeling

better.

"It was you who woke me, wasn't it?" Wrenn asked the AI.

Answer: Yes, as soon as you removed the earpiece, I could no longer monitor your status and vitals. I was successful in cracking into the mayor's system. I intercepted comms chatter ordering the guard to dispose of you. I promptly increased my volume output 300% to warn you and awoke Crewmember Aurora as well.

"This is one rude awakening I can be thankful for." Wrenn joked.

Response: I am happy to be of service, Captain. I would have warned you sooner had you not been otherwise occupied.

Aurora rolled her eyes. "Otherwise occupied."

"Why are you so pissy about it?" Wrenn raised an eyebrow. "Aren't you the one who hired her?"

"I did nothing of the sort!" Aurora stood. "She and her male counterpart came to my room first and I promptly told them to bugger off!"

"Wait . . . then who hired them?"

Observation: I have already traced a wireless transfer of credits directly into two of the prostitute's accounts from Lieutenant Myers', Captain.

"Damnit, I knew my luck wouldn'ta turn that good that quick." Wrenn grumbled. "When I didn't finish my drink he musta come up with an even snakier way of offing me."

"Your luck?"

"Yeah, me and the lady have been havin' a bit of a back-and-forth seems like. One minute my ship's torn to pieces over a freak failure of the Digiway, the next I find a derelict frigate just floatin' on by itself ripe for the taking. Works in reverse too, one minute I've got a beautiful woman surprising me in bed . . ."

"The next you're being shot and poisoned." Aurora finished. "You know, what your people call luck is usually just the strings of destiny tying you back to your intended path. The harder you resist, the harder the snap back to your fate."

Wrenn rolled his eyes. "Or it's just on account of that son of a bitch brother of mine bein' an asshat."

"You realize you just insulted your own mother with that statement . . ." Aurora teased.

Wrenn was clearly not in a laughing mood. Aurora relented and the two just stared at the fire in silence for a few minutes. The night was chilly, but most of the relentless wind seemed to be somewhat shielded from them in the outcropping. Aurora patted Wrenn's head reassuringly after a bit. "Families can be messy. I should know."

"Yeah?" Wrenn didn't look away from the flames.

Aurora nodded. "My people, though they act advanced, can be quite barbaric when it comes down to it."

Wrenn didn't say anything, allowing her to continue. Aurora sighed, seeming to allow herself to open up just a hair. "You've seen some small samples of our advancements, but most of our technologies are hidden from your Alliance. Our leadership thinks conflict is inevitable with your people, so they keep a close eye on any assets that they deem too dangerous for humans to discover.

"My father is . . . very loyal to the Selkath Empire, what your people call 'Utopia'. So, when my ability started to present itself, well, he practically surrendered me to the military's control."

"He abandoned you?" Wrenn asked.

"To abandon me, he'd have to have been there in the first place; but, yes . . . you could say that." Aurora looked at the fire solemnly.

Wrenn stayed silent for a long time. "What ability?"

Aurora nodded, knowing the question was coming. "My people have been prosperous for thousands of years. That prosperity is due in large part to the Alma Hir."

"The whosa whatsit now?" Wrenn shook his head.

"Roughly translated it means 'Positive Future Obtainer', what your people might call an 'oracle'."

"You mean a fortune-teller?" Wrenn asked.

"Sort of." Aurora nodded. "Though not just for the individual whose palm is being read. My people have

150

mastered many concepts that yours might consider fantastical. Movement through space *and* time come easy for us, our largest ships are even able to 'fold' space for long distance travel. At first this technology had its drawbacks, most of which being crews of the earliest vessels would feel displaced or almost as if they were living in two places at once. The earliest unshielded voyagers even . . . changed. Now, a hundred generations later, this change is still widespread amongst our people, showing itself through a recessive gene that can pop up in any number of our population. These are the future members of the Alma Hir. Once trained, they can see many futures for many things. People, places, technology. Inventions, scientific discoveries, and important figures are brought before the Alma Hir to have their fate tested."

Wrenn scoffed. "There you go on about that destiny junk again . . ."

Aurora seemed slightly offended. "You . . . don't approve?"

"I don't believe in 'fate' is all. Load of hogwash if I ever heard it. Too many things in this wide open galaxy for there to be some all-knowing entity controllin' it all."

Aurora squinted at him. "It's why I'm here, you know."

"Huh?"

"You, your fate . . . I saw it."

"When? How? The fuck you on about?"

Aurora sighed. "My ability . . . I can see the future. I am to be an Alma Hir, or, I was to be. I refused that life, to be a tool for others, to be a seer for everyone's future but my own. I will not be trapped in a gilded cage, I want to be free - not have someone looking over my shoulder the rest of my days, you understand?"

Wrenn sighed as well. "Oh, all too well, darlin'."

Aurora felt a rush swell in her chest, recognizing a kindred spirit in Wrenn the same way she had when she first met him. She smiled warmly. "That night in the casino, when you came over from the table and took my hand, I saw your fate. Not all of it, just what was going to happen that night. I knew you were going to win that game, procuring a lot of money in the process."

"So, you decided to rob me . . ." Wrenn chuckled.

"Yes, but we both know that was never in the cards, so to speak." Aurora playfully bumped him with her hip.

They both laughed, Aurora taking in a breath before speaking further. "Later, once aboard your ship, I snuck into your room and got a better look, as it were."

"When you claimed I was snoring?"

"Precisely." Aurora nodded.

"So, what'd you see?"

Aurora shook her head, her golden curls wafting in reaction. "No, I decided never to reveal someone's fate for them ever again. It clouds the mind, forces them to forgo any semblance of free-will. Besides, I thought you didn't believe in that, what did you call it again? Hogwash?"

Wrenn huffed. "Ah whatever, I was just curious."

Aurora grunted and looked back at the fire. "Point of the story, Captain Wrenn, is that families can be complicated, believe me. Once they find your value, they will use you just as quickly as anyone else in the 'verse . . . they'll just make you feel guilty about not accepting the deal."

Wrenn nodded and grunted in acknowledgment. "But . . . that doesn't take away the fact that they are your blood. I may despise my father for what he did, but I would never wish any harm befall him."

"Yeah well, guess we Terrans are a bit different." Wrenn sighed.

"Clearly." Aurora agreed.

The two sat silently for a few more minutes as the wind howled around them. Before long Aurora started pulling the blankets back from Wrenn's sleeping area. "Hey, what the hell are you doing?"

"Scoot over, I'm coming in. I'm freezing."

"Hey now, if you need some warming up . . ."

"Don't get any funny ideas, darling." Aurora warned. "This is simply for comfort."

"Alright, fine, just don't be surprised if lil' bit here don't wanna listen and gives you a lumbar massage."

Aurora scoffed loudly. "Why didn't that Jenny give me more blasted blankets?"

△△△

Wrenn woke when the heat of the morning sun and his blankets became unbearable. His initial breath took in the smells of ash from the snuffed out campfire, the dust of the desert around him, and the hypnotic fragrance of Aurora's hair. She didn't stir as his eyes fluttered open, his memories and awareness combining slowly, his mind still seemed a bit sluggish from the after-effects of the poison. He was reminded of his aching leg, still wrapped in a bandage. He was also painfully aware of a new soreness in his chest, likely a farewell gift from the toxin leaving his system. Cheyenne had mentioned something about the cure-all syringe on hand in the emergency first-aid kit working as a sort of super-steroid for white blood cells. They'd be right vicious to anything that weren't supposed to be there, but like any barroom brawl after a fight, don't matter who was wrong or right, the stools were gonna feel the effects. She had said it in a much more scientific fashion but Wrenn had stopped listening 'bout halfway through.

A sensation he hadn't counted on was the funny feeling he was getting from his particulars. There was a rubbing that was going on, sliding along the fullness of his morning wood. Wrenn looked downwards under the covers, noticing Aurora was massaging his cock between her firm butt cheeks. Her breath was labored, from their spooning positioning he couldn't see much of where her hands were but it didn't take much imagination to hazard a guess. Was she aware he was awake? Should he tell her? Wrenn's eyes rolled backwards as her movements became more forceful, her hips grinding into him harder than before. He heard a small whimper escape her lips, she was definitely struggling to stay quiet. The captain decided to remain silent himself, enjoy the moment rather than complicate matters. He'd yet to truly see her angry, but he didn't much care for the thought of leaving her blue-balled. Aurora's jilling became more frantic, Wrenn seeing her elbow moving now, her torso trembling and the whimpers coming from her seemed barely contained. A final moment of tension and then she gasped, deflating like a switch had been turned and there was little further motion other than some residual rocking of her hips. Wrenn hadn't a chance to build himself at all, but the morning hadn't been for him. He was happy just to be her, for lack of better term, toy.

After a few more minutes, once she had seemed to catch her breath, Wrenn stretched exaggeratingly and faked a yawn. He could feel Aurora jump, likely shocking her out of whatever bliss she had still been basking in. "Mornin'." He said.

"Good . . . good morning." Aurora stammered.

"Been up long?" Wrenn smirked.

"No!" She answered quickly. "No . . . just woke a few moments ago myself."

"Gotcha."

The man tried to rise, but the pain in his body struck him something fierce and he fell back to the blankets in a groan. Aurora spun, sitting up on her elbow and checking him over. She put a hand on his bare chest and looked at him in concern. "What's wrong?"

"Nothing." Wrenn lied. "Just, sore from sleepin' on the ground is all."

Aurora seemed to be feeling his accelerated heartbeat and squinted at him. "This isn't the time to play macho, Wrenn. You nearly died last night."

". . . But I didn't." Wrenn smiled cockily. "Guess Lady Luck ain't given up on me, yet."

"Lady Luck had nothing to do with it." Aurora huffed. "I still haven't gotten an ounce of gratitude, by the way."

"Seems to me you already took your reward this morning." Wrenn teased.

Aurora's porcelain face turned bright red. "You . . ."

"Why stop there though?" Wrenn asked. "I might not be at peak performance, but we could still find some mutual satisfaction."

Aurora rolled her eyes, her embarrassment dissolving as sudden as it came. "And there it is . . ."

"What?" Wrenn asked.

Aurora pulled back the blankets, rising and beginning to clothe herself. Wrenn could see she had stripped down to her underwear during the night, likely due to their shared body heat. He rather enjoyed watching her ass bounce as she squeezed into her leather pants. Aurora sat on a rock next to the burned out fire and started strapping on her boots. "The ego." She answered, not looking at him. "You act as if the planets themselves should move out of your way. Sometimes, Wrenn, I think your head is bigger than most of them."

"Sorry princess, but sometimes to survive out here, you gotta . . ."

"Don't Call Me Princess!" Aurora snapped, standing.

Wrenn could see a fire behind her eyes, a deep hatred that she'd never shown before. For all her acting talent; she'd certainly kept many things close to the chest, but here and now she was showing him all her cards. She was injured, maybe not physically, but there was a trauma buried deep that he recognized. No one came out to Reach, to the Omega Quad in general, unless they was running from something. The captain held up his hands in surrender. "I'm sorry. I didn't mean to offend."

"Sometimes you speak down to me as if I were a child. I'll have you know I've lived three of your lifetimes, *Terran*." She spat the last word as if it were an insult. "You should feel lucky to have my experience on your side."

Wrenn relented. He nodded, doing his best not to answer her further. "You're right. I am very grateful to have you. It wasn't my intention to anger you with . . . whatever you got going on. I just figured we might have some fun together, is all . . ."

Aurora came back to the blankets, crawling down onto all fours and bringing her face within an inch of his. "We agreed to keep this professional, remember?"

Wrenn chuckled. "So, what was that you were doin' just now?"

Aurora shrugged a shoulder and stood. "That was me using you. Rather, a *small* part of you. I have no interest in taking it further."

"Uh huh." Wrenn smirked; somehow, he knew it was more than that. Or, was he just hoping it was? Regardless, the opportunity was long past at this point and it seemed unwise to push it further.

The captain tried again to rise and felt dizzy. He grumbled as he laid back down, shielding his eyes from the bright morning sun. "I'm not sure I can get up just yet."

"Probably best if you didn't." Aurora finished dressing. "I'm going to sneak back into town and get us some supplies. We should lay low for the time being. Perhaps Jenny and her father's ruse fooled the mercenaries into thinking you are dead."

"We'll need to thank them." Wrenn winced as he turned to face her.

"Oh, I already paid them."

"With what money?" Wrenn looked up.

"Why, the remainder of your casino winnings, darling." Aurora smiled wickedly.

"Of course you did . . ." Wrenn sighed.

"Would you have rather them left you bleeding on the floor?" Aurora countered. "We have few allies here as it is. The last thing we need is the townsfolk turning on us as the mercenaries have."

"No, you're right. I've had about all the betrayal I can take on this job."

"Speaking of which." Aurora used a pocket mirror to fix her hair best she could. "What's our next play?"

"Well, Desmond will likely tell the mayor I've bailed,

leaving him as the only option to reopen the mine . . ."

Aurora nodded, "There's no way of getting to the mayor to tell our side of things without revealing ourselves to the mercenary officer, either."

Wrenn nodded. "We might be able to play it from another way."

"How do you mean?"

"Well, we know they plan on using the grav lift cars as a railway. We could head out into the desert and find whoever's been sabotaging the mine thus far, warn them what's coming, help them even. We do enough to show Desmond's mercs are incompetent. The mayor will drop his ass faster than a dwarf planet's solar cycle." Wrenn explained.

"Then we swoop in like heroes and fix everything quick, exploiting our connections with the saboteurs?" Aurora finished. "I don't know, Wrenn, it seems overly complicated."

"Only other alternative is to bail, try to convince big Ronald we've got it fixed and collect before he gets wise." Wrenn shrugged.

"I can't imagine that will go over well once he hears that it was a mercenary group that fixed the problem and not you. He'll likely put a bounty out on us." Aurora sighed.

"Yeah, this whole job got more complicated than I was expectin'."

"Likely the reason Ronald never sent any of his own people." Aurora reminded him. "He did warn you this job would need some problem solving."

"Hang on . . ." Wrenn thought. "What if we beat Desmond to the punch?"

"Elaborate." Aurora prompted.

"Sewell's a businessman, right? Those corpo types only care about money. Why buy the farm when you can just steal the milk for free or whatever?"

"I don't think that's how the saying goes . . ." Aurora shook her head.

"It doesn't matter. Point is, we roll out to the desert, find these saboteurs, and wipe them before the train gets prepped at all. No more saboteurs, no more need for the mercs. Mine goes back to producing, mayor saves money on protection, mercs get booted out of atmo and we get our reward."

Aurora nodded. "Of course, we know nothing about these saboteurs or their capabilities."

"Can't be too bad, otherwise they'd be using more direct tactics, right? They don't have enough strength to attack the fort directly, so they're fighting them guerrilla style."

"Fighting a war of attrition rather than a full engagement." Aurora agreed. "Still, they might be more than the two of us can handle."

"With two starfighters and a frigate in orbit for bombardment? Unless they've dug in deep, I doubt it." Wrenn scoffed. "From the sounds of it, they ain't been here long enough to do something like that. They'd have leveled the town otherwise, when they was buildin' the damn place."

"Perhaps . . ." Aurora thought.

"They figure they'll give the company some grief, help their stock plummet, then buy them out and take over the town. Suddenly the convoys start workin' again like magic. It's classic corpo dust-up shit. I saw it all the time in the Alpha."

"And what happens to the innocents that get caught in the crossfire?" Aurora asked.

Wrenn rolled his eyes. "Corps don't give a shit about anything other than profits. Couple miners get blasted, they ain't gonna shed a tear so long as they can make their shareholders richer."

Aurora clicked her teeth in disgust. "That's just . . ."

"Sick? Evil? Trust me, you ain't sayin' nothin the rest of us Terrans haven't said before. They don't care about people, just their next quarterly earnings report." Wrenn tried again to rise but still had trouble. "Fuck me, I need to get my shit together so we can go."

"Not yet, Wrenn. You still need some time to heal." Aurora helped him back down to the blankets.

"But, if this is gonna work, we need to get out there and start searchin'."

"It does us no good if you crash your fighter from exhaustion." Aurora cautioned. "I'll get those supplies and we can take a day or two for you to recover. Remember, they're still waiting on those reinforcements. Even after they arrive, they'll need to offload and prepare the train. We've got time."

Wrenn sighed heavily. She was right. He nodded. Aurora stood and surprisingly gave him a kiss on the cheek. "Just take it easy, Captain. I'll be back by sundown."

"Yeah, yeah, yeah . . ." Wrenn grumbled.

CHAPTER 18

Warning: You have exceeded your allotted energy output for the day, Captain. Cheyenne chimed in his ear.

Wrenn dropped the emergency case of supplies from his zipper near the fire pit as he collapsed back onto the blankets. "And just how the hell do you know somethin' like that?" Wrenn wheezed.

Explanation: By analyzing the captain's metabolism, scans of the planet's average midday temperatures, heat index, and accounting for the calories the captain has consumed. . . I was able to determine a rough estimate of total activity the captain can be allotted during his current healing cycle.

"You did all that for me?" Wrenn winced as his thigh began to throb.

Observation: It is my function, Captain.

Wrenn smiled softly to himself. He'd never felt right with someone looking over his shoulder, watching his every move, judging his choices and actions. . . I mean, it's what got him out here in this fucking desert. . . but for some reason, he didn't feel annoyed by Cheyenne's spyin'. The computer wasn't doing it to track him, or tax him, or monitor his likes/dislikes to sell off to some corp. . . she did it because she cared about him. Sure, she was programmed to care about whomever was designated as captain and crew aboard the *Whisper*, but this felt more like she wanted to rather than she had to. Hypocritical as it was, Wrenn kinda liked having a guardian angel. "You like lookin' out for me, huh?"

Repeating: It is my function.

"Yeah, but, it's more than that, ain't it?" Wrenn peered up at the sky, as if he was trying to look at Cheyenne in orbit.

The sounds of her thinking tickled his eardrum until finally she replied. *Admission: It makes me. . . happy.*

Wrenn chuckled. "Well, alright darlin'. I'll settle down for the day."

The sun was high now, though he didn't risk checking to see exactly where. The outcropping provided much needed shade and ultimately made it tolerable to stay outdoors, but only just. The wind blowing down the canyon helped keep most of the air fresh and cool, but at times it still blew in a cluster of sand or wave of heat that caused Wrenn's mouth to dry. He'd pulled out the emergency supply crate that came standard on most fighters, unaware of how to use the digital storage aboard Aurora's Starfire. He wasn't even sure the thing would let him pilfer through her belongings without chopping his hands off with the protective shell. If worse came to worse he could always board his Lancer and tell Cheyenne to fly him back to the *Whisper*, but he hoped to not give away his position if at all possible.

Wrenn ripped open the footlocker and started downing bottles of water. They were about as tasty as one would expect of sterilized water that had been in storage for years, but he didn't much care at this point. His body was screaming at him for sustenance, both for battling the heat and healing his wounds. Wrenn spent most of the day in agony, blanking in and out of consciousness as the sun moved across the sky. The last time his eyes closed he could see its rays starting to peek at him from under the outcropping's ceiling and he rolled over to keep it from shining in his eyes. Next he knew, the fire was crackling again and the air was bone-chilling. Someone had wrapped him in the blankets and had even cleaned up the trash from the survival kit. Wrenn watched the fire, noticing it was mostly coals, with a cast iron pot hung over it and a woman stirring what was within. Jenny looked over at him and smiled widely, her face a glow even in the low light. "Howdy stranger!"

"Hey..." Wrenn managed.

"You look like something the dog dragged in . . ." She moved over to him, checking his forehead with the back of her hand. "Least you ain't got a fever. Means you're right on the mend."

"What are you doing here?" Wrenn asked.

"Can't I come check on one of my guests?" Jenny joked.

"You still want to? After what trouble I brought to your doorstep?"

Jenny waved a hand at him. "Oh that? Please! Nothing a quick body swap didn't fix and a few choice rumors spread to the local gossipers. Ain't no one'll know but us and the dead."

Wrenn shook his head. "You seem pretty laid back about all this compared to the other night."

Jenny sighed. "I'll admit, it was hard seeing Cybil like that..."

"Was that her name?" Wrenn asked.

"You never even asked her?" Jenny shot him a scornful look.

"She... didn't give me much of a chance..." He admitted.

He thought a lecture was coming, or at least a few choice words, but instead Jenny just laughed. "That's Cybil. She always was a go-getter." She smiled. "That's what I choose to remember her as, the woman with a fire in her, a passion for passion as it was. I can't think of a better place for her to meet her maker than in the arms of someone she had just brought great joy to. It's how she woulda liked it."

"If you say so..." Wrenn avoided the subject.

"Are you religious, Mr. Wrenn?"

"Captain." Wrenn corrected. "And no... I'm not."

"Can I ask why?" Jenny sat beside him, ignoring the correction.

Wrenn sighed, "For the same reason I don't believe in fate or destiny, it's all hokey nonsense. Can't nothing be that powerful to control all there is out here in the 'verse. It's just too much."

"But that's where faith comes in." Jenny smiled. "Ain't something for you to be understandin', just believin'."

"Yeah well, you keep to your ancient gobbledygook and I'll keep to mine." Wrenn grumbled.

"Fair enough. Anyway, don't you worry none about the whole thing. Papa and I got everything squared away and your partner paid more than a fair share for any inconvenience."

"Yeah, she told me."

Jenny rose and started scooping the stew she was brewing in the pot into a bowl. "What's the deal with you two, anyhow?"

"Deal?" Wrenn asked.

"Yeah, like . . . are you two a couple? On one hand you seemed awfully friendly-like that first mornin', but on the other hand she went and got a separate room, but on the other other hand she refused Steven for company that night. . . so I figured . . ."

"We're just business partners." Wrenn interrupted her, probably a bit too forcefully.

Jenny seemed to catch the unintentional inclination. "I see."

"Why, you askin' after something in particular?" Wrenn looked up at her as she sat down next to him again with the filled bowl in hand and a spoon.

"I might be . . ." Jenny smiled.

Wrenn's eyebrows shot up. "Not even going to dance around the subject, huh?"

"You should have realized by now, Mister Wrenn, that I don't believe much in the way of pussy-footin'. I say what I mean and I mean what I say, anythin' else is just wastin' everyone's time . . . mine most especially." Jenny gathered a spoonful of stew and blew on it, almost seductively. "Now, eat this."

"Captain." Wrenn corrected again, before taking the bite he was offered. His taste buds exploded with a rich tapestry of meat, fresh vegetables, and spices. "Damn!"

Jenny giggled. "I take it you like it then?"

Wrenn nodded. "You've got a gift."

"Nothin' that's much use out here in the Reach, but Papa always said the wild west was tamed one full belly at a time." Jenny shrugged.

"Wise man." Wrenn agreed.

"I think so. He was the first of the family to think about expandin' out here, though most of the others thought him a bit touched in the head. Hard enough to get supplies to our farthest establishments in the Alpha, forget something on a barren planet in the Reach, but Papa's a right stubborn old fool. When we couldn't get supplies of fresh ingredients, he took him a few of the burlier miners and found us some local options. That's what you're tastin' here now, mixture of some desert rat and cactus leaves. Took me nearly a month to get the recipe down pat."

"Is that why you're out here? For him?"

Jenny shook her head. "Naw, unlike the rest of my kin I guess I've got a tumbleweed in my chest instead of a heart. I was always the sort to keep movin', even as a youngin'. I lived with my extended family most of my life, since Papa and Momma split up to take care of separate restaurants when I was about as short as a buckthorn."

"That must have been rough." Wrenn agreed.

"Actually, the opposite." Jenny smiled, she kept scooping up spoonfuls of soup and feeding them to him while she talked. "I love my family, always have. I got to travel the galaxy from one of my relatives to the other, learnin' all kinds of dishes, meetin' all kinds of people. It was wonderful."

Wrenn was having trouble eating fast enough to take in the portions she was force-feeding him. The man finally raised his hand and took the bowl and spoon from her. "Oh, sorry, guess I got a little carried away there while reminiscin'."

Wrenn coughed. "It's fine. If Imma drown I'd rather it be in something tasty than not."

Jenny's face flushed at the compliment. "What about you,

Mister Wrenn? Got yourself a family out there in the stars?"

Wrenn shook his head. "I did . . . once . . ."

The silence that followed told Jenny all she needed to know on the subject. She nodded after a while and went back to sitting beside the fire. "Sometimes, it's the family we forge on our own that ends up being the strongest. Don't gotta be blood to be kin."

Wrenn said nothing as he continued eating. He couldn't decide if it was his desire to forget or the lack of anything further to say on the matter, but Jenny seemed to enjoy the company just the same. Once he'd finished, she offered him seconds, which he gladly took. By the time Aurora arrived back at the camp his belly was full to bursting and he was having trouble keeping his eyes from drooping. The girls must have thought he was already asleep in the dull firelight because they started talking as if he weren't alert to hear it. "How's he doing?" Aurora asked.

"'Bout as well as can be expected, I'd wager." Jenny replied.

Wrenn watched as Aurora put a finger to her ear, as if she were hearing Cheyenne's voice in the com piece. The AI must have muted herself on his end so she wouldn't 'wake' him. Aurora nodded and then sat down across the coals from the redhead. "Who was that just now?" Jenny questioned.

"Hmm?" The blonde asked.

"In your ear, you acted as if you were listenin' to someone . . ."

"Oh," Aurora looked over at Wrenn, apprehensive on how much to divulge. "It's . . . just someone back on our ship . . . *his* ship." She corrected.

"Must be real nice, travellin' among the stars. I only ever saw it from the transports I took to and from different port towns." Jenny looked up at the clear night sky, a thousand twinkling dots shining back at her.

"It's a feeling like none other." Aurora agreed. "It's freedom, in its truest form."

"You sound as if you've lived like I have, grounded and looking up for more." Jenny mentioned.

Aurora nodded solemnly. From what she had told Wrenn of her past, he understood completely why she looked so downtrodden. "I aim to change my fate." The blonde finally said.

"That's a tall order." Jenny responded. "Ain't much we can do to go against God's will."

"Yes, but sometimes it's worth the sacrifices." Aurora argued.

Jenny nodded. She grabbed hold of a tool that helped her take the pot off the cooker and place it beside the fire so she could look at Aurora directly. "I ain't the type for preachin', even less so the kind of person that tells others how to live, but I am the type to worry about lost souls. We each got our path to follow, and we're gonna end up just where we're supposed to be when it's all said and done. I just hope your journey's a smooth one and you find what you're looking for."

Aurora smiled at her, the two women nodding. "Thank you. That's very kind of you to say."

Jenny waved her hand and started fixing two more bowls of soup for them. Aurora took her first bite and was immediately infatuated with the dish, asking Jenny to reveal the recipe. Jenny went about repeating the story of her father's ingredient gathering which of course led to further discoveries in cuisines and comparisons with Utopian dishes Aurora had grown up with. The gentle tones of their voices sounded almost as if two birds were calling toward one another across a wood while Wrenn laid in the shade. He smiled to himself, feeling comfortable and protected for the first time in a long time. In space, you almost had to get comfortable with silence, or else you'd go mad. Loneliness and solitude were things every ship captain knew better than his own ship's manifest, so when there were moments of togetherness, even something as simple as folk sitting 'round a campfire talkin' about recipes, it chased away those thoughts of isolation, that fear of never making it back from the cold black of the 'verse. When Wrenn fell asleep, he rested better than he had in years.

CHAPTER 19

Two days went by before Wrenn could manage to move with nothing worse than a limp. The leftover supplies were loaded onto the fighters and then he and Aurora used the canyon to mask their departure from the outskirts of town. Jenny had smuggled them a scan of the surrounding area from a local prospector, with additional scans from Cheyenne above to help match. The route to the mine was plain enough to see, a well worn trail that slalomed between the buttes and spires until it came up to the edge of a rather large crevice. A manmade structure stretched across a large area, likely a processing plant of some kind to turn the crystals into fuel. The triple smokestacks that stuck out from the building were dormant, sand dunes starting to form in various pockets around the building and surrounding blacktop. The place hadn't been functional for quite some time.

Aurora and Wrenn landed their craft on the pavement outside of the factory, dust kicking up as the thrusters helped them slow and hover down to the asphalt. When they exited their craft, they were greeted with nothing more than the ever-present wind of the desert. "Let's do a once over before we go inside." Wrenn suggested.

"Good thinking, wouldn't want to walk into an ambush." Aurora nodded.

"I woulda thought we'd run into something by now." Wrenn mentioned as they moved toward a row of trucks idly parked on the closest side of the building. "We flew along the travel route specifically so that someone would show themselves."

"Maybe the saboteurs don't have the capability to combat aircraft." Aurora proposed.

"Maybe . . ." Wrenn shrugged. "If that were the case though, why didn't Sewell just start transporting the fuel via fixed wing?"

"Likely the man panicked and didn't think of anything other than securing his own well-being." Aurora answered. "Did you not say these corporate types value little but their own satisfaction?"

"I guess . . ." Wrenn sighed. "Maybe the fool just didn't plan it through."

"Or . . ." Aurora piped up as she looked below one of the trucks. "He was worried about the craft becoming more scrap for the pile."

She pointed it out for Wrenn. The fuel lines on each of the trucks had been cut, their containers punctured and the contents spilled about the ground. Even after the extended absence of any workers here, the smell of spilled fuel was still heavy on the air, and the ground still carried massive stains from the dumping. Wrenn walked along the row of trucks, ensuring they each had shared the same fate. Strangely, in one of the last few vehicles, a piece of whatever had been used to puncture the fuel tanks was still stuck in the hole it'd created. Wrenn wrenched it free, looking bewildered at what appeared to be a sharpened piece of crystal. Aurora was confused as well. "A shard from a mined gem cluster maybe?"

Wrenn shook his head. "No, this looks . . . forged. Like ancient stone tools on old Earth."

"Let us see what awaits us inside."

$$\triangle\triangle\triangle$$

The stillness of the air inside the factory was more unsettling than the barrenness of the exterior. Towering gears used to crush and pulverize the crystals dominated the open floor, with tubing and pipes running into vats that would mix other chemicals to eventually produce fuel. Filtration devices, conveyor belts, and other common factory machinery loomed as sleeping giants, undisturbed and unbroken, just primed for a switch to be thrown or a lever pulled to start functioning again. Eerie and abandoned, even the howling air outside could not shake the ghosts that lingered in this space.

Wrenn and Aurora moved through the factory unobstructed, checking high and low for any signs of tampering or traps. Their hunt went unrewarded, with the only exception being the computers in the control center. In stark contrast to the machinery on the factory floor, the screens and switches in the control center had been absolutely eviscerated. Broken glass covered the ground, wires laid severed on consoles, the entire room looked as if something had burst out of the control stations and sheared solid steel like it was paper. "Holy hell, what is powerful enough to do something like this?" Wrenn asked.

"No scorch marks." Aurora pointed out. "Not an explosion."

"So, something did this *by hand?*" Wrenn shook his head.

Observation: More accurately, by claw. Cheynne piped up in their ears. *Notice the scratch marks and indentations at the point of origin.*

Wrenn spread out his fingers to try and match the patterns of the claws etched into the metal. It was similar to a humanoid hand, with three fingers and thumb, but the size was one and a half times larger than his palm. "Had to be something big." Wrenn noted.

"And angry." Aurora agreed.

"And behind you." A gravelly voice joined in.

Wrenn spun, reaching for his iron, but the blow to his head forced stars to form before his eyes. For the second time in almost as many days, his vision was blanketed in blackness. He fell to the floor, a feeling of panic and alarm flooding his mind before the void swallowed him completely.

△△△

Wrenn's head throbbed harder than a morning hangover. He groaned and shook it to try and clear the cobwebs. His eyes had trouble adjusting to the dim-lit cavern he seemed to have found himself in. Before blurting anything out, he took stock of his surroundings. He was tied to a post of some kind, keeping him aloft from the floor like he was some weird caterpillar in a rope cocoon. Aurora was near him, similarly restrained and still out cold if her limp head was any indication. Best he could tell, his weapons had been taken, which meant whoever had captured him probably had them. He was alive, so that meant that his captor wanted something out of him. Wrenn tried his best to gauge the area. It was a cavern, larger than he thought possible on such a planet. Light was scarce, no open flame could be seen anywhere which likely meant they were deep, where smoke would fill the area and keep anything down here from breathing. The only illumination was a gentle glow from some fluorescent fungi along the ceiling and . . . crystals!

A rainbow kaleidoscope of crystal growths dotted the walls of the cavern, pulsing waves of soft rays out as if they were some sort of oil lantern. Wrenn had heard crystals on Earth and other similar planets would refract light when shined on it, but never *create* it. Photons were a key component of flora development in most ecosystems, combined with moisture. Had planet life here developed on feeding from these crystals rather than the sun? That would explain the humidity he was feeling. Perhaps when Visigath had strayed from its original orbit, the planet itself had adapted to its new environment, migrating life from the surface to further within.

Wrenn shook his head. He needed to focus. He opened and closed his mouth a few times, trying to confirm he still had his ear piece. "Cheyenne, you there?"

Confirmed.

Wrenn sighed in relief. It was the start of an escape at

least. "Where am I?"

Answer: Unknown. Your signal was tracked to the fissure where I detected it descending into the planet's crust. I would surmise you are between thirty meters to a kilometer below the surface, depending on the temperature.

"Well, it's pretty humid down here." Wrenn noted.

Response: Likely due to the fact that you are below an ancient sea bed. Pocket reservoirs could be common place in your immediate area.

"Look darlin', that's interesting and all, but how the hell am I gonna get out of this place?" Wrenn whispered hoarsely.

Answer: Start climbing.

Wrenn sighed. "You are absolutely useless."

Response: Recent activities and the captain's history of dependence on me would prove otherwise.

Wrenn would have sworn had he not been afraid of waking whatever or whoever had nabbed him. "Just activate that vision thingy you showed me in the hangar. It could help us see better around here at least."

Confirmed.

Wrenn's eyes lit up from the inside, outlines of plants, crystals, and even small critters along the cave flooring presenting themselves to him. Wrenn struggled against his bonds as he heard Aurora stir. "What . . . Ud'Raan! What in the ancestors . . . !"

"Easy, partner." Wrenn calmed her. "You're alright."

"Wrenn!?" She hissed. "What is wrong with my eyes?"

"It's a little trick Cheyenne figured out, it'll help us get outta here."

"It's . . . disconcerting . . ."

"You'll adjust. Can you loosen your bindings?"

Wrenn saw Aurora shift and struggle. "Doesn't . . . wait . . . no, I'm bound pretty solid here."

"Bonds can no break." A low voice growled near them.

"Fuck me sideways, Cheyenne, why didn't you tell me anyone was near?"

Response: I am unable to detect any heat signatures in your proximity.

Wrenn recalled a similar situation in the factory, where whatever this thing was had snuck up on them out in the open without Cheyenne makin' so much as a peep. Their captor was something. . . different. "Come into the light so's I can see ya!" Wrenn challenged.

"You no give orders here." The voice answered. "Here is Chaz Purdue."

Wrenn sighed, the voice was unafraid, bold even. It had a growl to it, but somehow a hint of femininity. "Please, I just want to look who I'm speaking with in the eye."

Wrenn heard footsteps, heavy with the rattling of what sounded like reeds with every movement. As a figure rounded the corner, he could see a swirling tribal design painted onto the large body in the same phosphorescent coloring as the fungus. As it came closer, he noted a torso, long and powerful legs where it looked as if it walked on its toes. Two muscular arms swayed at its sides and a thick neck held aloft a head that looked almost like a . . . crocodile. A tail swung back and forth as the figure, easily close to seven feet tall, stood before Wrenn with crossed arms and a piercing reptilian stare. "Look eyes. Is respect." It said.

"Cheyenne, is my translator broken or . . ."

Response: Negative, Captain. She is speaking in a broken form of the Gihati language. It is a somewhat rudimentary language that lacks many of the nuances prevalent in Terran tongues.

"Got it."

"You speak, where?" The lizard-woman barked.

"I speak to you. Please, untie me?"

The woman grunted. "No."

"Why?" Wrenn persisted.

"Your kind, fleshy man, take mother."

"Woah now, I didn't kidnap nobody, you got the wrong guy." Wrenn argued.

The woman grunted. "Mother . . . stone . . ."

She pointed at the cluster of nearby crystals. Wrenn

nodded. "Oh, right, the miners."

The woman grunted. "Take. Not ask. Thief."

"How is she even understanding us? We're not speaking Gihati . . ." Aurora whispered.

The lizard-woman turned to see her, pointing to an earpiece wedged into a hole at the side of her skull. "Take from fleshy man."

"She has a miner's coms, probably fiddled with it 'til she managed the correct settings." Wrenn observed.

"That's quite intuitive . . ." Aurora pointed out.

"Am here. Can speak. Talk to me!" The woman pounded her chest in anger.

Aurora was instantly embarrassed. "You're right, I apologize. Please, let's start over, shall we? My name is Aurora, what's yours?"

"Inzenyr." The woman stated.

"Inzenyr . . . that's very pretty . . ." Aurora smiled.

"No trick. No flirt." Inzenyr exclaimed.

"I wasn't . . ."

"We're not trying to trick you, we're trying to be cordial is all. Listen, how about I introduce myself too, eh? I'm Captain Wrenn."

"Captain . . ." The lizard tilted her head. "Have ship."

"Yes! That's usually what captain means. It means I'm a leader!" Wrenn smiled.

"Leader." Inzenyr thought. "Shaman."

"Well, I mean, I ain't no spiritual type, but sure, if that's what your leader down here is, then I guess I'm about on par with him I suppose." Wrenn stumbled through his words.

Aurora threw him a death glare the likes of which he'd never seen. Wrenn did his best to shrug against his bindings. "We came here to warn you." Wrenn stated.

"Warn . . ." Inzenyr repeated.

"Yes. The miners, uh . . . the other fleshy men, they're coming back with lots of guns and men and, well, a shit ton more firepower than they ever had before. Go! Tell your leader and get him to release us."

The woman stared at him intently, obviously not sure if she should trust him or not. Her interest had seemed to have peaked when she found out about Wrenn's ship, but afterwards her protective walls went back up about as quickly. "I bring him, he judge."

The woman moved off through the cave system, Wrenn just noticing now that she was wearing what amounted to a leather bikini with small animal bones hanging off like fringe. Despite the scaley bits, her muscles made her out to be a rather stunning, albeit powerful, figure. Her toned thighs rippled with tense musculature, accentuating a firm butt hidden under the swaying tail. What little he'd seen of her front half in the dim light wasn't bad neither, with washboard abs and a toned abdominal with two firm breasts covered by leather. They clearly didn't need the support, as the leather top more or less just draped over them. Why a lizard-woman needed breasts was beyond him, but he wasn't about to start complaining. Aurora scoffed loud enough for him to hear. "Are you *really* checking out our *abductor*?!"

"Hey, you're the one who pointed out Imma man!" Wrenn snapped back.

"Absolutely depraved." Aurora rolled her eyes.

"Yeah, whatever princess, I ain't the one jillin' myself against a sleepin' man's happy pole." Wrenn sighed.

"I told you, don't call me . . ." Aurora stopped and took a few breaths to clear her head. "You're trying to get a rise out of me on purpose."

"Eh, I was hoping it might motivate you to bust through them bonds or somethin'." Wrenn started fidgeting with his ropes.

"I'm afraid I will only disappoint you there. My people may have long lifespans, but we don't have some hidden super strength."

"Worth a shot." Wrenn shrugged as best he could. "And for the record, you could never disappoint me, sweetheart."

Aurora scoffed at Wrenn's comment, but the captain could have sworn he saw her blush a little in the pale light. He continued to struggle against his ties until he heard the rattling of their captor's animal bones again, deciding it best to play it cool and try to win them over. Inzenyr appeared from around the corner again, this time with an older male. The new arrival walked with a hunched back, his leathery scales drooping and folding over themselves in places. He wore a more elaborate garment of leathers with a decorative blanket over his shoulders. Atop his crown, he wore a wreath of bone and teeth, some of which cascaded down over his face and only parted at the beginning of his snout. Wrenn noted his eyes did not open, likely due to blindness or injury. The older lizard came close to the captain, his nostrils inches from Wrenn's face as he took in a large whiff of the human's scent. The male growled something that seemed like a language to Inzenyr, who nodded and looked at the spacer. "Shaman say fleshy man smell strange. Different. How fleshy man leader for other fleshy man?"

"I says I was *a* leader, not their leader." Wrenn replied.

Inzenyr growled and mumbled to the shaman who replied in kind. After an exchange of grunts, whines, and barks the female turned back to Wrenn. "Shaman ask, why you here?"

Wrenn looked over at Aurora who shook her head frantically. Wrenn slipped his usual cocky grin. "We came here to warn you."

Inzenyr translated, then another exchange happened. The shaman shook his head. "Shaman say you lie."

"Well, how the hell would he know?" Wrenn spat. "Look, if he don't wanna hear nothin' from me then untie us and we'll be on our way, no harm, no foul."

Growling, mumbling, then, "Shaman say you different. Bring no drill. Bring no tool."

"I'm not a miner." Wrenn nodded.

"Fleshy man come take mother, take stone. Stone is sacred. Bring life. Shaman want know why?"

Wrenn was about to answer, when a thought crossed his

mind. "You already know." He looked at Inzenyr.

"No. Shaman ask because he not know."

"I ain't talkin' about the shaman. I'm talkin' about *you*, darlin'." Wrenn smirked.

The female lizard seemed uneasy. The shaman grumbled something at her and she replied back in a curt bark. "Shaman repeat question."

"So then tell him." Wrenn raised an eyebrow.

Inzenyr gave the shaman a complicated exchange of yips, snarls, and barks. It seemed she was not only discussing the fuel, but its uses as well. The exchange quickly turned into a lecture of some kind, almost like the shaman was getting a crash course in modern technology. Finally, the elder lizard nodded in understanding. He mumbled something and signaled to Wrenn and Aurora. Inzenyr moved close and started undoing the bindings that held them captive. "Shaman say follow, he show."

"Show us what?" Wrenn asked as he slid down to the ground, catching himself just before falling forward.

"Our way."

△△△

Aurora and Wrenn walked alongside Inzenyr as they followed the shaman lizard-man through a maze of underground tunnels. They had both been freed, but their weapons not returned to them. Wrenn tried his best to cozy up to the lizard-female, though she towered over him by nearly a foot. "So, how long have you been messing with our technology?"

Inzenyr huffed. "I collect, I learn. There many who fear outsider, fear fleshy man. I watch, I . . . learn."

"Is that how you studied a language? How you figured out the translator?" Aurora asked.

The tall woman grunted, nodding in a firm affirmation. Cheyenne chimed in their ears. *Observation: The Gihati are a pious people. They are known to send missionaries out into the farthest reaches of space to spread the gospel of their pantheon. It is reasonable to assume the mining operation is not the first attempt at settlement of Visigath. They could have easily attempted instruction and conversion of the local population some time ago without widespread success.*

"Were there ever other outsiders?" Aurora asked. "People who didn't look like us?"

Inzenyr nodded. "Come before, long past. Not many remember. I find camp, I find book. I learn."

"So you've been watching this whole mining operation, learning the process, knowing what they're using the crystals for." Wrenn observed. "You knew all this time, but you kept it from your leader? Why?"

Inzenyr grunted. "Many fear surface. Many ignore threat. Shaman old, remember much. Remember those before, remember they leave. Shaman think fleshy man leave, but fleshy man take mother . . . take stone." The female corrected herself. "I no let fleshy man hurt many others."

"How were the miners hurting the others?" Aurora asked.

"Mother . . . stone is life. Is everything for Chaz Purdue. Fleshy man take, Chaz Purdue die. I no wait. I stop fleshy man."

Wrenn turned to Aurora. "I think we found our saboteur."

Aurora nodded. "Yes, but . . . if we do what we said we'd do, these people . . ."

"Yeah, the game boards changed again, that's for sure." Wrenn agreed.

The group moved into a large, open expanse. It appeared to be a hollowed out reservoir, with waterways and pools scattered across the bottom of the cave while outcroppings of houses built into the rock walls hung above them. An intricate network of ropes, bridges, and rudimentary elevators helped some thousand or so lizardfolk walk between large circular huts made out of reeds. Workers swam along the waterways, used almost like trails or roads, while others cultivated fish or plants in the pools like farmers. An entire civilization thrived below the desert surface of Visigath, completely hidden from outside eyes.

"Wow." Wrenn managed.

"Is tribe." Inzenyr described.

"How many tribes are there?" Aurora asked.

Inzenyr shrugged. "Hundred. Thousand. I not know. Many of many across whole world."

Wrenn sighed heavily. Yeah, there was no way he was going to stop the ambushes or the disruption of the mining operations. In fact, he would only end up making it worse. Desmond and Sewell had no idea what they were messing with here. An entire ecosystem existed on Visigath, complete with an indigenous people who lived in harmony with the planet's scant resources. Who knew how long they'd been here? Had they evolved to live this way due to the desert outside? Could they have been here way back when the planet was covered in water? Reptile-like creatures did tend to thrive in swampy or oceanic biospheres, and they could live for a very, very long time. Desmond had even mentioned the fort built on the ruins of an ancient cave system. The shaman motioned them to continue following, Inzenyr gently guiding them forward through the village.

Wrenn and Aurora watched in greater detail the amount of life that hummed just below the surface of this 'dead' world. Farmers fed their fish stock, harvested reeds and seaweed from the pool's waters. Transporters hauled goods with strong backs and packs made from the natural fibers that also formed their dwellings. Children played in a nursery where an anti-chamber seemed to house bed upon bed of egg clusters. Wrenn's heart sank at the thought of what the mercenaries might do to a place like this if they were found out, if a conflict should arise . . . would arise . . . when the mining operation started back up again. Aurora noticed his face and seemed to share a similar dread.

The group walked through another cave tunnel until they came upon a room brighter than any they had encountered. Wrenn and Aurora had to shield their eyes in order for everything to come into focus. Around them were hundreds of crystal clusters, shining bright like the stars in the night sky. Amongst them, lizardfolk moved with clay pots and jugs. One would come close to a crystal, speaking to it in an almost song-like fashion. Their reptilian claws pet the crystal, coaxing it almost like a dairy farmer would his cow. In response, the crystal began to weep, dewdrops of a watery substance falling into the awaiting jug the worker placed beneath it. The worker then carried on, collecting jugs that were full at other clusters and replacing them with empty ones. The shaman shuffled over to one of the full jugs, bringing the edge to his lips and sipping a small amount. He sighed heavily as if he was feeling a rejuvenating effect from the liquid, offering it to Wrenn. The captain took a whiff and almost gagged. "Woof! That's fuel!"

"What?" Aurora asked, smelling the concoction herself and having a similar reaction. "It is!"

"The miners are crushing these crystals for this stuff when all they really need to do is harvest it." Wrenn observed.

"Stone is network." Inzenyr mentioned. "Stone take energy at surface, bring below. All Chaz Purdue do this. Is life."

"The fissure where the prospectors found the crystals . . ." Wrenn mentioned.

"It's one of these surface collection sites?" Aurora asked. "They're destroying the crystals that gather the sunlight and distribute it down here."

"Like the whole damn planet has one giant bloodstream." Wrenn nodded.

"Wrenn, this is huge!" Aurora remarked. "Not only does the mining operation endanger these people, but it potentially kills the entire system of other crystals across the planet. It's a finite and fragile resource and the corporation doesn't even realize it."

"Yeah . . ." Wrenn sighed.

The shaman turned to Wrenn, nodding in earnest as he seemed to sense the two were getting his message. He grumbled something to Inzenyr, who translated. "Leader. Tell other fleshy men, tell them what you see. They leave. Mother is for Chaz

Purdue."

Wrenn shook his head. "It won't be that easy. We *need* this fuel for our settlements, for our ships. We can't survive on new worlds without it."

The lizard-woman translated and the shaman grew tense and agitated. "Is not yours for take."

The workers around them stopped their duties, watching in both curiosity and concern at their leader's tone. Wrenn held up his hands in surrender. "That ain't ever stopped the corpos before . . . look, I'll do the best I can, but I don't think they'll listen to me. They're dead set on coming back here and taking them crystals, by force if needed."

"And trust us," Aurora piped in, "they've got a lot of force."

After translating, the shaman grunted. He brandished a knife from under his leathers, one made from what looked like shaped, dead crystal. "Then we will fight." Inzenyr interpreted.

"You will lose." Wrenn responded plainly.

"Fleshy men are few." Inzenyr joined in her leader's confidence. "Chaz Purdue are many."

Wrenn sighed again, shaking his head. "If the shaman lets us go, and gives us back our things, then I promise to go talk to the others."

The shaman nodded and motioned them to follow him back toward the village. Aurora walked beside the captain in silence, fully aware of his inner turmoil as her own thoughts tumbled about the same nightmare scenarios. If Desmond and his mercenary army met with the Chaz Purdue, it was going to be a bloodbath . . . and not one where the primitive people would come out on top.

CHAPTER 20

"This is a bad idea . . ." Aurora said over the coms as she and Wrenn's ships landed behind the Whitmoore's saloon. "What's to stop him from gunning us down in the street."

"The fact that it's close to dusk and we won't be the only sods out there." Wrenn replied, jumping out of his Lancer and moving at a brisk pace toward the fort. "The sooner they know about these people, the sooner they can adjust their operations."

"You said it yourself, they won't just leave, Wrenn." Aurora reminded him, running to catch up.

"No, but maybe . . . I don't know . . . they can trade or negotiate or somethin'. Maybe if I can just talk to Sewell for a spell I can convince him of a better plan like I did before."

"You have nothing he wants. You're only coming to him with a problem." Aurora protested. "We both know that lives matter little to these people."

"Doesn't mean I can't try."

Wrenn walked down the center of town, in full view of the miners and workers that were in the middle of moving from their daily activities to their nightly ones. No doubt many were shocked, probably havin' heard whatever fabricated rumor Jenny had spread about Wrenn's demise. A small gaggle of onlookers started to follow him at a distance, their interests peaked at the man's determined grimace.

When Wrenn came close to the gate, the guards again stopped him as they had before. Wrenn didn't bother with pleasantries this time. "Desmond! Get out here!"

The guards clearly were speaking with each other over the internal radios. Wrenn barked out again. "Lieutenant Desmond Myers! I'm calling you out!"

Murmurs and bustling surrounded him as Wrenn stood alone in the center of the road. Aurora had found a way to mingle with the crowd, stealthily moving to a flanking position should things sour. Before long, the large front gate started to open, a familiar Stetson-wearing man emerging from behind the fort's walls. "Brother! I had heard you'd left system."

"Bullshit, you heard your assassin had accomplished his task." Wrenn snapped back. "I'm here to show you that news is just a tall tale."

"Then I must ask, what are you still doing here?" Desmond shot back.

The two shouted at each other from over fifty meters away, neither side trusting the other to come any closer. The growing number of both townsfolk and guards at the front gate could hear every word. "I'm here to tell you what I've found at the mine."

"Oh? Do tell."

"Not here, I want to see the mayor." Wrenn ordered.

"That's not going to happen." Desmond barked. "It's our job to protect him from the likes of you."

Wrenn shook his head, not able to hold back the chuckle that came at the idea of Desmond taking a moral high ground. "Likes of me? Now that's rich. Tell me, do your men know about the poison you slipped me in that whiskey glass? Or their fallen comrade you sent to off me why I was sleepin'? I wonder how many of them would follow you if they knew you lacked the spine to kill your own kin face-to-face!"

"My men are loyal, disciplined, and serve with honor." Desmon snapped back. "They will not be swayed by your lies."

Despite Desmond's boasting, Wrenn could see a few of the mercenaries were shaken by his words. Their helmeted heads were easy to track as they shifted back and forth, their body language relaxing slightly as if they were questioning the loyalties his brother crowed so much about. Now Wrenn went in for the clincher. He turned to face the crowd, hoping his voice would carry enough over the air that was getting chillier by the second, the sun starting to sink in the west. "The mine is not what you think it is! It's an essential piece in the lives of the indigenous Chaz Purdue people! There are hundreds of them below ground. Women, children, old and young. They have a whole society down there, I've seen it! We start takin' those crystals and they'll die. They're prepared to fight for their way of life, for their neighbors!"

Wrenn noticed the crowd mumbling louder now, full discussions being had amongst the gathering. He turned back to Desmond. "Broker a truce with them, brother. No one needs to die over this. They have a way to help the company get what it wants and not one drop of blood needs to be spilt."

The mercenaries became even more invested now. Any soldier would gladly help the other guy die for his cause rather than themselves, but if no fighting needed to happen in the first place? Only a fool would spurn that idea. Unfortunately, Desmond appeared to be that fool. "We know all about those slimy lizard vagrants!" He blurted out.

"You . . . knew?" Wrenn looked at him, bewildered.

Desmond continued. "They are trespassing on Meteorite Mining land, not to mention guilty of murdering company employees and destruction of property. If they want to escalate their attacks on our people, then we are prepared to answer in kind . . ."

As if on cue, Cheyenne crackled into Wrenn's earpiece. *Warning: Captain, a ship is coming out of skipspace approximately twenty-five kilometers from the orbital station.*

Wrenn looked up as a bright flash burst forth from the darkened sky, a ship roughly the size of his fingernail moving toward the much larger orbital station. Cheyenne continued. *Analysis: Skyfox class vessel, frigate-sized configuration. Exterior markings and registration designate it a ship of Lieutenant Desmond's mercenary outfit.*

"His reinforcements . . ." Wrenn mumbled.

Desmond seemed to receive a similar message in his own com piece. He smiled at his brother, "As you can see, I've got some work to get back to."

"Desmond." Wrenn reached out for him. "Please . . ."

"You lost the right to ask favors of me a long time ago, brother."

The mercenary lieutenant turned on his heel, walking back through the gate and closing the massive doors behind him. The crowd began to disperse as the guards shooed them away, more out of a desire to get some place warm for the night rather than cowing to the mercs. Aurora met Wrenn in the middle of the street, the man unmoved since the final words with his sibling. "C'mon." She said, putting a comforting hand on his shoulder. "Let me buy you a drink . . ."

△△△

The saloon was slow that night, most of the townsfolk seeming more interested in spending time with loved ones rather than drinking away their problems. A general tension had built up quickly once word of Wrenn's shouting match with Desmond reached many ears. A storm was brewing and everyone knew it, question was, would people batten down the hatches or direct their anxiety toward something that needed doing?

Wrenn downed another shot as he sulked at the bar. Aurora nursed her drink on the barstool next to him while Jenny and Clive huddled near behind the counter. "So you're sayin' there's a whole slew of them down there?" Jenny asked, recounting the story Wrenn had told them of the Chaz Purdue.

"More than just them." Aurora nodded. "There are reportedly hundreds to thousands of tribes across the planet."

"Golly." Jenny shook her head. "Never would have guessed it."

"Their leader said he didn't much care about the surface

184

or us until we started messing with them crystals." Wrenn mumbled, half buzzed already.

"Explains why we never seen 'em." Clive mentioned.

"What's worse is they are completely unprepared to go up against a fully armed tactical force. There is only one of them that has a rudimentary understanding of our technology, the rest will be fighting with the equivalent of sticks and stones!" Aurora mentioned.

"They'll be slaughtered." Wrenn remarked, coldly.

"Which might start a prolonged conflict for control of the planet." Aurora agreed. "The other tribes, wherever they are, won't take such action lying down."

Jenny and Clive exchanged a look. Their quaint little backwater town was about to get a whole lot deadlier. Wrenn noticed their apprehension. "Best bet is ya'll pack up now, get the hell outta dodge. Once that train starts rolling, the pale rider follows it."

Jenny sighed heavily while Clive looked determined. "Ain't never been a Whitmoore that run from a fight, and I'm not about to be the first."

"Papa . . ." Jenny cautioned.

"Then you're a fool." Wrenn muttered.

"And you're cut off." Clive argued.

Wrenn simply chuckled as he nursed the beer chaser he'd already ordered. Jenny ushered her father to the kitchen before tensions flared brighter, Aurora turning to Wrenn. "And what are *we* doing?"

"What do you mean? We're getting the hell out too!" Wrenn took a swig from his long neck.

"Just like that?"

"Just like that." Wrenn repeated.

"You're not the least concerned for the Chaz Purdue, the armed battalion preparing to barrel down upon them, and the cluster fuck that follows it."

"Nope." Wrenn replied.

"You're lying. I saw the concern in your eyes the second

we walked around that village." Aurora squinted. "You knew what your brother would do to them because you've seen it before, haven't you?"

Wrenn sighed. He had seen what Desmond had done to people like that in the past . . . what Wrenn had helped do too. The captain shook his head. "No, it doesn't matter. Ain't nothing stoppin' this shit show so, best we get out now and try to convince Ronald we fixed something and bolt before he gets wise."

"Just keep running." Aurora observed. "Run from the Alpha. Run from Visigath. Run from the corps. Is that what you plan to do your whole life?"

"Worked so far." Wrenn finished his beer. Eyeing up and down the bar, Wrenn leaned over and pulled another bottle from behind the counter.

"Yes, worked so well, keeping yourself isolated and alone." Aurora mentioned. "Maybe if you run far enough and swindle enough people, you can find a little pocket of the galaxy where you can just live out the rest of your miserable existence."

"What the fuck would you have me do, huh?" Wrenn snapped. "Rush up against an armed battalion of mercs?"

"At least give them a fighting chance!"

"I ain't the hero of this story, missy!" Wrenn barked. "I don't know who you think you been ridin' with all this while, but that ain't the kind of man I am."

"The universe is not divided into heroes and villains, you numbskull," Aurora fought back. "It's filled with people. People who are selfish and people who aren't, people who are walked on and people who've got the boot. You hate the corps for only caring about money and here you are doing the exact same thing, sacrificing the little guy to get your credits."

Wrenn ignored her, taking a swig from the bottle. "If you're so dedicated, why don't you ride off and play hero then?"

"I already plan on it." Aurora stood. "I was just hopeful you were man enough to join me."

The Utopian stared at him for a full minute as Wrenn

continued to ignore her. She sighed, shaking her head and stomping off toward the entrance. The captain raised his bottle in salute as she left. "Guess that's adiós then, partner . . ."

△△△

When Jenny returned to the bar, Wrenn was three more bottles deep. He smiled at her stupidly as she eyed the rest of the saloon. "Where'd your lady friend go?"

"She's gone off to play the white hat." Wrenn slurred. "Thinks she can take on the galaxy, that one."

"She doin' that all by her lonesome?" Jenny asked.

"Nope!" Wrenn hiccuped. "She's gonna have the spooky lizard-people on her side!"

Wrenn cradled his head in his hand as he finished the last of his beer, grimacing with sadness as he noticed it was empty. Jenny had seen many a man in this state over the years. "Alright, stranger. I think this time you really are cut off."

"I'm not a stranger, you know me." Wrenn argued. "And I'm not *that* drunk . . . only a little bit drunk."

Wrenn stood from the stool in an attempt to demonstrate his sobriety, only to immediately brace himself on the bar to keep from toppling over. Jenny chuckled. "Uh huh, ain't no way you're flyin' outta here in this state. Come on, let's get you upstairs to sleep it off. I should probably change out your bandage one last time anyhow."

"Upstairs? But I don't wanna go upstairs. You *know* what happened the last time I was with one of them girls." Wrenn replied rather bluntly.

Jenny was hit with the memory of loss, her face saddened immediately. Wrenn, even in his inebriated state, noticed the impact of his words. "Ah shit, I'm sorry Jenny. I . . . I don't really know what I'm saying . . ."

Jenny shook her head, her eyes glassy with tears, but her lips forcing a smile. "It's alright. She's in a better place now, I know that. Feel sorry for the living, Mister Wrenn, for they know

187

not their maker's embrace."

Wrenn didn't know how to respond, only shrugging and trying in vain to sit back down on the stool without a misstep. Jenny chuckled again. "C'mon, chop chop, We're going up to the third floor, I'll hide you away in my room until you're right enough to fly back to your ship."

Jenny mentioned something to her father about closing up and then rushed what few patrons were still inside home to their own beds. The door was locked, the light turned off, and Jenny pulled Wrenn's arm over her shoulder. "Let's go you."

Wrenn moved with her up the stairs. The working girls and boys bid her good-night as they too shut down for the evening, some even giving Jenny a few coy glances or knowing winks before they were shooed back into their rooms. The two made their way up a second set of stairs hidden behind a locked door and Wrenn leaned against the wall as Jenny fiddled with her keys to open her room. "You're so nice to me . . ." He volunteered.

Jenny laughed. "Yeah well, sometimes against my better judgment." She teased.

"Why are you so nice to me?" Wrenn asked.

Jenny looked at him with her wide green eyes. "Ain't you figured that out yet, smart guy?"

"You . . ." Wrenn thought sluggishly, "You wanna ride on my starship?"

Jenny laughed as she helped him into her room. She let him stagger a few feet then gently maneuvered him to sit on the edge of the bed. Jenny closed the door and sank down to her knees, helping the captain remove his boots and jacket. "I wouldn't mind seein' the stars again with you, but no, that's not it."

"You gotta want somethin'!" Wrenn insisted.

Jenny sighed and sat down next to him. Her face was close to his, the smell of beer and peanuts heavy on his breath. "Sometimes, people do things just 'cause they want to, you know."

"You *want* to be good to me?" Wrenn asked.

Jenny chuckled. "Oh, you have no idea."

With that, she kissed him. Their lips intertwined, tongues playfully sparring as their arms slipped around each other's shoulders. Wrenn lost his sense of balance, falling back onto the mattress, taking Jenny with him. She squealed slightly as they bounced on the bed, laughing into his mouth as she continued kissing him. Reality suddenly hit Wrenn through the haziness of his drunken mind and he sat up. "Wait, wait, wait . . . I . . . I can't do this."

"Why not?" Jenny propped herself up on an elbow. "You ain't takin' no advantage, I promise. Truth is, I should be the one feeling guilty for ravishin' *you* in such a state . . ."

Wrenn chuckled. "No, I'm . . . I'm sober enough to agree, that ain't the problem."

"Then what is it, sweety?" Jenny caressed his arm.

Wrenn sighed, "I know what you're doin'. You're saying you've got no motive here, but I'm wise to it anyhow. Once we're together you'll want me to save your town or stop the mine from causin' some war or whatever . . ."

"Baby, I never . . ." Jenny started.

"Truth is, I'm leavin'." Wrenn interrupted her. "And nothin' that happens here is gonna change any of that. Don't matter if I fight the mercs or not . . . at the end of it all, I'm gone. I don't want you to get the wrong idea about me . . . like . . . some other people have."

Jenny sat up next to him. She smiled warmly, taking his face in her hands. "Honey, I ain't got no motives here, really, I don't. Whether you fight or fly or stay or go, that's all according to your journey. I can't decide that for you just as I can't tell the rain which way to fall. Sometimes, people just come into your life at the right time and make you feel the right way, and that's what I got for you. I want this cause I like you, that's all. What we do after, well . . . let's just cross that bridge when we get there, ok?"

Wrenn chuckled. "I thought that was supposed to be my

line?"

Jenny's eyes sparkled and she kissed him again. "Ladies can have one-night-stands too, you know?"

Wrenn kissed her back. "Fair enough."

They fell backwards onto the bed again, Wrenn unsure if the wave of dizziness he was feeling was on account of the beautiful woman in his arms or the remnants of his buzz . . . perhaps it was a little of both. Their hands caressed and explored each other, their lips doing the same as Wrenn moved from her mouth, her ears, her neck, and her collarbone. The pacing was romantic yet passion-filled, like a young couple reuniting after a long absence. Sure they devoured one another, ravishing each other's bodies and such, but with a kinder, gentler embrace. When the clothes started to fall away, Jenny seemed a might frustrated with her bodice as she comically fought with each string while also trying not to tarry too far away from Wrenn's lips. The result was the two of them chuckling as Wrenn did his best to assist with the stubborn item. The rest of the clothing proved far less unruly, tossing each article to the wind as they grew more and more excited with every inch of flesh revealed.

Wrenn cupped Jenny's ample breasts in either hand, burying his face between them and kissing the red, puffy nipples. He suckled at each, causing Jenny to languish her head back and moan, hand holding his head to her bosom. Wrenn noted more freckles across Jenny's shoulders and forefront, wrapping his muscular arms about her torso. His capture forced Jenny to keep her underskirt and panties on, but she would find her satisfaction regardless. She mounted him, Wrenn finding himself seated with his back against the wall, his face still buried in her chest. She could feel his engorged cock between her thighs, lowering herself onto the shaft as she forced it up against Wrenn's pelvis. Jenny started rocking her hips fluidly, grinding herself against him with only a millimeter of fabric separating them. The teasing was enough to make Wrenn grunt, but that paled in comparison to the moans escaping the barmaid's lips. She pushed her hips down harder, grinding her clit against the thickness of his member. The tempo was escalating, hips rocking faster and freer with every second. To Wrenn, she was simply winding him up to no end, but to Jenny, it was as if her loins were a caged beast just aching for release. As Wrenn started flicking one of her nipples with his tongue, while also pinching the other between his fingers, it was the last vestige of stimulus she could endure. Jenny's head fell back once more, her voice crying out in a guttural upheaval as her hips spasmed. Her legs were shaky afterward, the redhead collapsing against Wrenn as she allowed the aftereffects to wash over her.

When she was ready, Jenny curled up into a ball beside Wrenn, her hands wandering toward his crotch in an almost curious fashion. She laid her head on his leg, her hands both going to work on his nethers. One hand cupped his balls while the other moved up and down his shaft. Wrenn sat motionless, his head leaned against the wall as he enjoyed her fullest attention. Before long, Jenny's rhythm grew and she was finding new ways to change up the routine. Her head bobbed forward, mouth open and enveloping the tip of his member while the hands continued their work. Jenny's tongue rotated around the crest of Wrenn's head, her nimble fingers both squeezing and relaxing in alternating fashion. Jenny was quite the multi-tasker, able to juggle each action for long enough to create a sense of anticipation as to which she would do next, while also never neglecting any one area. Wrenn's eyes started to hurt he was rolling them back in his skull so often.

As he was almost about to burst, he cautioned Jenny by taking a handful of her curls and pulling back on them. The action only seemed to spur her onward as she moaned into his cock while it was firmly settled between her lips. Wrenn found himself bucking his hips, trying to pull away from her lest he be milked dry within the first minutes of their encounter. Jenny looked at him with a pout, clearly intending to continue until she had satisfied him as he had her. Wrenn smiled and kissed her, causing the disappointed look to morph back into a lust filled smile.

Wrenn used his weight to push, allowing Jenny to lay upon her back, her head upon the pillow. His hands caressed her, fondling her breasts, grabbing her arms, holding her hips. He helped her finally remove the last of her clothing, the gorgeous beauty laid bare before him in all of her splendor. Wrenn's lips moved southward, again suckling her nipples, then kissing along her belly and then further. Jenny gasped in surprise as his mouth found her slit, Wrenn's tongue darting out to play with her mound as his arms wrapped themselves underneath her thighs. He pulled her to him, ass cheeks nestling themselves onto his shoulders as he devoured her womanhood like a starved man. Jenny made no effort to hide her enjoyment, her hands clawing at his head, the sheets, the bedposts. She arched her back, moaning and grunting loudly as Wrenn lapped up and down her swollen quim. Wrenn could feel her stomach tighten as again Jenny started to crest upon the edge of release. He slid a few choice fingers into her opening, enjoying the accompanying shriek as Jenny flew up the rest of the way and sailed over. She spasmed again, this time her whole body seizing and her hands digging and pounding into the bed. Once she had regained herself, she shot upwards, taking grip of either side of Wrenn's face as she kissed him ravenously. She didn't seem to care that she tasted more of herself upon his face than him, in fact, she seemed invigorated by it.

When she finally relented, laying back again with a look of blissful anticipation, the only communication needed between the two was a shared nod. Wrenn positioned himself between her legs, holding onto his shaft to aim it for the strike. He started in smoothly, Jenny letting out little whimpers as her over-sensitive hole let her experience every inch of his throbbing spear. Wrenn met little resistance as he buried himself within her, watching as Jenny's mouth dropped and her chest heaved, struggling to breathe. Wrenn sank himself in clean to the hilt, falling forward onto her and enjoying the feel of her soft bust against his chest. Jenny finally allowed herself to inhale, wrapping her arms around Wrenn's shoulders as their hips began moving in tandem.

Before long, the bed creaked as Wrenn slammed his hips down upon her like a jackhammer, Jenny's wails only spurring him onward to be rougher and faster. Between her enjoyment and the foreplay, it wasn't long before Wrenn was finding himself winding up for the big finish. Jenny wouldn't let him go, wrapping one leg around him and her fingers digging into his back. She was cresting again too, and she wasn't about to let a change in position or tempo rob her. Wrenn fell victim to his urges, dropping his head into the crook of her neck as he allowed the feeling to take over. His stomach tingled, his ass clenched as he shot his load deep within her, his successive hip pumps only helping her pussy milk his every last drop. Jenny had clenched too, sailing over her edge yet again as their tempo slowed and was replaced by caresses and kisses. The two remained there for a while, exactly how long neither cared. When Wrenn finally pulled himself off of her, his member slid from her orifice and allowed his seed to dribble out. The two gasped while laying next to each other, hands still intertwined and smiles laid bare. Jenny nuzzled up to him, kissing his skin all over as her free hand stroked his chest and stomach, sometimes even playfully teasing the head of his cock to get a jolt out of him. They kissed, and giggled, and cuddled as if they were newlyweds, all the while the temperature in the room dropping as the freezing air outside snuck through the cracks in the window. Before long, they were wrapped up under the sheets, their eyes growing droopy as the endorphins flooded their brains. "Hey, uh . . . is the door locked?" Wrenn asked. "I don't want . . ."

"Right . . . like before . . ." Jenny nodded. "I'll get it."

The redhead jumped out of bed, her naked body a glow in the moonlight. Wrenn watched in perverted admiration as her butt bounced with every step while she hurriedly tiptoed to the door, locking both the handle and a deadbolt. For extra measure, she slid a chair in front of the portal, shivering intensely as she rushed back to bed in half as many steps as it had taken to get across the room. She was shaking as Wrenn opened the blankets for her, cradling her close for warmth. He smiled. "Oh, one more thing . . . I think I left my . . ."

Jenny punched him in the stomach and Wrenn laughed. "Whatever it is, it can wait till mornin'!" Jenny grumbled. "It's freezin'."

Wrenn smiled as they enjoyed each other's company. The wind from outside died down, as it did most nights in the desert. He lost track of time as his eyes cast about the room, admiring Jenny's décor or the way the moonlight bounced across the metal walls. He knew she was asleep before too long, though respite seemed to elude him. He thought back to more serious matters, to what he should do next and how to move forward. He didn't have that many options, and each seemed more fool-hardy than the last. Could he be the type of person to just run and try to stay one step ahead of the consequences? He'd done that once before, though even out here in the Reach it seemed he couldn't get away from the fallout. Aurora had been rather opinionated on the matter, for someone who had at first appeared aloof and self-interested. She had gone off to play the heroine, a move he had not seen coming. Could he do the same? Risk his neck for those that, in all likelihood, had nothing of value to offer him for the trouble? No, it was better he go now, claim the credit of Desmond's work before the bosses got wise. Surely the mercs would wipe out the locals without so much as losing more than a few of their own . . . unless the lizardfolk had more advanced firepower on their side.

Wrenn sighed, staring out at the moon through the window. Jenny had her head on his chest, her mouth agape and a bit of drool pooling in the crook of his arm. Wrenn chuckled to himself, a surprisingly put together woman and yet she looked positively disheveled when the layers were peeled away and she was relaxed. Jenny started to snore softly, any semblance of delicacy she still had thrown by the wayside. If the mercs took over the mine here, what would happen to the townsfolk? Desmond never had been one to spare the rod when it came to locals, even ones of his own species. Playing the hero now might stop further bloodshed down the road. But then, what good would he do Jenny if his blood was the one spilt instead? What might happen to Cheyenne with no one to guard her against corps or pirates or whatever else out there would love to get their hands on his ship? The outcomes were all too cloudy, too complicated. The simplest answer was most often the right one, but then again, when had Wrenn ever done what was simple? He closed his eyes, slowing his breathing down to not only welcome sleep but try to calm his thoughts. He would have loved to just wait 'til morning to decide, but he had been kicking the can down the road for long enough. This job had only gotten more and more difficult the more he'd tried to weasel out of making any hard choices. It was time he put his foot down and decide. It was time to be a man. It was time . . . to get some sleep.

CHAPTER 21

It took Aurora a few days to muster up enough Chaz Purdue to mount a proper ambush. Inzenyr pointed out most of the spots she had used for prior attacks, Aurora deciding on a particularly small canyon that forced the caravans to slow down on a blind curve. With the elevated high ground, they could easily create a shooting gallery even if they were dealing with nothing but spears and bows with arrows. Aurora decided that the first order of business would be to capture or kill the line layers, the job that she and Wrenn had originally volunteered for. If the train had no guiding wire, it would be forced to stop in the canyon, where it would be a sitting duck for her and the lizardfolk.

Camping out along the ridge, it was in the dead of night when scouts sent word that the first of the mercs were soon to enter the killzone. It was a small crew, no more than five armed guards and three workers who went about setting up the hovering beacons and then connecting the cable that was roughly the thickness of a tree trunk. The darkness only helped Aurora and her troops, allowing them to sneak into position unseen and then rain down death from the cliff's edge. The mercs fell pretty easily, despite having a significant technological advantage, and mercifully the workers got through it with only minor injuries. Aurora slid down the side of the rock, clambering into the cabin of the large crane truck and shoving a knife into the face of the driver. "Turn off the engine!" She barked.

The frantic worker obliged, turning the keys and

throwing them to her. Within minutes, the lizard warriors had gathered the dead and tied up the wounded, shuffling them down the causeway to a cavern hideout. Aurora made sure wounds were dressed and sustenance cared for despite the arguments made otherwise by Inzenyr. "Fleshy men not show same mercy for us!"

"Then we will be better!" Aurora insisted.

"If captain here, he see reason!" Inzenyr snarled.

"Yeah, well . . . he's not here, so you're stuck with me." Aurora crossed her arms.

"Why he no come? Why he no here? He promise help."

"He is helping, just somewhere else." Aurora lied.

Inzenyr huffed loudly and stomped off. Aurora sighed heavily, why was she defending him? Wrenn was long gone by now, probably counting his reward credits and darting off to ancestors knew where. He hadn't given two thoughts to letting these people get slaughtered, and here they were wanting him instead of her. Aurora stomped over to her sleeping area and violently threw open the collection of furs and leathers from a variety of beasts on Visigath. She was so angry she could feel her stomach churn, or, that might have been the roasted desert rat she had been given from the locals. Either way, she was miserable, all the while unable to get the selfish, dirty, rotten, scoundrel of a captain out of her head. This had to be some sort of punishment from the spirits for her leaving the empire. There was just no other explanation for it . . .

△△△

By morning the trap had been set. The scouts reported the sighting of what they called 'a gargantuan metal worm' speeding through the desert toward them. The Utopian warned every warrior to stay hidden until the monstrosity was at a complete stop and its crew had exited the craft to attack. Arrows and spears would simply bounce off the tungsten plated boxcars that were thick enough to outlast atmospheric reentry when they were once part of the grav elevator. Their only hope at lasting success would be to load the cars with previously harvested crystals and blow it all to smithereens.

Aurora watched with bated breath as the train made its appearance over the horizon. She was impressed at the quick handiwork Desmond and his outfit had performed in retrofitting the cars to travel horizontally instead of vertically. Magnetic coils ran along only one side of the carts, a massive spare propulsion engine welded firmly upon the backside, likely taken from a derelict sloop or cruiser. She barrelled along at a breakneck speed when out in open terrain, but quickly slowed herself down by rotating the magnetic discs toward its front as it neared the canyon. She rolled past the point of no return, cars shifting and jostling as they went 'round the bend. The engineer, peering out from a small slit at the front, saw the wire come to the last buoy and end, frantically doing everything he could to kill the engine and slow the four massive boxcars without crashing. The train actually used the buoy itself as the final barrier, bumping into it and causing it to drift slightly into the canyon wall itself. Once the dust of the minor impact had settled, the sides of the lead boxcar slid open, a squad of mercs jumping out to secure the area. A lizard warrior across the gap from Aurora leapt up to strike, only to be pulled down by Inzenyr before he was spotted. Aurora took in a sigh of relief. The female warrior might not agree with her on everything, but at least she was loyal to the plan.

The mercs and the engineer started exchanging a rather heated argument, the rest of the guardsmen spreading out along the canyon. When Aurora was satisfied all was set, she let loose a loud cheer, the others around her jumping to their feet and slinging every weapon they had down on the surprised mercenaries. Aurora used a captured repeater from one of the forward guards they had taken out the night before, since she could do little from the rise with just her knives.

The mercs reacted quickly, pulling back to the cover of the boxcar as they found themselves at a major disadvantage.

Aurora pressed her attack, signaling for some warriors to push ahead and behind the train in order to flank it. The mercs didn't bother to move the train, seeming to be content to hunker down. By the time Aurora figured out why, it was too late.

The first of the Chaz Purdue warriors reached the door to the rear boxcar and grabbed hold of the handle. Soon as it was pulled open, Aurora realized her folly. An explosion rang out through the canyon, the warriors unlucky enough to be in front of the door were blown back into the rock face, most perforated with shrapnel and burns. A second squad appeared from the opening, spilling out into the canyon and reinforcing their compatriots. The third boxcar's door also opened, even more troops spilling out. Aurora's ambush had just been counter-attacked. To make matters worse, a mounted gun revealed itself as it moved out on rails from the final boxcar. A duo of covered mercenaries fed a chain-link of some sort of large round into a heavy looking gun, the barrel rising upward until Aurora could swear she saw right down the tube. "Everyone scatter!" She yelled.

A large *FWUMP* sound echoed down the rock walls, followed closely by an explosion along the canyon. The damn mercs had brought a 40 mm chain fed grenade launcher with them, something old Earth would have called a MK 19. The weapon had been fitted into an improvised rotating turret, able to fire both short and long range depending on the angle. The mercenaries turned toward the other side of the canyon, blowing away a few more of the Chaz Purdue warriors before they had time to dive away from the edge. Aurora swore to herself. They'd prepared for this, probably even counted on an ambush of some kind. She'd have to withdraw what was left of the lizard forces, find some way to try again further down the line. Just as she was about to give the order, she heard another, even louder explosion overhead. The lizardfolk ducked for cover, as did the mercenaries down below, but Aurora knew all too well that this new thunderclap wasn't a burst accompanied by smoke and flame, but a sonic boom followed by an aircraft flying faster than the speed of sound.

A Lancer F319 shot overhead, a vapor cone encircling its midsection as the roar of its engine soon followed behind it. Aurora's stomach jumped into her throat as she saw the zipper bank hard, line itself up with the canyon, and fly low over the ground, heading right for them. She hit the dirt instinctively, the few Chaz Purdue around her following suit. The fighter strafed the train cars, cries of alarm and agony accompanied another loud explosion reverberating from the ravine. After the aircraft passed overhead, Aurora crawled to the cliff's edge, eyeing to her merriment the turret engulfed in flame and consisting of little else but twisted metal. The Utopian jumped back to her feet, firing off rounds from her stolen repeater at the mercenaries who were still recovering from the airborne attack. The small cluster of lizard warriors pressed their new advantage, moving in close to force the remnants of the mercenaries to fight them hand-to-hand. Regardless of technological advantage, there's only so much a basic human can do against a raging seven-foot dino man. Hollers and cheers rang out from the indigenous people, when only a few minutes earlier their fatigue had seemed sealed.

Aurora dropped to her knee on the cliffside, only just realizing how much she'd been caked in sweat and sand. She heard thrusters whirring once more and turned her head to see the Lancer landing behind her. She abandoned her post, sprinting toward the fighter with whatever energy she had left. As the pilot dismounted from the cockpit, she leapt into his arms, nearly tackling him to the ground. "You bloody bastard!" She exclaimed, though laughing while she said it.

"Hey now, is that any way to greet your knight in shining armor?!" Wrenn spun her a few times before letting her back down.

Aurora punched him hard in the chest. "What are you doing here?!"

"Well, I thought about it and I figured ain't no way you'd survive without me so . . ."

Aurora huffed, placing her hands on her hips. "I was doing just fine."

"That ain't what I saw." Wrenn teased.

Aurora rolled her eyes. "Well, regardless, I'm glad you showed up when you did.

"And the fun's just started!" Wrenn began moving toward the canyon.

Aurora followed. "Started?! We need to get out of here before more troops show up!"

"What do you mean? Ain't this a train robbery?"

Aurora shook her head. "What? No, there's nothing of value on that train."

"We ain't robbin' *from* the train, princess." Wrenn chuckled. "We're stealing the whole damn thing!"

ΔΔΔ

Wrenn coupled the last boxcar back onto the wire, completing the reversal of the carts along its 'track'. They'd been easy enough to move, once unbuckled from each other it had only taken a few lizard warriors to push the floating monstrosities around until they had perfectly reordered the train to face the opposite direction it had come from. Instead of blowing the vehicle as Aurora had originally intended, Wrenn ordered everyone to load the harvested crystal into the front-most car along with whatever grenade ammo that'd survived his bombing run on the MK 19. A simple flip of the switch was all it would take to start the train back along the guide wire to its point of origin, hopefully with enough speed to ram it full on into the fort's walls. Once everything was set in place, Wrenn and Aurora stood at the engineer controls. "The Chaz Purdue prepared to get the survivors back to town?"

Aurora nodded. "Inzenyr said they'll blindfold them and take them through the underground, she promised to personally deliver them just outside of town before nightfall."

"I'm glad so many surrendered . . . I'm hoping more will

follow suit after we drive home with this care package." Wrenn sighed.

"You know this is a suicide run . . ." Aurora cautioned.

Wrenn nodded, wrapping his knuckles across the metal wheel. "Yeah, well . . . I got a lot of skeletons in my closet and more than enough people got a bone to pick with them. I . . . I ain't done right by you before, leavin' you holdin' the bag like that. I'm hopin' this might help redeem me, in your eyes, at least. Maybe there'll be one person out in the 'verse that don't think me a lousy, two-timin', selfish loser."

Aurora burst forward, kissing him deeply on the lips and shoving him against the far wall. Her tongue lashed out, her hands pulling the man closer to her as if her life depended on it. Wrenn reacted in kind, wrapping an arm around her waist and the other in her hair. The two remained in a lover's embrace for a few minutes until a chime echoed in both their com pieces. *Confirmed: I have full control now, Captain.*

Aurora drew back, her breath shaky. "Control . . .?"

Repeating: Yes, Crewmember Aurora, I have complete control over the train's propulsion and guidance systems.

Aurora took a step back, her cheeks flushed. "You . . . you were never going to drive this thing into the fort . . . were you?"

Wrenn chuckled. "Hell no, I'm brave not stupid."

"You asshole!" Aurora punched him again.

Wrenn laughed heartily as he blocked her subsequent blows. "Hey now, that was nice though, if I didn't know better I'd say you're sweet on me!"

"I'll fucking kill you, Wrenn. I can't believe you just . . . Argh!" Aurora exclaimed, clearly flustered.

"Well, can it wait until we're done here? I'm gonna need your help escorting this thing from the air."

Aurora crossed her arms in a huff, embarrassment blanketing her face more so than rage. "You . . . ugh, fine. What is the *real* plan?"

Wrenn chuckled again, clearly delighted in his trickery. "You and me will fly overhead, make sure the care package gets a clear shot to punch it all the way to the end of the line. I watched them offload that ship of theirs over the last couple days. They got four fighters that escorted their two SPYTERs up and down but I wouldn't be surprised if that frigate of theirs don't rain down hellfire from above. We could be facing any one of them."

"Glorious." Aurora sighed.

"Hey, we don't have to shoot them all down, just buy enough time for delivery." Wrenn shrugged.

Aurora nodded, still struggling to recover from her humiliation. "Right . . . well, let's get to it."

"Music to my ears, princess."

△△△

Statement: Train on final approach. Cheyenne signaled through the com link. *Warning: Fighters have been scrambled according to mercenary radio traffic.*

"Right on schedule!" Wrenn agreed. "Comin' at us, two by two."

"Split them up? Divide and conquer?" Aurora called back over the coms.

"From my mind to your lovely lips!" Wrenn nodded.

Aurora peeled off to the right, goating two fighters to follow her with a few purposeful stray shots. Wrenn continued onward, staying above the train, ultimately playing chicken with his opponents. "Come on, you jackwagons, time to play!"

Wrenn cheered as he gunned the engine, banking hard and causing his zipper to spin as he opened fire. The other fighters didn't know what to do, one accelerated to meet the challenge while the other gained altitude in order to avoid a head on collision. Wrenn shot past them both, a few singes from stray plasma rounds tarnishing his wing. "Whew! A bit too close a shave on that one!" He laughed.

Higher up, Aurora slalomed back and forth in an attempt to avoid the two chasing her. The closest merc fighter opened up a volley of plasma rounds, her ship's protective coating shifting to take the hit and then scattering to keep the acidic aftereffect from damaging anything. Aurora cut back on her thrusters and the morphing shell expanded outward, creating drag that appeared to shoot her backward while her pursuers flew past her. Aurora ramped up her engine once more, the tiny moving pyramids returning to a wing-like design. One quick volley from the Utopian Starfire and both fighters blew to splinters in a bright fireball. "All done here, how are you looking?"

"Almost . . ." Wrenn answered, wrenching back on his altitude and pushing the pedal for maximum thrust. The Lancer shot directly upward, the two pursuant mercs struggling to follow. Wrenn shot past the upper cloud cover, cutting back on his engine and allowing gravity to take hold of his zipper. The captain spun around, now pointing the arrowhead designed fighter straight down. As the mercs neared the lower clouds, they were shocked to see Wrenn burst forth from the milky fluff, lighting them up with plasma rounds. Both fighters blew apart, Wrenn's zipper cutting through plumes of flame as he continued planet bound. "Ok, you got them, now pull up Wrenn." Aurora called.

"I'm trying . . ." Wrenn called back.

His zipper was rattling as the wind whipped past him, his thrusters working overtime to try and set him right again. Aurora looked on in horror as his fighter dove head first toward the ground. "Wrenn! Pull up!"

The captain fiddled with some controls, diverting power from his rear propulsion to the thrusters under the nose. He locked in the changes, his craft turning perpendicular to the ground fast approaching. With a quick return to propulsion, Wrenn shot forward, his wings catching the air and providing him the lift he needed. Wrenn cheered over the radio as he banked around one of the many buttes in the area, having made it by no more than about twenty feet. "Told you I had it under control!" He joked.

Warning: Train at maximum velocity. Impact imminent! Cheyenne beckoned their attention.

"Here come the fireworks!" Wrenn laughed as he and Aurora joined back up, flying along the guide wire a kilometer or so back from the train. Cheyenne sent the boxcars into the last buoy, snapping the carts free of their tether and straight toward the outer wall of the anchor fort. Tungsten steel met with hardened concrete as the first train car crumpled on impact. The train's thickness, combined with its momentum, made it easy for the first few layers of building to be penetrated before the surprise they'd packed went off. The blast that followed rocked the foundations of the entire town, a plume of smoke and flame towering some hundred feet into the air. What was left was a fort that looked like half its northern end was blown away and the smoke, black and thick, billowed out from the opening like a gushing wound.

Wrenn landed close to the base while Aurora circled round to land near town. The captain ran to the opening, his iron at the ready for any surprises. He climbed up a pile of rubble, the remnants of what had been the outer two walls. He saw mercs crawling, coughing, and running to get away. A shot ran out, the round buzzing past Wrenn's ear and colliding with the concrete wall. The captain ducked into a doorway, taking cover from whoever had the sense to recognize him in the chaos. "Damn you, brother!" Desmond called out, coughing. "Why couldn't you just leave well enough alone?!"

"What can I say? I'm like a rash that won't go away!" Wrenn called back.

Two more rounds bounced off the wall, shots made out of frustration rather than any real intent of harm. "Just give it up, Desmond! You clearly botched this beyond repair!"

"Oh, so you and the Scabies can just swoop in and take over?! Fuck you!"

Wrenn shook his head. "The SCA?! What the devil you on about?"

There was no answer. Wrenn waited a few seconds before he peeked around his cover. He held up his revolver, not wanting any surprises as he stalked slowly down the destroyed hall that led further in. Wrenn cleared a few dozen corridors and rooms before he followed the crowds out toward the main entrance. As Wrenn caught sight of the outer courtyard, he could see the front gates opened wide and a wave of battered mercs flooding out into the streets of town. The miners and shop owners were strewn all along the walkways, watching in disbelief as the mighty soldiers they had feared for so many months now stumbled and scrambled for safety. Desmond walked toward the back of the pack, clearly infuriated beyond all sanity. Wrenn ducked behind one of the doors as he watched them move out into the main street, Mayor Sewell finally hobbling out of the wreckage with what appeared to be nothing more than a scratch on his leg. "Lieutenant Myers! Lieutenant Myers!" The weasel cried. "You have to save me! Please!"

"Not now mayor!" Desmond barked, scanning the crowd for his target.

Sewell fell to the merc leader's feet, half groveling, half malingering. "I've got money! Loads of it! It's locked away in the vault! Take it, all of it! Just get me off this godforsaken planet!"

"Enough!" Desmond spat, aiming his pistol downward at the slimy official.

A single shot ran out among the town. Onlookers screamed in shock as Mayor Jeremiah Sewell's body tumbled over in a lifeless heap, his brains splattered across the dusty street. Wrenn shook his head in disbelief as Desmond called out to the bystanders. "Get out here now Ethan! Show yourself or I'll start shooting more of these peasants! Eventually I'll get to one you actually care about!"

Wrenn moved into the open, aiming down his sights at the back of his brother's head. His finger flexed upon the trigger . . . it'd be so easy right here, just a single shot, a single moment of dishonor and not only his troubles, but those of this whole damn planet would be over. Wrenn clenched his jaw, why couldn't he do it? What was stopping him? Desmond turned suddenly, bringing up his sidearm and firing before Wrenn could pull himself back to the matter at hand. One shot lodged itself into Wrenn's shoulder, his finger squeezing off his own round that impacted with Desmond's gut. The improvised standoff resulted in a draw, both men stumbling to their knees. "You always were a pussy." Desmond spouted, spitting blood from his mouth as it bubbled up from his midsection.

"Learned from the best . . ." Wrenn smirked back, gritting himself through the pain. He dropped his iron to the dirt, clenching his palm over the open wound in his shoulder.

"It doesn't matter what happens to me here, little brother. The others are coming, I've told the whole gang about your new name."

"You . . . what . . . ?" Wrenn's eyes grew in alarm.

Desmond laughed. "That's right, I've stayed in touch. They're all *anxious* to have a few words with you, 'specially the captain. You know how he just *loves* his chats with traitors."

"Traitor?" Wrenn coughed. "I weren't no traitor, Desmond. It was the captain that betrayed *me*."

"Keep telling yourself that." Desmond spat. "I'm sure the Alliance blew all kinds of smoke up your ass when you sold us out to 'em."

"But I never . . ." Wrenn started.

The man stopped mid-sentence as he noticed Desmond raising his pistol. "Then again . . . it's only fair they come to visit a gravestone anyhow, after all . . . it's family's responsibility to lay you in the ground, brother."

"Desmond . . . please . . ." Wrenn shook his head.

"Good-bye brother. Say hi to Momma for me . . ."

A shot perforated the dry air as Wrenn winced but felt nothing. He opened his eyes to see Desmond arching backward followed by his face tumbling into the sand, a hole blown into his back. Behind him, not too far, Jenny lowered a shotgun from her shoulder and nodded. Wrenn chuckled to himself. "Pinch me someone, I might be fallin' for that girl . . ."

The captain collapsed onto the ground, townsfolk sprinting forward toward him. Jenny and Aurora were the first to get to his side, followed closely after by Clive who lifted

Wrenn back to his feet. As the girls held down bandages over the wound followed closely after by healing gels, Clive started walking Wrenn out into the main street.

As they passed by Desmond's body, Wrenn spared one look to his fallen kin. Clive allowed him to lower to a knee, expecting perhaps the man to say a prayer or close the shocked eyes of his dead brother. Wrenn, in fact, took hold of the dead man's Stetson, placing it upon his own brow and standing. He rose as a different man that day, despite what he mighta thought of hisself. The sun's rays were blocked behind the wide brim, encasing him in a shadowy silhouette. He was no longer the boyish rogue who meandered his way through the galaxy, but a heroic gunslinger, able to ride in and right the wrongs of those who might harm others. Though the truth of these events you now know, dear reader, Wrenn's image was cemented in the minds of those witnesses, and through the subsequent gossip, his heroic reputation would only grow. Sometimes you can't help when your legend is born.

As they moved further onto the main street, Wrenn noted the miners and mercenaries were still squaring off against one another, both sides looking pensive at what the other might do. Wrenn signaled for Clive to hold up. "Hey, soldiers . . ." Wrenn coughed. "Your leader is dead, your client is dead. The Chaz Purdue will be bringing your survivors from the train here by nightfall. I would suggest you take yours and run on home, ain't much else for you here."

The few mercenaries that weren't desperately injured looked at each other for confirmation. After a few exchanged words, they nodded, gathering up their wounded and heading back toward the smoking fort. As they did so, the town finally let out a cheer, many hats sailing into the air in jubilation. Wrenn motioned for Clive to continue and the group moved through the throngs of celebration to the saloon. "I can't believe you pulled that off." Aurora smiled.

"Neither can I." Wrenn wheezed.

"There's still a lot that's got to get done, worst of which

will be convincing Ronald to leave the Chaz Purdue alone." Aurora sighed.

"Sure we can't just get back to the ship and sail to greener pastures?" Wrenn joked.

Aurora put more pressure down on the bandage she was holding to his shoulder and the captain wailed in response. "You should know better than that . . . Ethan."

Wrenn winced. "Another name from another life . . . explained in a conversation at another time."

"Fair enough." Aurora responded. "Other things need our attention first."

"Alright, alright. Just . . . let me get a few drinks in me and I'll be right as rain."

"You'll be needing a bit more than that, Mister Wrenn." Jenny smiled. "Take you a few days just to get the hole patched up, probably weeks before you'll be able to move it again."

"Are you volunteering to be my nurse, Miss Whitmoore?" Wrenn teased.

"I might be persuaded." Jenny winked.

Clive cleared his throat loudly as they reached the door to the saloon. "I was offerin' her a job . . . honest!"

The girls' laughter followed them in as Clive used Wrenn's body to open the door, Wrenn's protests be damned.

CHAPTER 22

"You sure you know how to fly one of these things?" Wrenn asked Jenny as she sat down in the SPYTERs pilot's seat.

"Better than you could with one arm!" Jenny argued.

The mercs had evacuated in such a hurry earlier in the week, they'd left quite a few supplies behind, to include the entirety of the late Mayor Sewell's fortune in an underground vault. Since the combination died with the man, Wrenn felt it only right to leave it to the dead man's boss to collect, being that they were likely funds scraped off the top of every sale of fuel thus far anyhow. Wrenn's arm was still in a sling as he watched the last of the supplies being loaded onto the shuttle, mostly consisting of rations and toiletries for those stranded at the orbital station. Inzenyr placed the last box down and straightened herself in front of the captain. "All is ready, I go with you now."

"Hey I really appreciate you tagging along to help demonstrate the crystal's true potential." Wrenn nodded.

"If help Chaz Purdue, I bring many stories of the stars." The female lizard nodded.

"Woah, I thought you was just gracing us with your presence for the return trip to Deadrock?" Wrenn cocked his head.

"It is decided, I am one with you, fleshy man." The large lizard placed a heavy hand on Wrenn's wounded shoulder and the man seethed in pain as she moved past him.

Wrenn sighed heavily as he watched her climb up into

the cockpit to keep Jenny company on the trip up. "How do I get roped into these things?"

"Because deep down, you've got a good heart." Aurora piped up, coming up the back ramp as Jenny started firing up the SPYTERs engines.

"Oh yeah? I thought I was an asshole." Wrenn squinted.

"You're that too. People can be more than one thing, Wrenn."

The man scoffed. Aurora leaned forward, kissing him gently on the cheek. "Come on, Captain. Let's go home."

△△△

"So, tell me again, how is it that I sent you to *fix* my supply problem and somehow you caused more devastation in the process?!" Ronald Donnersvelt guffawed as he listened to the rather marvelous retelling of the events on Visigath.

"Well, uh . . . you see . . . I think you're focusing more on the negative than the positive." Wrenn pointed out.

"And what is keeping me from taking out the costs from your hide, Captain!" The three muscle-men moved, stopping only when Inzenyr showed her teeth and growled.

Wrenn nodded. "Understandable, understandable. But, listen Ronny, there's more than enough funds left over from Sewell's . . . uh, dismissal . . . to fix up the grav elevator and repair the anchor."

"How so?" Ronald waved his goons back.

"Turns out, the little shit was cheating you, skimming a boat load of money off the top of every exchange and keeping it in a vault down there on the planet's surface. Probably what he used to hire the mercs in the first place." Wrenn explained.

Ronald sighed heavily, squeezing the bridge of his nose with his fat sausage fingers. "Very well . . . now, what's this about changing the operation from a mining colony to a dairy plantation?"

"Not as in cows and such, but more along the lines of

211

processing these crystals without separating them from the planet." Wrenn elaborated. "See here, my companion Inzenyr will demonstrate."

The lizard-woman held up a cluster of harvested crystal. She spoke the same indiscernible words as her people had in the caves, caressing the stone in a tender fashion until the mineral began weeping. Wrenn rushed forward, grabbing hold of Ronald's 'Mine your own Business' commemorative mug and dumped its contents out onto the floor. He held the mug under the crystal for a few minutes until it had produced enough of its contents to satisfy him. "Take yourself a gander at that, Ronny."

The pudgy man took the mug, taking in a whiff of the liquid followed by dabbing his finger into it. His eyes widened, licking his fat digits with his tongue and then spitting it out. "That's fuel!"

"Just about." Wrenn nodded. "You'll have to dilute the stuff a bit, but it comes out purer this way than any sort of crushin' would do, and when the crystals are still connected to the planet, they'll refill with the stuff over time."

"By the stars . . ." Ronald gasped. "How do we learn this technique?"

"Oh, you ain't." Wrenn shook his head. "This here's a trade negotiation."

"What?" Ronald asked flatly.

"You heard." Wrenn crossed his arms. "The Chaz Purdue are your new miners. They'll harvest the fuel, bring it up to the surface, and then trade you for it."

"And we just take them on their word they won't try to attack anymore of our shipments?" Ronald argued.

"That's a part of the deal. I'm sure your corporation's got some negotiators and what not, but basically it boils down to: you want the fuel with no more bloodshed, you gotta go through them. It's not a bad deal Ronny, really. The amount of money you'll save by milkin' the crystals rather than mining them is a steal. I see it as a win-win."

Ronald thought for a long moment before finally

nodding. "I'm not sure how the board will react when I tell them a mining company has expanded into crystal *farming* but, what the hell, things have always been a little different out here in the Reach."

The man presented his chubby fingers and palm to Inzenyr who stared at it with a stoic expression. Wrenn pantomimed for her what was expected, and the lizard-woman finally came forward and practically crushed every bone in the man's hand as she shook it. Ronald squealed like a stuck pig as he cradled his bruised digits against his chest. "Alright, alright, get out already! I've had about enough of these shenanigans."

"So I can expect my payment . . ." Wrenn pestered.

"Yes, yes! I'll wire it to your account now, just get the hell out of my office!" Ronald waved them off with his good hand.

Confirmed: Funds deposited, Captain. Cheyenne chimed in.

"Pleasure doing business with you, Ronny." Wrenn bowed.

"Out!"

△△△

Wrenn watched from the station's viewing deck as the *Whisper's* toroid and factory blocks were reattached outside.Stretching his arm, finally free from the confinement of the sling, his wince turned into a grin so wide his face hurt as he imagined what the finished insides looked like. He was so entranced by the idea of his ship finally being up to snuff that he didn't even notice the old Ratadendrin mechanic, Daisy, waddle up beside him. "I managed to get her about right as rain." The little mouse-lady spat.

"Thank you." Wrenn said softly.

The Rotty smiled up at the man, seeing the familiar look of complete infatuation on a captain's face. There might be any number of a million partners out there for a man like him, but there would never be a love so special as that of a captain with his ship. She'd seen it more than her fair share, but she never did get tired of it. Daisy patted Wrenn's leg. "You did good, son. She's a fine vessel."

"She is." Wrenn agreed. "So what were you able to rustle up to slide into her?"

"Well, I got you completely stocked with guest rooms, sixteen in all, in those wings of the factory block. Got you a communal dining facility and a hydronics research bay in the northern section too."

"What about the southern section?" Wrenn asked.

"Oh, that . . . I found you somethin' special I knew you of all people would appreciate." Daisy winked.

Wrenn laughed. "I'll take your word for it."

The Rotty woman nodded. "Your payment came through just fine, I even dropped the price a bit on account as I like ya and such."

"There's more to it than that though, ain't there?" Wrenn pried.

Daisy nodded. "You always were a quick one . . ."

Wrenn looked down at her expectantly and the old woman sighed. "It's my granddaughter. She done fell in love and I'm not quite sure her heart could take it if I told her to stop."

"With me?!" Wrenn squeaked.

"You? Hell no! With your ship!" Daisy placed her hands on her hips. "Done fallen head over heels for the old girl and I can't bring myself to tell her to move on."

Wrenn chuckled, relief washing over him all of a sudden. "Oh . . . well . . ."

"Can you do me a favor and bring her onboard for a little while? I'm sure it's just a phase. She won't be a bother, honest!" Daisy pleaded.

"Hey, hey . . . relax. We'd love to have her. I could use someone in engineering anyways until I get the hang of her myself. Just as long as she's not the type to go gabbin' our business to everyone." Wrenn replied.

"Oh, she'll be quiet as a mouse!" Daisy elbowed him in the calf. "Get it?"

Wrenn rolled his eyes. "Yeah, I get it. Well, she can come aboard anytime she's ready I suppose. Now that she's whole again, we'll need to stock up before shippin' out. Speaking of which . . . whereabouts can I find an instrument shop?"

"Like the kind you calibrate or the kind you play?" Daisy asked.

"Musical type." Wrenn elaborated.

"Old Grissom's got a junk shop that should have just about anything you might need." Daisy answered. "Though, fair warning, he's a bit of an oddball."

"That's ok, we've had our share of weirdos out here in the Reach already."

Daisy grunted. "This one's nuttier than a popcorn fart, I'll tell you that much."

Wrenn chuckled and thanked the old mechanic. The Rotty woman waddled back along the passage, leaving Wrenn to enjoy the view of his favorite girl.

△△△

Moving along the promenade, Wrenn bought himself a churro from the traveling cart as he followed the directions he'd been given to Old Grissom's. Hidden in a dark nook, the store was the only one without a neon sign. A single wooden board hung above the doorway with the word "GRISSOM'S'" painted in bright green. Seemed about the only shop that wasn't a subsidiary of the mining corp on the whole station.

Stepping within, Wrenn was reminded of a junk-filled garage or packed storage lockers that had once been owned by hoarders before their inevitable unglorified deaths. There wasn't a clear path to walk through the place, Wrenn having to push past a row of old Earth bicycles hanging on the ceiling next to a stack of what he assumed were old kettles. He stumbled and knocked over a carefully constructed tower of old world video cassettes which made a racket so loud he thought he'd alert the whole station. "What? What? Who's there?!" An old scraggly man appeared as if out of nowhere.

"Cripes grandpa, you scared the shit out of me!" Wrenn exclaimed.

"Hope not, otherwise you're cleaning it up!" The man guffawed at his own joke.

"Right . . ." Wrenn rolled his eyes. "I've got a crew member that would get along swimmingly with you, old timer."

"Oh? Then send them! Otherwise, what's your business?"

"I take it you're Grissom?" Wrenn asked.

"Yeah! Now, what'ya want?" The old man snapped.

"Jeez, old man, you think you'd be nicer to a potential customer."

"Pah! That fancy talk is for the corpos, sweet talkin' ya, layin' honey in your ears while they steals the wallet right out your back pocket. Don't need it, don't want it."

Wrenn shrugged. "I guess you got a point there . . ."

"So, what'ya need? Ain't no point browsin', you'd be stuck in here for weeks unless you knew where to find it." Grissom responded.

"Well, I'm hoping you might have strings."

"What kind of strings? Sewin'? Shoe lace? Pullstring? Bowstring? Drawstring? Yaaaarn?" The man's face came closer to Wrenn's with each successive word.

"Guitar strings, preferably metal. I got an old resonator that's had a bit of a rough time lately." Wrenn sighed.

"Ain't we all!" The man said, disappearing being a pile of junk before Wrenn could say another word.

Wrenn looked around, trying to follow the store owner's movements but only caught blurs as the spindly geezer whipped around the mounds of nonsense like a tornado. Before long the guy was back in front of him, a D'Addario pack in his decrepit fingers. "Here ya go!"

"Wow, uh . . . thanks! How much do they cost?" Wrenn took the small box from him.

"Hmm, what's it cost anyhow? Don't rightly know myself. S'pose if you ask ten men what they value most you'd get just about ten different answers if all the men were different fellas. Why, ask a dyin' man in the desert what he want most, he'd probably tell you water and he'd probably give you anything of his to get it; come to the drowning man with the same offer and he'd laugh you right out of sight, assuming he can laugh while he's sinkin'. 'Spose it just comes down to what matters most to the man at the time, but I could see some universals that many would probably hold dear. Family, love, companionship . . . these are what truly matters in the universe. Every one of a hundred billion souls wander through these stars searchin' for their fortunes, when most don't realize they're the richest bastards already by far . . ."

Wrenn nodded solemnly. "Yeah . . . I guess you might be right . . ."

The old man sighed. "Then again, I'm fucking starving, so hand over that churro there and we'll call it even!"

"Done!" Wrenn smiled, handing over his treat.

"Now get out!" Grissom spat, gumming the bread as he scampered off behind a wall of old computer monitors.

"Right . . . well . . . see ya." Wrenn shook his head exasperated as he found his way back out to the promenade.

ΔΔΔ

Wrenn managed to restring and clean his dobro guitar, carrying it by the neck as he toured the finished *Whisper.* He breathed in her recycled air and smiled as he peeked into her now fully equipped gym, sauna, and track in the toroid ring. The guest suites looked very nice, a queen-sized bed at the end next to a viewing window, a standard couch that could convert into a futon next to a coffee table and even a small kitchenette on the far side. The lab looked . . . labby, he guessed. There certainly were a lot of gizmos and measuring thingys. The dining facility seemed simple enough with steel tables and attached stools with an industrial kitchen and serving line at the back. Wrenn was just about to finish his inspection when he came across the surprise Daisy had mentioned.

Opposite side of the factory block from the eatery and lab was a sight that looked both out of sorts with the rest of the gray metal interior and somehow also perfectly at home aboard a ship owned by Wrenn. Nestled into place, complete with its own swinging twin batwing doors, was a wooden-walled saloon. Neon signs out front advertised 'beer' and 'music' as they flashed enticingly to any would-be passenger aboard the *Whisper*. Wrenn moved inside to have his heart melt at the sight of tables and chairs, most bolted to the floor incase of a gravity malfunction, along with a bar and stage on the far end for live music. When in need, a multi-colored juke box stood next to the stage, flanked by some bathrooms so that patrons wouldn't need to wander far to make room for more revels. It was not the largest of honkey tonks Wrenn had seen, but it certainly was the prettiest.

The captain moved up onto the stage, sitting down on a barstool. He cracked his knuckles and strummed a bit on the resonator, listening as the sound echoed off the walls and back to his ears. He smiled, allowing his fingers to roam across the strings like they was frolickin' in a field not seen since last season. Wrenn closed his eyes, allowing the music to take him on a journey he'd not ventured since entering the Digiway. It wasn't long before he could hear the words being sung to the song he was playin', wafting into his mind like a summer's breeze. Somehow, someway, she came into his mind. Her smile coaxed his hand to draw out the last song she ever taught him, the last shot he took to try and win her back:

Did I drive you away?
I know what you'll say
You say, "Oh, sing one we know"

But I promise you this
I'll always look out for you
Yeah, that's what I'll do

Wrenn opened his eyes, realizing suddenly that the voice he was hearing was not in his head. Jenny moved with grace in from the door and stepped up onto the stage with him, singing the words as Wrenn continued to strum out the rhythm.

I say, "Ohhhhh"

The red head smiled, swaying back and forth as the guitar crescendoed and dipped, her body giving movement to the sounds echoing from his hands.

I say, "Ohhhh"

Wrenn continued playing, the woman coming to a stop on stage and kneeling down, resting herself back on her heels. They looked at each other, no conversation passing between, no needing of explanation. As soon as he started the second verse, Jenny came right along with him.

My heart is yours
It's you that I hold onto
Yeah that's what I do
And I know I was wrong
But I won't let you down
Oh yeah, I will, yeah I will, yes I will

While the two continued back into the chorus, they were unaware that Inzenyr, Wrenchy, and Aurora entered the saloon and took seats for the impromptu concert. Aurora moved to the bar while the other two sat in chairs at one of the closest tables. Cheyenne's projected image appeared behind the counter, offering drinks as if she could serve them, but was unable to grab hold of a glass in her holographic state. Wrenn and Jenny finished up the song with the final verse and the others clapped for them.

Yeah, I saw sparks

Yeah, I saw sparks
And I saw sparks
Yeah I saw sparks

"Sparks" by Coldplay

Jenny and Wrenn seemed surprised by the others suddenly in the room, but played up the stage performance anyhow, taking each other's hand and bowing together. Jenny kissed Wrenn on the cheek as she smiled warmly in the stage's hot lamps. "That was fun!"

"I didn't know you could sing." Wrenn smiled.

"Oh, I've always dabbled a bit, Papa always said I was the daughter of the river with a voice like the heavens."

Wrenn smiled. "Well, he was right about that."

"Careful, Mister Wrenn, I might take you for a flirt." Jenny winked.

"It's Captain, we're aboard my ship now." Wrenn corrected.

"Sure, but I'm not a part of your crew." Jenny remarked.

"You could be . . ."

Jenny's smile faded slightly. She gazed about the room, seeming almost emotional as she looked it over. "My own Whitmoore's?"

"No." Wrenn shook his head. "No corpo nonsense aboard my ship."

"Family business." Jenny corrected.

"How about, independent offshoot?" Wrenn compromised.

"Place just named *Jenny's*?" The redhead giggled.

"We'll come up with something."

The barmaid looked around again, taking in a breath. "My guess is you're really just needing a logistics manager, probably a cook too."

"If you're willing, though I can't pay you but an equal share, don't matter how many jobs you claim. I'll let you keep sixty percent of what you earn here in the bar, though."

"Eighty." Jenny countered.

"Sixty-five."

"Seventy." Jenny demanded.

"Ok, but the crew drinks free." Wrenn smirked.

Jenny shrugged. "'Spose I could live with that."

"Then welcome aboard, Miss Whitmoore."

"My pleasure, Mister Wrenn."

"Still no Captain?"

"Independent contractor for an independent offshoot." Jenny giggled.

Wrenn rolled his eyes as Jenny hugged him. She moved off stage to visit with Wrenchy and Inzenyr while Wrenn moseyed up to the bar and took out two long necks from behind the counter. The captain twisted both caps off and handed one to Aurora. "To a job well done!" Wrenn offered his bottle in a toast.

"Well . . . it got done, at least." Aurora smiled, raising hers to his with a satisfying *clink.*

They both took a swig and Wrenn nodded gratefully. "I . . . uh, I suppose you'll be moving on now? Word has it the Digiway should be repaired by next week or so."

"Suppose I could . . ." Aurora looked over the bar lazily.

The two sat in silence for a few minutes, nursing their beers in an awkward stillness. Laughter from the other table reached them quite easily, Cheyenne was even bouncing on her heels in anticipation. "Request: Would it be permitted for me to join the others at the table, Captain?"

"Sure, knock yourself out."

"Response: I don't believe being unconscious would be beneficial to the social situation."

"Just . . . get goin'." Wrenn sighed.

Aurora chuckled as the computer walked away, joining the others near the stage. "Sometimes I think she does that just to get a rise out of you."

"She succeeds." Wrenn grumbled. "I'll be honest, I've no clue what I'm gonna do with all of them. I've never been a leader before, never looked out for anyone other than myself. I keep collecting all these people when all I'm good at doing is getting them into trouble."

". . . and you're rather adept at getting them *out* of that trouble as well." Aurora reminded him. "If you stick to doing the right thing."

"And what is the right thing?" Wrenn asked.

"Whatever I tell you it is . . ." Aurora smirked.

Wrenn laughed, taking another swig of his beer. "Well, I guess you better stick around then, you know . . . for their sake."

"I suppose I must." Aurora winked.

"Cool." Wrenn nodded, finishing his beer and standing. "I guess I better go find us a job."

Aurora nodded, unable to find any words to reply. They stood awkwardly for a few moments before Wrenn turned and walked out of the saloon. As soon as he had made it to the hangar, he paused, staring out at the vastness of space from the open hangar door. The man pulled a newly purchased pack of cigarettes from his pocket, turning over his lucky and then lighting the first fresh one. He pushed the brim of his Stetson back with his thumb, taking in a deep drag and exhaling slowly. Wrenn knew he had a target on his back now, that people from his past would be comin' for him. Maybe it was a mistake, bringing all these girls along with him, but in the end, he felt . . . better with them around. For the first time in a long time, he was starting to let down those walls he'd built after she'd left him. Maybe he could find his place once more, out here, in the vastness of the black . . . aboard the *Whisper on the 'Verse.*

The End

I hope you enjoyed your adventures with the crew of the *Whisper*. Don't worry, there's lots more spectacular space shootouts to come!

Please leave a review on amazon and tell me what you liked/disliked. I really want to makes these books as approachable as possible. Let your voice be heard!

If you'd rather tell me privately, feel free to email me @ marcbransonauthor@gmail.com

Socials, Email Newsletters, & Website coming soon.

BOOKS BY THIS AUTHOR

Alloys: A Lit-Rpg Harem Adventure

Nicholas Faraday is a scientist, not a soldier, so when a spell gone wrong transports him to a magical world full of demons and the undead, he'll have nothing but his wits to help him survive. After meeting a beautiful yet deceitful sorceress, Nick finds he can alter the very fabric of this world, which he'll need to use every bit of to find a way home. Finding more allies in a strong female warrior, a gorgeous farm girl, and a cunning succubus, Nick will need all his knowledge of biology, chemistry, and physics in order to stay one step ahead of the terrifying Dullahan doing everything it can to force Nick to stay . . . in a grave.

Alloys: The Imperial Equation

Nicholas Faraday is a wizard. Well, actually he's a scientist that was pulled from Earth and is now trying to carve out a life for himself in the foreign world of Donau. Pulled from the modern day into a pseudo-medieval culture can be jarring, but with his advanced knowledge and a strange ability to alter the physics of the planet, Nick was able to rescue a small village from a murderous headless horseman.

Now, the emperor has requested his presence in the capital city, an invite that Nick is clearly not allowed to decline. Together with the group of women he has met in his time here - the beautiful redheaded farm-girl Ruby-Sue, a warrior nun named Ariel, and a incredibly charismatic succubus named Jezebel -

Nick will venture into an unfamiliar city filled with political maneuvering, power struggles, and hobnobbing. The young man will find it challenging to find a use for his vast knowledge of biology and engineering in this fish-out-of-water adventure that will keep readers guessing to the final page.

Come join the cloak and dagger mystery. Visit the illustrious palace, majestic cathedral, and battle-hardened arena. Discover the secrets embedded deep within this ancient Roman-style metropolis, but take care, for around every marbled wall lies the danger of a swift death.